ALREADY CHOSEN

(A Laura Frost Suspense Thriller —Book Seven)

BLAKE PIERCE

Blake Pierce

Blake Pierce is the USA Today bestselling author of the RILEY PAGE mystery series, which includes seventeen books. Blake Pierce is also the author of the MACKENZIE WHITE mystery series, comprising fourteen books; of the AVERY BLACK mystery series, comprising six books; of the KERI LOCKE mystery series, comprising five books; of the MAKING OF RILEY PAIGE mystery series, comprising six books; of the KATE WISE mystery series, comprising seven books; of the CHLOE FINE psychological suspense mystery, comprising six books; of the JESSE HUNT psychological suspense thriller series, comprising twenty four books; of the AU PAIR psychological suspense thriller series, comprising three books; of the ZOE PRIME mystery series, comprising six books; of the ADELE SHARP mystery series, comprising fifteen books, of the EUROPEAN VOYAGE cozy mystery series, comprising four books; of the new LAURA FROST FBI suspense thriller, comprising nine books (and counting); of the new ELLA DARK FBI suspense thriller, comprising eleven books (and counting); of the A YEAR IN EUROPE cozy mystery series, comprising nine books, of the AVA GOLD mystery series, comprising six books (and counting); of the RACHEL GIFT mystery series, comprising eight books (and counting); of the VALERIE LAW mystery series, comprising nine books (and counting); of the PAIGE KING mystery series, comprising six books (and counting); of the MAY MOORE mystery series, comprising six books (and counting); and the CORA SHIELDS mystery series, comprising three books (and counting).

An avid reader and lifelong fan of the mystery and thriller genres, Blake loves to hear from you, so please feel free to visit www.blakepierceauthor.com to learn more and stay in touch.

BOOKS BY BLAKE PIERCE

CORA SHIELDS MYSTERY SERIES
UNDONE (Book #1)
UNWANTED (Book #2)
UNHINGED (Book #3)

MAY MOORE SUSPENSE THRILLER
NEVER RUN (Book #1)
NEVER TELL (Book #2)
NEVER LIVE (Book #3)
NEVER HIDE (Book #4)
NEVER FORGIVE (Book #5)
NEVER AGAIN (Book #6)

PAIGE KING MYSTERY SERIES
THE GIRL HE PINED (Book #1)
THE GIRL HE CHOSE (Book #2)
THE GIRL HE TOOK (Book #3)
THE GIRL HE WISHED (Book #4)
THE GIRL HE CROWNED (Book #5)
THE GIRL HE WATCHED (Book #6)

VALERIE LAW MYSTERY SERIES
NO MERCY (Book #1)
NO PITY (Book #2)
NO FEAR (Book #3)
NO SLEEP (Book #4)
NO QUARTER (Book #5)
NO CHANCE (Book #6)
NO REFUGE (Book #7)
NO GRACE (Book #8)
NO ESCAPE (Book #9)

RACHEL GIFT MYSTERY SERIES
HER LAST WISH (Book #1)

HER LAST CHANCE (Book #2)
HER LAST HOPE (Book #3)
HER LAST FEAR (Book #4)
HER LAST CHOICE (Book #5)
HER LAST BREATH (Book #6)
HER LAST MISTAKE (Book #7)
HER LAST DESIRE (Book #8)

AVA GOLD MYSTERY SERIES
CITY OF PREY (Book #1)
CITY OF FEAR (Book #2)
CITY OF BONES (Book #3)
CITY OF GHOSTS (Book #4)
CITY OF DEATH (Book #5)
CITY OF VICE (Book #6)

A YEAR IN EUROPE
A MURDER IN PARIS (Book #1)
DEATH IN FLORENCE (Book #2)
VENGEANCE IN VIENNA (Book #3)
A FATALITY IN SPAIN (Book #4)

ELLA DARK FBI SUSPENSE THRILLER
GIRL, ALONE (Book #1)
GIRL, TAKEN (Book #2)
GIRL, HUNTED (Book #3)
GIRL, SILENCED (Book #4)
GIRL, VANISHED (Book 5)
GIRL ERASED (Book #6)
GIRL, FORSAKEN (Book #7)
GIRL, TRAPPED (Book #8)
GIRL, EXPENDABLE (Book #9)
GIRL, ESCAPED (Book #10)
GIRL, HIS (Book #11)

LAURA FROST FBI SUSPENSE THRILLER
ALREADY GONE (Book #1)
ALREADY SEEN (Book #2)
ALREADY TRAPPED (Book #3)
ALREADY MISSING (Book #4)

ALREADY DEAD (Book #5)
ALREADY TAKEN (Book #6)
ALREADY CHOSEN (Book #7)
ALREADY LOST (Book #8)
ALREADY HIS (Book #9)

EUROPEAN VOYAGE COZY MYSTERY SERIES
MURDER (AND BAKLAVA) (Book #1)
DEATH (AND APPLE STRUDEL) (Book #2)
CRIME (AND LAGER) (Book #3)
MISFORTUNE (AND GOUDA) (Book #4)
CALAMITY (AND A DANISH) (Book #5)
MAYHEM (AND HERRING) (Book #6)

ADELE SHARP MYSTERY SERIES
LEFT TO DIE (Book #1)
LEFT TO RUN (Book #2)
LEFT TO HIDE (Book #3)
LEFT TO KILL (Book #4)
LEFT TO MURDER (Book #5)
LEFT TO ENVY (Book #6)
LEFT TO LAPSE (Book #7)
LEFT TO VANISH (Book #8)
LEFT TO HUNT (Book #9)
LEFT TO FEAR (Book #10)
LEFT TO PREY (Book #11)
LEFT TO LURE (Book #12)
LEFT TO CRAVE (Book #13)
LEFT TO LOATHE (Book #14)
LEFT TO HARM (Book #15)

THE AU PAIR SERIES
ALMOST GONE (Book#1)
ALMOST LOST (Book #2)
ALMOST DEAD (Book #3)

ZOE PRIME MYSTERY SERIES
FACE OF DEATH (Book#1)
FACE OF MURDER (Book #2)
FACE OF FEAR (Book #3)

FACE OF MADNESS (Book #4)
FACE OF FURY (Book #5)
FACE OF DARKNESS (Book #6)

A JESSIE HUNT PSYCHOLOGICAL SUSPENSE SERIES
THE PERFECT WIFE (Book #1)
THE PERFECT BLOCK (Book #2)
THE PERFECT HOUSE (Book #3)
THE PERFECT SMILE (Book #4)
THE PERFECT LIE (Book #5)
THE PERFECT LOOK (Book #6)
THE PERFECT AFFAIR (Book #7)
THE PERFECT ALIBI (Book #8)
THE PERFECT NEIGHBOR (Book #9)
THE PERFECT DISGUISE (Book #10)
THE PERFECT SECRET (Book #11)
THE PERFECT FAÇADE (Book #12)
THE PERFECT IMPRESSION (Book #13)
THE PERFECT DECEIT (Book #14)
THE PERFECT MISTRESS (Book #15)
THE PERFECT IMAGE (Book #16)
THE PERFECT VEIL (Book #17)
THE PERFECT INDISCRETION (Book #18)
THE PERFECT RUMOR (Book #19)
THE PERFECT COUPLE (Book #20)
THE PERFECT MURDER (Book #21)
THE PERFECT HUSBAND (Book #22)
THE PERFECT SCANDAL (Book #23)
THE PERFECT MASK (Book #24)

CHLOE FINE PSYCHOLOGICAL SUSPENSE SERIES
NEXT DOOR (Book #1)
A NEIGHBOR'S LIE (Book #2)
CUL DE SAC (Book #3)
SILENT NEIGHBOR (Book #4)
HOMECOMING (Book #5)
TINTED WINDOWS (Book #6)

KATE WISE MYSTERY SERIES

IF SHE KNEW (Book #1)
IF SHE SAW (Book #2)
IF SHE RAN (Book #3)
IF SHE HID (Book #4)
IF SHE FLED (Book #5)
IF SHE FEARED (Book #6)
IF SHE HEARD (Book #7)

THE MAKING OF RILEY PAIGE SERIES
WATCHING (Book #1)
WAITING (Book #2)
LURING (Book #3)
TAKING (Book #4)
STALKING (Book #5)
KILLING (Book #6)

RILEY PAIGE MYSTERY SERIES
ONCE GONE (Book #1)
ONCE TAKEN (Book #2)
ONCE CRAVED (Book #3)
ONCE LURED (Book #4)
ONCE HUNTED (Book #5)
ONCE PINED (Book #6)
ONCE FORSAKEN (Book #7)
ONCE COLD (Book #8)
ONCE STALKED (Book #9)
ONCE LOST (Book #10)
ONCE BURIED (Book #11)
ONCE BOUND (Book #12)
ONCE TRAPPED (Book #13)
ONCE DORMANT (Book #14)
ONCE SHUNNED (Book #15)
ONCE MISSED (Book #16)
ONCE CHOSEN (Book #17)

MACKENZIE WHITE MYSTERY SERIES
BEFORE HE KILLS (Book #1)
BEFORE HE SEES (Book #2)
BEFORE HE COVETS (Book #3)
BEFORE HE TAKES (Book #4)

BEFORE HE NEEDS (Book #5)
BEFORE HE FEELS (Book #6)
BEFORE HE SINS (Book #7)
BEFORE HE HUNTS (Book #8)
BEFORE HE PREYS (Book #9)
BEFORE HE LONGS (Book #10)
BEFORE HE LAPSES (Book #11)
BEFORE HE ENVIES (Book #12)
BEFORE HE STALKS (Book #13)
BEFORE HE HARMS (Book #14)

AVERY BLACK MYSTERY SERIES
CAUSE TO KILL (Book #1)
CAUSE TO RUN (Book #2)
CAUSE TO HIDE (Book #3)
CAUSE TO FEAR (Book #4)
CAUSE TO SAVE (Book #5)
CAUSE TO DREAD (Book #6)

KERI LOCKE MYSTERY SERIES
A TRACE OF DEATH (Book #1)
A TRACE OF MURDER (Book #2)
A TRACE OF VICE (Book #3)
A TRACE OF CRIME (Book #4)
A TRACE OF HOPE (Book #5)

CHAPTER ONE

"I can't believe you would do this to me," Isabella said, or rather screeched, stumbling a few steps away from Harry and shaking her head in open disbelief.

"You're being ridiculous," Harry scoffed. He looked annoyed. Like he was close to being done with her. That alone made her all the angrier. How dare he look like that when she was the one who had been wronged?

"I saw you," she insisted, swinging her arms wide. The weight of her purse made it swing out on the thin bejeweled strap, almost setting her off-balance, even though the only things in it were her ID and her cell phone. "You were making eyes at her. And you said something to her when she gave you the drink!"

"Yeah, I said thanks," Harry scowled, rushing towards her with an outstretched arm to guide her away from the road. "Like, thank you for the drinks? I was just being polite."

"You're never polite to bartenders," Isabella threw back, nearly tottering over on her heels as she lunged away in the opposite direction from his arm. She almost collided with the wall of the next building, saving herself just in time only by crossing her legs at an awkward angle.

"Don't be ridiculous!" Harry fumed, that word again. "Come on. Just – look, you're too drunk for this. *I'm* too drunk for this. Let's just go home."

"No way!" Isabella exclaimed. She had planned to go home with him tonight, but there was no chance now. Not now that she knew he'd been flirting with someone else. Maybe it was over between them. She'd figure that out once she had a chance to sit down. And pee. She needed to pee.

But she needed to get away from him even more.

"Well, what are you going to do, then? Walk around the streets all night?"

"Don't be ridiculous, Harry," Isabella said, far too pleased with herself for coming up with the retort and dimly aware in the back of her mind that her voice had sounded far more slurred than his. "I'm going home. Just not with you."

"Fine," Harry sighed, scratching the back of his head and shoving his hands in his pockets. It was a cold night, still winter and without a cloud above to trap some heat, but Isabella didn't feel cold yet. She still had the alcohol in her system, and the fire of rage to keep her warm. "I'll walk you back, then."

"No!" Isabella shouted, pushing him away with a desperate flail when he tried to come closer. "I don't need your help. I'm going home on my own. You do whatever you want, just not anywhere near me."

"It's too dangerous," Harry said, shaking his head. "You know that. You can't walk alone here at night. You *do* need me. Or at least let me get you a taxi."

"So I can owe you the fare?" Isabella shook her head angrily. When he tried to come towards her again she swung her purse in a vicious arc, and he stumbled back, almost tripping on an empty glass bottle that rattled noisily along the sidewalk.

He was distracted; she took that chance to start walking away a bit faster.

It wasn't so easy with her heels, especially at speed. She just kept putting one leg in front of the other, and every time she thought she was going to fall forwards, she put the next leg in front and somehow managed not to fall. She thought she'd heard Harry behind her at one moment and then the sound of him being sick, and she turned down an alleyway on her right as soon as she did, thinking he would look up and not know where she'd gone.

She almost chuckled out loud at the idea of his face. Magic Isabella, disappearing right in front of his eyes!

But she didn't, because she was being *quiet*, because she had to get away without him knowing she was gone.

Isabella clopped through the alley in her heels, looking up ahead. It was a long alley, actually. She paused for a moment, her skin beginning to crawl. Even through the alcohol, she had this strange feeling that she wasn't alone.

She turned and looked over her shoulder, wondering if Harry was following her.

There was no one there.

As she kept watching, Harry stumbled past the entrance of the alleyway without looking in, and then he was gone out of view. She stifled another chuckle, this one of victory. She'd done it. That idiot was probably giving up and going home, himself.

She swallowed, feeling the chill in the air a little more.

He was right about it not being entirely safe to walk home on her own.

But what was she going to do? Go back out to the brightly-lit street and call out for him to come and save her?

No, he'd flirted with someone else right in front of her. There was no way she could trust him now. She took a breath. She would carry on.

Isabella turned around quickly, and the rest of the alleyway was still empty, too.

She took one more deep breath and started to walk again, trying harder this time to keep her feet steady so she didn't trip on any of the debris scattered around. It was mostly broken or empty bottles and other kinds of trash, probably left here by other people who used the alley as a shortcut from the bar.

She scanned the ground carefully but then ended up having to stop and lean on a stack of crates, thinking she was going to fall over because she was leaning further and further forward. The crates themselves wobbled dangerously under her weight, and she careened away from them, landing with her back against the opposite wall and still just about upright. Isabella slumped, letting the wall take her weight for a moment. Ugh. It was such a long walk home. Maybe she should have grabbed a taxi after all; but now she was halfway down the alley, and it seemed to make as much sense to keep going forward as to go back…

Isabella moved to push off the wall, but then froze.

There were two people on the ground in front of her, right on the other side of the crates, across the alley against the other wall.

Isabella swallowed. "S-sorry," she stuttered out first, thinking she was intruding – it looked like the two of them were spooning each other, maybe to keep warm. They were probably homeless, she thought. There was barely any light in the alley except what came from the lights of the streets at either end, and Isabella strained her eyes in the darkness – but what was strange was, they hadn't responded or reacted in any way to what she'd said.

She took a small step towards them, wondering if they needed anything. If they had even heard her. If they were asleep, she should just keep walking and get out of there instead of disturbing them. But if you were sleeping in an alley, wouldn't you be so alert you'd wake at any sound…?

Isabella stepped closer again, and then…

Oh, God!

She recoiled backwards, almost toppling the stack of crates again. Blood! She was sure of it! There was blood on the young woman's face, and… she rooted around desperately in her purse for her cell phone, grabbing it and switching on the flashlight, and then –

Dead. She was dead.

The people Isabella had thought were sleeping were dead.

She moved the beam of light with a shaking hand onto the second person, the man as she'd thought, but – but, no, it wasn't a man at all, and he wasn't dead – he was –

He wasn't even human. He was a mannequin, like the kind you saw in clothing stores.

The dead woman was being cradled by a mannequin.

Isabella stumbled backwards two more steps, screamed, and threw up against the wall.

CHAPTER TWO

Laura Frost tried to center herself, to get some kind of stability into her hands so they wouldn't shake so much. She flipped down the overhead sun visor and checked her makeup in the mirror, then flipped it back up out of the way. She looked fine. Her blonde hair was neatly tied back, and the red lipstick she'd chosen as a kind of power move to reinforce herself was intact.

She just wasn't sure it was working.

She looked down at her hands holding the car keys, one of them still bandaged from the burns she'd sustained to the side of it two cases ago, and sighed. This was stupid. She wasn't going to get anywhere sitting in the car. She had to get out. Go into the café. Meet him.

She'd spent her whole life trying to find another person who had real, bona fide psychic visions like she did, and now that one had found her, she was too nervous to go and see him.

That was true irony, wasn't it?

She took another deep breath and this time, an image of her daughter's face floated into her head. Lacey. Her little girl was only five. She looked to Laura as a role model, someone who showed her how to live. Laura wanted to set the example that you had to be brave, take life by the reins, and never allow it to beat you down – the way it had when she'd succumbed to alcoholism and nearly lost Lacey in the first place.

No, Laura needed to be brave. She got out of the car and walked resolutely towards the café, trying to ignore the way her legs felt, like they were going to give way. She headed inside, glancing around for only a moment before seeing him sitting at the other end of the café in a booth that was right in the far corner. He saw her looking and raised a hand, and now she had no choice but to go over to him.

Zachariah Kingston. She'd had time to look into him, since he turned up at her apartment unannounced in the middle of the night. That was why she'd asked him to meet her today, after asking him a few questions that night to make sure he really was a psychic like he claimed to be. She'd seen her fair share of charlatans, after all. She wasn't about to get caught out by another one.

She had asked him to leave then and meet her later under the pretext of it being a late night, but the reality was she'd wanted to look his name up in all systems the FBI had access to, to make sure there was nothing on his record that would serve as a red flag.

And there was nothing. Not a parking ticket, not a caution for jaywalking, not a single instance in which he'd been taken in for questioning even as a witness.

Which, in itself, somehow, only served to make her more suspicious.

"Laura," he said, warmly, as she approached. His voice matched his appearance, with a kindly, grandfatherly face framed by white hair. He was still slim and fit, though, and his blue eyes had a twinkle to them that made him seem younger than he looked.

"Zachariah," Laura said cautiously, taking a seat opposite him and sliding across the booth. Not too far. She wanted to be able to make a quick exit if necessary.

"Zach, please," he said, making a small movement of wry self-deprecation with his mouth. "The only people who call me Zachariah are my doctor and my mother, and I'll be honest with you – I haven't seen either of them in years."

Laura's mind was working overtime, analyzing and over-analyzing. He hadn't seen his mother in a long while – well, at his age, that probably meant she had passed away. But the doctor? Was he trying to tell her that he was in excellent health? That he was poor, unable to afford insurance and therefore getting by and struggling on his own like so many people were forced to? Something more sinister that she hadn't worked out yet?

Or, was she being too much of an FBI agent – and he was really just telling her that he hadn't seen his doctor or his mother for years and he felt the use of his full name was too formal?

"Zach," she conceded, figuring it was better to play ball until she could figure out more about him. She wasn't sure how to start the conversation, now she was there. What did she say? There was so much she needed to know. Starting with niceties felt fake when she didn't really care yet – she was still too preoccupied with figuring out if he had an ulterior motive.

"I can't believe I've finally found you," he said, his eyes creasing and his face relaxing into a relieved smile. He shook his head, wiping a finger under one of his eyes – whether to wipe away a tear or show that he couldn't believe what he was seeing, Laura didn't know.

That was a completely different tone than what she had expected.

"You've been looking for me for a long time?" she asked. When he'd turned up at her apartment, they hadn't gone much into it. She'd just asked him to prove that he really was psychic by telling her something he wouldn't have known otherwise, which he had, and then asked him a lot of pointed questions about who he was.

"Not for you, precisely, but for someone like you," he said, waving a hand in her direction that he then turned towards himself. "Someone like me. Someone who could do what I could do. It's been a lifetime's search. I always felt that I couldn't be the only one – but until now, I never found a single other person."

Laura took this in for a moment, blinking. A whole lifetime. She'd also spent a long time searching, but he was older than her. If he'd gone all this time and never found anyone else…

What if they were the only two people out there?

It should have made her feel hope that she could find another. Maybe it would feel that way later, when she had processed everything. For now, though, all she could focus on was the fact that it seemed too desperate. Just two of them, after a whole lifetime. Not exactly the community of like-skilled individuals who could help her learn everything about her ability that she really craved.

Still. Maybe it would be enough.

Maybe he could teach her what she needed to know.

"Why me?" she asked. "You said you had a vision which led you to me. Why do you think that happened? Why me, why here, why now?"

Zach leaned his chin on his hands, clasped together with his elbows on the table, and seemed to muse on the question for a moment. "It's hard to say," he said. "I didn't really get any clear information from the vision – just where you were and where I could find you. I don't know if there's a reason that I get certain visions at certain times, but these ones showed me what you could do and then led me to you, in a sequence."

"Explain," Laura said, staring at him intently.

"Can I get you some coffee?"

Both of them jumped, looking up to see a bored-looking waitress staring down at them. She was overweight and dressed in a frumpy uniform, her hair piled messily on her head, grays breaking through the mahogany color she obviously dyed it.

"Um, yes," Laura said, scrambling for a thought. She'd forgotten where they were. What people did there. "And a couple of slices of toast, please."

"I'll have a stack of pancakes," Zach said with a smile, as if he was already pleased just imagining his order. "And a coffee too. Laura, are you sure you don't want pancakes? I'm getting this."

Laura shook her head no. It wasn't the cost of the pancakes that bothered her. She didn't want to stay here too long, and she definitely didn't want to eat something that would sit heavy in her stomach. She needed to stay alert.

"Alright, then," the waitress said, pouring them both out a coffee at the table and then wandering off. Laura tried to make a mental note that she was going to return with the food. It would be a good idea not to say anything incriminating or weird when the waitress was bound to drop by.

"I'm explaining," Zach said, tapping the table as if remembering where they'd left off. "Right. Well, I first saw you solving a case – you were phasing out, having a vision, and then when you came out of it I saw you'd got some kind of idea. You were looking for a man, and you knew who he was. I saw it in your face. That kind of… the spacing out for a split second, the new realization, the figuring out how to conceal it. I know that look. I've worn it enough times over my life."

Laura nodded. So far, it made sense. That must have been during the case she'd just come home from, where a man who heard the voice of his ancestor in his head was killing modern-day descendants of the man who had killed his family. A complicated case – one she would have been a long way from solving if it hadn't been for the visions giving her a nudge in the right direction.

"Then, I saw another vision of you getting off a plane at the airport here in Washington, D.C.," Zach continued. "After that, a vision of you entering your home. It was a very immediate vision – my head pounded afterwards. I knew you were there and you'd be ready for me when I knocked on the door."

Laura nodded. Much of it was similar to what she'd already heard from him when he showed up and she needed proof of his abilities – but to hear it all explained in full made so much more sense. It was the same way that her visions worked.

"The headaches," she said, leaving it as an open question. She felt almost shy, strangely. Talking about a deeply-held secret she'd only ever spilled to one person in her life, and now finding someone who could identify with what she was saying – it felt truly strange.

"Yes, with every vision," Zach nodded. "It's a pain, but I can tell the timing of the vision by the severity of the headache. A light ache means it's not going to happen too soon, and a migraine means it's happening right now. Is it the same for you?"

Laura nodded slowly, looking down into her mug of coffee. "Yes, it's the same. It's funny how you get used to that constant pain."

They were interrupted again by the waitress, who placed down two plates in front of them: two slices of dry toast with a pack of butter on the side for Laura, and a pile of pancakes with a jug of maple syrup for Zach. Laura busied herself with scraping a thin quantity of butter onto the bread, even though she wasn't fully sure she wanted to eat it after all.

"Constant?"

When she looked up, Zach had a strange expression on his face, kind of querying.

"Yes," she said. "There's so little time between the visions – multiple a day usually, and then only a short while between the cases when I might drop down to one a day or one every two days. Then I'm back on the road and it starts again."

Zach frowned, re-steepling his hands thoughtfully. "You seek out the visions?" he asked. "I mean, you try to trigger them on purpose?"

"Yes, of course," Laura frowned, but a moment later, the reality of the situation became clear to her. A terrible vision of the future, something you couldn't control or always understand, that brought on pain – why would you want to embrace that, unless you had a very good reason? "I mean, being an FBI agent – the visions help."

"Right," Zach nodded. He gave a light shrug. "Unfortunately, I've only had a few occasions in my life when it was useful to have these visions of mine. Most of the time, all they have done was to make me aware of a disaster I couldn't prevent. Although I am still proud of the fact that I convinced my late wife, who passed away a few years ago now, not to book a vacation to New York back in September 2001."

Laura blinked at him. "You knew about the Twin Towers?"

He nodded sadly. "I did. I saw it before everyone else. It was truly horrific."

"And you didn't try to warn anyone else?" Laura demanded. A sense of anger flared in her. The senseless loss of life. Could it have been prevented? She'd never been physically connected to anyone in the attacks, and she hadn't seen it in advance herself.

"Who would have believed me?" Zach asked softly. "A high school English teacher from some nowhere town – someone with no proof, no details. Just the knowledge that an explosion would happen *somehow, sometime*. I couldn't have warned anyone even if I thought I had a chance of being heard."

Laura tried to swallow down the indignation that wanted to overwhelm her. He was right, of course. And how many times had she been in a similar situation – knowing something would happen but powerless to really do anything about it? Even her own father's death from cancer had been something she had seen before it happened.

"What were the other times?" she asked, instead of continuing to argue.

"Well, one of them was a little darker," Zach said. A wry smile passed his lips, perhaps at the knowledge that 9/11 had been dark enough. "As I say, I was a high school teacher. One night I had a terrible vision of one of my female students being attacked on the school premises after hours. I realized she was signed up for a club, so I made sure to pretend I was marking papers at the school the next day and happened to hang around where the club took place as the students were leaving. I was able to step in and prevent it from happening. Of course, no one knew I had prevented it – but the man responsible was a fellow teacher, and with that knowledge, I was able to start watching him more closely. Before the end of the school year he'd been arrested and sentenced to jail time for his interest in violent films featuring young children."

Laura felt something stir inside her heart. Although the age group was different, she'd also used her visions to protect a young girl from an abuser – little Amy Fallow, whose violent father had been poised to take her life. The fact that Zach had used his visions to undertake similar protective work put her more at ease in his presence.

"What do you think drives all of this?" Laura asked. "I know I use my visions to solve crimes and catch killers, but is that why I have them? Is there some kind of greater purpose to all of this, or is it just random? Why would we have these visions in the first place?"

Zach shook his head. "Your guess is as good as mine," he said. "I've never been able to figure it out. At times it feels like a blessing, at times a curse. But as to a deeper meaning, I've no idea."

Laura nodded slowly. She took one bite of her toast and then put it down, finding she didn't have much of an appetite. Zach picked up his own cutlery as if that was permission, and started to make his way through the considerable stack of pancakes.

She considered him while he tucked in, taking a sip of her coffee instead of eating more. He was benign enough, she thought. There was nothing threatening about him, from his avuncular manner to his grandfatherly appearance. If he'd dedicated his life to teaching children, that was as much a service as the one she provided. Perhaps he was someone she could trust.

And even if she couldn't trust him, they had a lot in common – and he could tell her a lot about the things she could do.

Laura checked her watch. It was halfway through the morning already, and she felt drained from their conversation. Even though she'd been waiting to meet someone like Zach for a long time, this was a lot to take in – and she still wasn't sure she had processed it properly. She needed time to marshal her thoughts, to figure out what to ask him, what to talk about. She needed time to clear her head before she got overwhelmed and started feeling like she needed a drink again.

"I'm going to have to head out," she said, pushing her toast to one side. "We should meet and talk again soon. You have my number?"

Zach nodded. "And you have mine," he said. "I'm an old man, Laura. Retired, no wife, my children grown and leading their own lives. I'm at your disposal. You call me when you want to talk again."

Laura nodded. "I will," she said, which was a promise.

She got up, turning to face the road and her car again. She had another person to see today, and she didn't want to wait around too long before she saw him – because, as strange as it was to admit it to herself, she needed him just then.

CHAPTER THREE

Laura walked through the smart reception of the hospital, feeling like she was entering some start-up's swanky office block rather than a medical facility. The place where Chris Fallow had chosen to practice medicine, since returning from his work with Médecins Sans Frontiers, was perhaps the opposite of that charitable work. Slick, state-of-the-art, and definitely not affordable for the masses.

The fact that he took a designated one patient a week from the inner-city hospital who wouldn't have been able to make their insurance payments there, just to help save a life, was the only thing that made her feel comfortable with it all – the only thing that made her secure in the knowledge of how different he was from his violent brother, Governor Fallow. Now that he was Amy's guardian, being sure that he was not just about money and appearance had been one of Laura's first concerns.

She walked right past the desk with only a smile and a wave to the woman behind it, who returned the gesture and flagged her right on through. Chris always took a short break at this time of day, usually to go over paperwork and make sure he was up to date with the admin of his job. When she wasn't out on a case, Laura knew she could come here easily and find him.

"Hey," he said, looking up with a grin when she entered his office and then standing up. "Laura! I didn't know you were coming."

"I wasn't sure I'd have time," she said, walking right to his open arms and receiving his kiss of hello. The office matched him: modern, light, and airy, but not too stuffy. There were little touches here and there, like a framed card drawn by a young child to thank him for helping to save their father's life during his work in Africa, that made it clear this was not the office of the average cardiologist.

"Well, it's good to see you," he said, smiling down at her from his slightly taller height. His brown eyes were full of affection, a look she could never imagine seeing on his brother's face. "A very welcome change to staring at the paperwork, anyway."

Laura chuckled. "I brought your gym bag," she said. "You left it at my place yesterday."

"Oh!" Chris exclaimed, taking it from her hand. "I wondered why it wasn't in my car. And why you had it. For a moment when you came in, I thought Gina had just given it to you on your way in."

Laura laughed. Gina, out in reception, had been flipping through a magazine – Laura doubted she would even have noticed the presence of the bag. "No, it was behind my sofa. You should really leave it somewhere you can see it when you're on the way out, so you don't forget."

"I will," Chris said, and leaned down to kiss her again. "Still, I don't mind the excuse of having you come over here in the middle of the day. And I didn't mind the rest this morning either, when I got to the gym and realized I was going to just have to come to the office early instead. I had a quick nap on my couch."

Laura shook her head in amusement. "Did I really wear you out that much?" she asked. "You're a lightweight."

"Hey!" Chris exclaimed in mock hurt, leading her over to the sofa so they could both sit down together. "I'm a single dad, you know. Having the night off while Amy was staying at a friend's house was the only break I got this week. It's not my fault my stamina might be a bit, well, suffering."

"The lucky thing is, I didn't have any problem with your stamina," Laura grinned. They'd had a good night, after all. It was only the fact she knew she was meeting Zach in the morning that had cast a shadow over anything, but she hadn't been able to mention anything about that to Chris.

How could she? He had no idea about her abilities. The only person who did know was her partner at the FBI, Nate – and that was only a very recent development. There was a part of her that wanted to tell him, now that their relationship was getting more involved, but…

She'd only just learned to trust her partner of several years of close work. Trusting Chris might not take as long, but she definitely wasn't ready for it yet.

Not given the risk that it could destroy their relationship before it even fully blossomed.

"You didn't?" he asked. There was a little hesitance in his voice even as he sat, as if he wasn't sure about the question he was going to ask. "Only, you did seem a little distracted. Normally, I wouldn't take it personally – but I thought you'd wrapped up your last case and sorted everything out with Nate."

"I did," Laura nodded, inwardly cursing herself. Evidently, she hadn't done a good enough job of hiding her inner emotions. "I was just a little tired, myself. That's all."

Chris nodded. At least he seemed to be convinced easily enough. "So, what about this weekend?" he asked. "Still on for the girls' playdate?"

"Of course," Laura smiled. Amy and her own daughter, Lacey, had become fast friends. They would probably have led their own miniature revolution if either she or Chris tried to cancel their weekly visits. For a five-year-old and a six-year-old, they had a lot of foot-stomping power between them.

"Did you want to stay a little later?" he asked. "I was thinking we could make a full weekend of it and let the girls have a sleepover. And, you know. So could we. If you wanted."

Laura smiled. "Yes, that would be great," she said, although she was inwardly marking off those days on her internal calendar as dates on which she would not be able to secretly meet with Zach again. Chris might find it suspicious if she snuck off halfway through the weekend to meet a strange man who she wasn't willing to tell him anything about. "I'll have to check with Marcus. He might not be okay with Amy staying over at another man's house, and I don't want to cause an argument by doing it without permission. She's bound to say something, isn't she?"

Chris nodded. He seemed a tiny bit crestfallen about the idea they might not be able to go ahead with it, but of course he had to accept that Lacey's father would have a say in things. Even though Laura and Marcus were long since divorced, he had full custody – and she only had visitation rights. She may not have been happy about it, but he had the final say over where Lacey did and didn't go, and it had to remain that way until one day she might be able to get herself a better custody agreement.

She'd have loved to have her daughter full-time again – but since that would also represent a huge upheaval in Lacey's life, she didn't want to push it just for her own sake.

"Well, enough about me," he said, even though they hadn't really been talking about him at all. "I've had a boring morning. What about you? How do you spend your time when you're between cases? Are you in the office today?"

"No, thank God," Laura said. "I've finished all my paperwork since the last case, so I managed to fit in a day off."

"You didn't just sleep in all morning, did you?" Chris teased. "If you did, I'm going to have to demand an apology for making me feel bad about skipping the gym!"

"No, no," Laura laughed, but she knew she couldn't tell him the truth. The lie came out of her mouth almost automatically. "I was just doing some chores, you know. General to-do list stuff that doesn't get done when I'm working. I've got some grocery shopping planned for after this."

"So exciting and glamorous," Chris said with a grin. "You know, I don't actually have an appointment for another half-hour. You can always stay with me a little later, if you think your groceries can wait a bit."

"I just might," Laura smiled. It was good to take time out from her job, which constantly threatened to consumer her whole life. If it weren't for Lacey and Chris, Laura had no doubt the job would *be* her life. She would have probably ended up going into the office today even though she had nothing to do, offering to help out someone else with their case or something. That was how some agents ended up – so dedicated to the work that there was no room for anything else. She knew more than a few colleagues who were divorced, just like she was herself.

Though, in her case, it had been the alcohol abuse that had driven Marcus away, not the long hours of work.

Chris opened his mouth to say something about a patient he'd been working with, but he didn't even get through a full sentence before Laura's phone started buzzing in her pocket, making her quickly fumble to get it out and check the screen.

"Sorry," she said, and winced. "I think they heard us. It's my boss."

Chris sighed, leaning back and taking his arm from behind her shoulders so she was free to escape. "Go ahead," he said, with a weary smile. The kind of look that said, 'I wish you didn't have to go, but I get it.' After all, the nature of his own job meant he knew all about getting called up at the last minute to deal with an emergency.

Laura leaned down and kissed him on the forehead, then answered the phone as she walked out of his office with a wave. "Special Agent Frost."

"Ah, Laura," Division Chief Rondelle's distinctive sharp tones came over the speaker. "I'm glad I've caught you. I know it's your day off, but…"

"Don't tell me," Laura said, flashing a smile at Gina on the way out. "You want me to come in so you can brief me on a new case."

"Got it in one," Rondelle said. "Can I bribe you with the fact that Nate is also coming in and this will be your first case back together as partners again?"

"Bribe accepted," Laura sighed, ending the call in favor of hustling to her car so she could get to the FBI headquarters faster.

CHAPTER FOUR

Laura rushed along the corridor, seeing Nate right up ahead of her and wishing she had slightly longer legs to allow her to catch up. At the sound of her shoes on the floorboards he glanced over his shoulder and then slowed his steps, waiting for her.

"Good timing," he said, as she caught up. He looked like himself, like she could always rely on him to be: tall, Black, and handsome, with the kind of muscles that didn't occur too often outside of law enforcement and Hollywood stars. Not all FBI agents spent half their downtime in the gym, but Nate was one of the ones who did, and it meant he was always someone who could be relied upon for the heavy lifting.

He was even casual, laidback, not at all surprised or awkward about seeing her here in the hall on the way to Rondelle's door. He must have known she would be on the way, but that wasn't why she would expect him to react a little differently than he used to.

They hadn't spoken much lately. There had been their grand falling-out, in which he got to a breaking point about whatever she'd been hiding from him for years and called it quits on their working relationship. Then there was the subsequent falling-out in which she told him the truth about her abilities and he refused to believe her. Finally, there had been the awkward distance between them when he did believe her but didn't know how to accept it.

But now here they were, back together for their first case since all of that, and he was looking at her like they'd been working together just like normal as recently as yesterday.

"Yeah," was the incredibly articulate answer that Laura managed to wring out of her brain before it shut down. It was probably for the best – she didn't want to say something that would make the awkwardness return.

"You know anything about the case yet?" Nate asked, as they started walking down the hall again.

Laura shook her head. "When he called, I just told him I'd get over here quick to cut down on the delay."

Nate shrugged. They were approaching the door now. "Guess we're about to find out," he said, and knocked.

They heard the muffled but still infinitely audible voice of Rondelle bidding them to enter, and Nate turned the handle before stepping aside to let Laura in before him. She did so, ducking under his outstretched arm to find Rondelle eyeing them both with dry amusement.

"The dream team back together again," he said, grabbing a file from a stack on the side of his desk and opening it to check the contents before tossing it forward. Laura moved to grab it before it slid off the edge of the desk and onto the floor, flipping it open reflexively and holding it where she and Nate could both read it. "This one isn't too far from home, you'll be pleased to know. No flights – you can drive over there within a few hours. You're headed to Mariesville."

"Are we still getting a hotel?" Nate asked. "It's a long drive to make back every night when we never know if we'll be called back for new evidence."

"I have booked a *motel* for you within the city limits," Rondelle said, tilting his head along with the emphasis to stress the downgrade. "It's a bit of a curious case. Not that there's such a thing as a 'normal' murder, when it comes to you two. You know I like to make sure I have my best agents tackling the weird ones."

"So grateful for that," Laura muttered, flipping through the pages loosely until she came to a photograph. There were a few of them, part of the limited materials they had available to them before they actually got on the ground and saw what the local cops were dealing with. It *was* pretty odd, she'd give Rondelle that. There was a female corpse in the photograph, quite clearly positioned with a mannequin behind her as though they were spooning.

"Is that a mannequin?" Nate asked, with a look of disgust. It was true that they always dealt with the odd cases – but that didn't mean each new one wasn't shocking. That each new one didn't erode their faith in humanity just that little bit more.

"I'm afraid it is," Rondelle replied. "This is the second such case which has come up for them in as many days. The mannequin element is very interesting, but it's also a signature – and I'm sure I don't need to tell you that it's the kind of signature that often points to a serial killer in the making. To put it bluntly, if you don't get over there and stop this from turning into a rampage, I believe the victim count could start to spiral rapidly over the next few weeks."

Laura sighed. Wasn't it always like that? That was part of the curse of being one of the best-performing agents in the FBI. With every difficult case they solved, it made it that much more certain that they would be assigned to the next difficult one as well.

"Look, I won't go too deep into it," Rondelle said. "You know the drill, and I'd rather have you get over there soon. The locals are way out of their depth, and if you don't get over there fast, I'm afraid we might end up seeing some lost opportunities to nip this in the bud before he really gets started."

"Right," Laura said, and looked up at Nate as she closed the file. "Guess we'd better get on the road, then, hey? Are we taking your car, or mine?"

Nate gave her a horrified look. "You think I'm driving my car hours across country to a crime scene?" he asked, and she laughed.

With any luck, it seemed like things between them were going right back to normal – which was perfect, because any awkwardness would have got in the way of their investigation, and it sounded like they had lives to save.

***

Laura yawned and reached for the file, tucked up high on the dash, pulling it down to take a look at it. "Right. Better start taking a look at these details," she suggested.

"Hit me with them," Nate agreed, keeping his eyes on the road. In the end, they'd agreed on neutral ground: taking one of the FBI cars from the compound and leaving both of their own behind. It was just like having a hired car, except there was considerably more paperwork. At least their own vehicles wouldn't take the brunt of what would hopefully be limited to a few days of driving around madly.

"Right," Laura said again, as she tried to scan down the first page to grab the salient information so she could start translating that into narration. "So, we've got two victims already, like Rondelle said. The first one found was a man. He was also with a mannequin. Neither of the victims have any kind of link between them that the local PD could find, and at first glance their profiles are pretty disparate. Different ages, home addresses aren't close by, different body statistics. Nothing that immediately jumps out as a pattern."

"Wonderful," Nate said with heavy sarcasm. "I do love it when they give us a challenge. Where were they found?"

Laura turned the page. "Our male victim, John Wiggins, was found in an alleyway. It was a secluded spot, and he was found in the morning, with the initial report suggesting he was left there all night. Then the second victim, Kenya Lankenua, also in an alleyway but in a different part of town. She was found late last night – it looks as though she may have been discovered not long after being left there, by a young woman who was just stumbling home from a bar."

"Method of killing?" Nate asked. It was like he was ticking off a mental list of the important facts – which, to be fair, he maybe was.

Laura consulted the file. "Blow to the back of the head with a heavy object, in both cases. Blunt force trauma."

Nate grunted in response, and then there was a period of silence. Laura flipped through the rest of the file and found nothing worth mentioning, shoving it back up onto the dashboard.

They were out of D.C. now, out on a nice smooth and open road that would take them a long way before they needed to think too much about directions or turn-offs. Nothing to focus on.

Nothing to talk about.

Laura cleared her throat quietly and looked out of the windscreen. Only another three hours to go before they arrived.

They would be able to think of something to fill the silence before then, right?

"So," she started abruptly, right at the same time that Nate said "Hey," leaving them both silent again as they each waited for the other continue. They shared an awkward chuckle that broke some of the ice, though not enough for Laura to feel as though it wouldn't reform easily.

"Um, you go," she said, gesturing loosely towards him.

"It was nothing," Nate said, shaking his head. "I was just wondering how things are going with that doctor."

"Oh, great," Laura said, smiling briefly. It was kind of odd for them to talk about it. When they'd first partnered up, Laura had been in the throes of divorce. She hadn't dated anyone since then – not until Chris. There hadn't been anyone for her to tell Nate about, and it wasn't as though she'd spoken much about Chris either, given the recent turmoil between them. "If we can get this case wrapped up before the weekend, we're hoping to spend it together with our girls."

Nate smiled without looking away from the road. "Sounds very domestic."

Laura hadn't meant it to sound like that. It was true, though, she supposed. That was the reality of it when you had a couple of kindergarteners in tow at all times. Even if she wanted their relationship to be sexy and exciting and romantic, it was kind of destined to be – yes, domestic.

"We have a lot of fun," she said, which came out as more defensive than she had intended.

"Have you, um," Nate started, and then stopped.

"What?" Laura asked. There was only one end she could think of for that sentence, but since Nate wasn't a teenage girl, she was sure she must have guessed wrong.

"Had any visions about him?"

That was not what she had expected at all.

Laura looked down at her hands. Why did it feel so uncomfortable to talk about this? "No," she said, at length. "No, I haven't."

"Is that a good sign?" Nate glanced at her for a moment and then back at the road.

"It's not anything," Laura said. "I don't control when the visions come and I don't really think there's any particular rule about when or why they happen. At least, I haven't noticed one in all these years. It could mean that I'm just not seeing the bad thing that's about to happen."

"Right." Nate said. There was an uncomfortably long pause, then: "So you haven't seen that he's going to die, like you saw with me?"

"No," Laura said immediately. "No, I haven't. The shadow of death is – it's very rare. I probably come into contact with people all the time and never see anything threatening them, even though they might die not too long after."

"That's kind of creepy to think about," Nate said, and Laura regretted bringing it up.

God, she wished this elephant wasn't in the room. Even when it wasn't an elephant anymore because they were addressing it directly, it seemed to be hanging over their heads and changing every dynamic between them.

She just wanted it to feel the way it had before all of this. When they were just partners. Yes, she'd had to hide a huge part of herself from him – but at least it hadn't been awkward most of the time.

She stared out of the window, not sure what to say next or where to take the conversation. What was she going to ask him about? His love life? It had been weird enough talking about hers, and last she knew, he was still in the recovery period after his longest-lasting girlfriend had broken it off. What he'd been up to lately? Probably researching the place he was supposed to transfer to when he decided not to be her partner anymore, and looking for a new place to live. The cases she'd worked on lately? That would just be a reminder of the fact that they hadn't been working on them together.

And what else was there?

Was she supposed to start telling him all about Zach – a new discovery she hadn't even really processed or understood herself yet?

"I didn't really mean creepy," Nate said, after another long silence. He sounded guilty, like he'd messed up. But he hadn't messed up. It was Laura who had messed up. She was the one making all the problems here. If she just didn't have this ability in the first place, none of this would have happened. "It's just weird to think about. I'm still getting used to it."

"I know," Laura said quietly. "I'm sorry I dumped all this on you."

"I asked you to," Nate pointed out. "I wanted to know so that we could work together better as partners. I still feel that way. It's a good thing that I know, so I can help you out with it and you don't have to pretend about your leads anymore. We're going to be better at solving this case."

"Yeah," Laura agreed, even though she had so many doubts spiraling through her head that it was a wonder he couldn't hear them out loud.

For a start, her visions hadn't exactly been playing ball lately. She'd started seeing visions of the past, not the future, and she had no idea why. She'd been unable to trigger the visions when she needed them. She'd seen the same thing over and over in tiny, unreadable fragments, instead of getting new insights that would help her progress her understanding of the case. She'd even had visions trigger in instances that she couldn't explain how or why they'd set off. None of it made sense anymore.

She had no idea what was going on with her head or why, and she couldn't be sure that anything she saw was actually going to help her with the case.

But that was something she was going to keep to herself, because she didn't want Nate to realize that not only had she thrust a monumental secret on him and asked him to keep it from their superiors – but she'd also done it at a time when her visions were less reliable than they'd ever been.

She just had to hope that by some miracle, everything worked the way it was supposed to this time – and they caught the killer fast, so Nate could see he'd made the right choice to come back as her partner.

CHAPTER FIVE

Laura stretched her arms above her head, getting out of the car and then rubbing the aching muscles in her shoulders. There was something about sitting in a car for hours that made you feel cramped and sore in ways that just sitting in a chair for hours didn't. Maybe it was the lack of freedom, the knowledge that you couldn't get up and move even if you wanted to.

Or maybe it was the tension that had simmered in the air between Laura and Nate for the whole journey to Mariesville that had her feeling stiff and sore.

"This must be it," Nate said, nodding a short way down the road. It was unmistakable: crime scene tape across the entrance to the alleyway, a police officer in uniform standing against it with sunglasses covering his eyes and his arms crossed over his chest, and at least three marked and unmarked vehicles that Laura would have bet a lot of money were law enforcement.

Laura shaded her eyes for a moment and nodded in the same direction. "Guess we'll have to head inside the alley to see if we can spot some kind of chief around here."

Nate nodded in response, already starting to lead the way. They had their badges out and ready to show the cop guarding the tape by the time they had walked over to him, and he nodded them through with only a spark of interest at the FBI insignia. He must have already heard the FBI were on their way.

It was obvious as soon as they entered the alley that the person in charge was standing right in the middle of the long, narrow space, looking down at something on the floor with his hands on his hips. He was talking with what looked like someone from the forensics staff in white overalls, both of them gesturing towards a spot on the ground a few times as Laura and Nate walked over.

Before they were in earshot of the quietly-spoken conversation, the Captain turned and looked at them. He wore the blue uniform of the police force, the insignia of his rank clearly visible and his hat tucked under his arm. He was probably in his fifties, with black hair that was graying at the temples and piercingly sharp blue eyes that made Laura shiver involuntarily. He was not the kind of detective she would have liked to go up against if she was a criminal, herself. She imagined he would be quite effective in the interrogation room.

"Agents," he called out, obviously clocking them before they had the chance to introduce themselves. "We're just looking over the scene. I'm afraid you've missed the body."

"That's alright." Nate came to a stop in front of the Captain first, holding out a hand to shake. "Special Agent Nathaniel Lavoie."

"Special Agent Laura Frost," Laura added, when Nate made a slight gesture in her direction to prompt her instead of saying the words himself.

The Captain nodded, shaking Nate's hand and then Laura's. "Captain Ortega," he said. "I take it you're here to see what we already know about the victim."

"Yes, please," Nate said agreeably. He and Laura turned when Ortega did, looking down at the empty space in the alleyway which had clearly been home to a body not long before, conspicuous by its absence.

"Well, I can say it's not much," Ortega sighed, in a matter-of-fact way. "We've already processed the body and the mannequin through the lab – it's been top priority. There's not a lot of physical evidence that we can use. The mannequin was wiped totally clean, probably cleaner than it even was in the factory after it was made. There aren't any marks on it indicating where it was manufactured either, so we're not able to use that to track down the source. Looks like the killer wore gloves – we haven't found any fingerprints or DNA traces on the body or anything else that we could definitively narrow down to the killer. Of course, the public nature of this spot means it's tough to use much of what's here – any defense attorney worth their name would be able to argue that someone might have walked through here and touched those crates or those garbage bags for any reason."

Laura nodded. "What do we know about the cause of death? Our report says blunt force trauma. You have anything more specific than that yet?"

Ortega shook his head. "We haven't found a weapon or any indication from the wound itself as to the shape of the weapon," he said. "Just blunt object is what they're telling me. But there is one interesting thing about the head wound."

"Oh?" Laura asked.

Ortega pointed to the scene left behind in the wake of the body. "You see the blood? That would have pooled out from the head wound. There isn't any evidence of a blood trail or any drips that we've found coming into or out of the alley, and due to the amount of blood here, what I understand is that the victim cannot have been killed very far from here. In fact, it's possible or even likely that she was killed right here in the alley and then laid down. If she was killed elsewhere and then moved here, we'd see a lot less blood."

"But no spray pattern," Nate said, glancing around.

Ortega nodded. "That about sums it up. Lots of reasons why there might not be a spray pattern, of course. Something to do with the nature of the blunt object. Maybe the spray hit the killer and so their body blocked it from landing on other objects around them. Maybe the impact of the wound did not actually cause an initial blood spray, so to speak, but the blood began to pour out in earnest when she was then immediately laid down and gravity got to work. The first victim has a similar story – no blood spray, no indication of where the crime was committed."

"This is a meticulous kind of work," Nate said thoughtfully. "The whole scene with the mannequin had to be thought out carefully, especially to make sure there was no forensic evidence left behind. It looks to me as though he would have had to bring the victim here specifically, with everything already set up and waiting for her. That's the only way it would make sense to me."

Laura nodded in agreement. "Having to set all this up, maybe dragging a mannequin out of a parked car and bringing it here, would be a big risk if you were having to rush because the body was already in position. Stressful. I would imagine someone facing those circumstances would probably make more mistakes, leave something behind. The cleanliness of the scene itself suggests that rushing wasn't much of an issue. I think you're right. This was all in place, waiting for her."

"So, then, the question is whether she was the intended victim all along, or just the first person to walk into his field of opportunity," Nate said. "What do we know about her – the victim?"

Ortega gestured vaguely towards where the body would have been. "Kenya Lankenua. You've seen the pictures?"

Nate drew out the file from his pocket, unfolding it from the way he'd had to make it fit the space. He pulled out the photographs they'd seen during their briefing with Rondelle and showed them to Ortega. It was a grotesque scene, the mannequin posed as if holding her from behind.

"She's a single, unmarried woman, early twenties, working as an office administrator for a local firm here. Neither her workplace nor her home were at all connected with the alley and there's no reason for her to walk through here for either of them, but that doesn't rule out leisure activities. Obviously we've only made a few inquiries so far, but we haven't got an account of her movements last night before she was killed. Since she lived alone and wasn't in a relationship, and didn't seem to tell her family she was planning to go out, we don't yet know what she was doing. Whether she was lured here or came here by coincidence."

"Very unhelpful," Laura said with a sigh, then flashed Ortega a wry smile so he knew it wasn't him she was annoyed with--just the data. "Alright, so this positioning is very clearly meant to send a message. She's spooning with this mannequin. What's the meaning behind that? The killer made a very strong choice to use these mannequins, meaning there was a reason behind it."

Nate looked down at the empty scene as though he could still see the victim lying there, instead of just the remnants of the pool of her blood soaked into a flat cardboard box. "Spooning suggests something romantic," he said. "There could be an element of love in this – like a spurned lover or maybe a jealous one."

"This kind of rage could point to a perceived wrongdoing on her part," Laura suggested. "She cheats, so he hits her over the head and poses her in the alleyway in an incriminating position, imagining her with the other man."

"Who's the other man?" Nate asked.

"We have the male victim," Laura shrugged. "That could be a great place to start."

"We haven't found any link between them," Ortega interjected.

Laura nodded. She didn't say it, but they would have to re-investigate everything, including whether there was any way the two victims could have been connected. While Ortega and his team must have put their best efforts forward, they had, after all, invited the FBI to help them because they knew they were out of their depth. She and Nate couldn't take anything they had found out so far for granted.

There was always a link between the victims of crimes like these. Even if it only existed in the mind of the killer. The trick was finding out what it was.

"We need to talk to her family," she said. "Get some insight from them. I'm guessing you have an officer with them already?"

Ortega nodded. "I can take you right there."

Laura drew a breath and tried to think of some way to politely tell him not to come – but Nate beat her to it. "Don't worry," he said.

"We've got our own car. Just give us the address and we'll be on our way. I'm sure you have a lot of important work to do – let us do our thing, and we'll let you do yours."

Ortega nodded curtly, then extended a hand towards their car. "I'll walk you back and get it in your GPS. I'll give you my number, too, in case you need anything."

"Great, thanks," Laura said automatically, her mind already on the next thing.

Find the link between the victims. Understand the killer. Find the killer. Stop the killer.

Easy, right?

Except their cases never were – and Laura knew they were only about to take the first step in what could turn out to be a complex and brutal case.

CHAPTER SIX

Laura watched Nate get out of the car, resting for just one moment before she got out and joined him. It felt like she was already coming out of a long week. Even though she'd managed to recover somewhat from the last case she'd been on – which wasn't always a given – there was still a lot going on. Her burned hand, which still ached whenever she accidentally brushed it against something without warning, even though it was protected by the bandages. Zach and the revelation that she wasn't the only psychic in the world. Trying to find the new balance in her dynamic with Nate.

Even though she'd longed to have him back as her partner, she was already beginning to find that she needed a moment here and there to herself to breathe. Being with him felt like hard work, in a way it never had before.

Well, not never. She had to remind herself sometimes that, once, they hadn't known each other at all. They'd had to learn to trust one another back then.

She hoped they could do it again.

Laura walked behind Nate up the short path to the front door of the property, steeling herself for another interaction now: with the grieving family of the victim. That was never easy, either. So much heavy emotion, and it could easily become rage – and it could easily be directed at anyone. That was the thing with grief. Even those who tried to help could sometimes find themselves in the firing line.

Nate knocked on the door, and it was only a brief moment before it opened to reveal a plain-clothes detective – the badge hung around his neck made him obvious. Ortega must have called ahead to tell him to expect them, because all he did was look at their outstretched badges with a glance, nod, and then beckon them in.

They emerged into a home that was almost unnaturally quiet. Laura followed the detective and then Nate to the first door on the left and was thus the last person to enter the room, only seeing the group inside once Nate had stepped aside and she could move into her own clear space. There wasn't anywhere to sit; the small sofa and one armchair were occupied by an older man and woman as well as a girl who looked to be in her late teens.

The grieving family, no doubt.

"Mr. and Mrs. Lankenua?" Nate asked. There was a slow nod from both of them, and the girl looked up dimly at him through red-rimmed eyes.

"You're the agents we were waiting for?" she asked. Even though she was the youngest person in the room, she seemed to be naturally taking control. The older couple – the parents – were subdued and numb, hands clutching one another, tracks of tears visible on their cheeks. The woman was wrapped in what looked like a traditional print, brightly colored over her dress and a wrap over her hair, somehow incongruous with the atmosphere in the house.

"Yes," Laura said, speaking up in the hopes that a female voice would be reassuring for her. "We've just arrived in town, so please forgive us if we end up asking questions that you've already answered – we want to be as thorough as possible in finding out who did this to Kenya."

"*Keen-yah,*" the girl said, correcting Laura's pronunciation. She had a stern jut to her jaw, braided hair flying about her face as she shook it warningly. "I keep trying to tell these dumb cops!"

"Precious," the mother said in a low tone, a warning.

"It's alright," Laura said. "Kenya. I apologize. We won't get it wrong again."

"Shouldn't get it wrong in the first place," Precious muttered.

Laura glanced at Nate. This wasn't a good start. The parents were obviously too numb and lost in their grief to help much – the father hadn't even really reacted to their presence yet. The sister, meanwhile, seemed to have taken a knee-jerk reaction of anger to all of this. It did happen. But maybe Laura needed to step back and let Nate deal with this, because she'd already poisoned her own image in front of the girl.

"What can you tell us about Kenya?" Nate asked, his voice gentle, very careful to get the pronunciation correct. "What was she like?"

"She was a normal woman," Precious said in a bitter tone. "Normal. She had a job. She didn't like it very much, but it paid the bills. She had friends that she spent time with. She had dreams. She was a good sister. I don't know what you can possibly want to know that could explain why someone would do this to her."

"There's never a good reason for something like this," Nate assured her. "But the killer might not see it that way. They might have convinced themselves they were doing the right thing somehow, or that they were provoked. It's our job to figure that out, so we can catch them and put them away."

"That's not going to bring my sister back, is it?" Precious spat. The mother shifted on the couch again, pressing a tissue to her forehead and squeezing her eyes shut, but she said nothing.

"No," Nate said, taking a harder tone as he moved to sit on the edge of the coffee table. It was a power play, though in opposition to the expected direction: it put his huge frame lower than Precious, made him look up towards her, gave her the dominant position. "But it might stop him from killing someone else's sister. Or brother. Or daughter, or mother. That's what we're trying to do here. The quicker we catch him and get him off the streets, the better."

Precious seemed to stumble a little on this premise, realizing it was fairly hard to argue against. She wanted to, but she floundered for a moment and then rolled her eyes. "What do you need to know?"

"Kenya's relationships," Nate said, leaning in and getting to the point now that he had her grudging permission. "Did she have a partner at all?"

Precious shook her head, glancing at her parents as if this was a secret they were not supposed to know. "Her boyfriend broke up with her last week."

Her father muttered something under his breath, something Laura couldn't understand, rolling his head from one side to the other like he couldn't bear to hear of it.

"He was a nice boy," her mother said, in a strained and almost broken voice, as if she needed to say it. Needed to reassure her husband that things were not as they seemed – that the 'boy' wasn't a predator or the one who had done this to her daughter. She had no suspicion of that, Laura could see easily. Not that it mattered. She wasn't professional law enforcement, and even if she had been, she was too close to the situation. Laura and Nate would have to make up their own minds about this boyfriend.

"What was his name?" Nate asked, looking at Precious for the answer as he had been doing so far.

"Pete Yalling," Precious said, glancing at him through round eyes as if warning him to be cautious. "She's right, though. He doesn't have anything to do with this. He was alright. They didn't even fight or anything. It was a pretty good breakup, the way Kenya told me. He suggested that they weren't the right fit for each other anymore and she agreed. No one got hurt."

"Why weren't they right? What had changed?"

Precious shrugged. "I don't know. Just grew apart, I guess. Pete's doing a master's but Kee decided to start work. Or, had to. Wasn't like she could afford to get herself in even more student debt."

Nate nodded sympathetically. "What about others?" Nate asked. "Was she back on the dating scene already? Was there maybe someone from before? Someone she'd grown interested in, or who had an interest in her that she didn't return?" Laura could feel him digging for information about the potential idea of Kenya having cheated on her boyfriend, but he couldn't come out and say it. Not to Precious. She would probably explode.

"No, there wasn't anyone," Precious said. "Kee and Pete have been a thing since forever. Since high school. She never got interested in anyone else and she kept her head down at college. They both went to the local college here, so she was with him all the time. Not like she was going to meet anyone else with him watching."

Laura made a mental note of the language, the way Precious said it. Was it just that her sister was a good girl, the kind who would never dream of cheating on a partner because it would hurt them? Or was she saying that Pete was controlling, that he wouldn't let Kenya out of his sight and got jealous if she spoke to other men? That was something to explore when they spoke to him later.

"Any disputes with friends lately? Or colleagues, at the office? Did she fall out with anyone?" Nate asked, checking off all the usual questions.

"No," Precious shrugged. "It's stupid. Kee always kept herself to herself. She was quiet. She didn't interfere in things that were none of her business, not like other people do. She didn't get into conflict. She would much rather just accept whatever someone else wanted and give in. She wouldn't get involved in office politics or fall out with a friend – that just wasn't what she was like."

Nate glanced up at Laura, checking whether she had any further questions. Laura shook her head slightly. They weren't getting a great deal of information here. It would have been ideal to hear from all members of the family, to get more insights, but Precious was the only one who was keeping it together enough to talk. Her answers were still leaning more on the verge of hostile, too, even if she was cooperating for now.

It would probably be better to come back here later if they hit a brick wall or needed more information to back up a theory.

"Alright," Nate said. He drew out a business card from his pocket and held it out to Precious, who took it cautiously as if expecting it to burst into flames. "We've got a lot of different avenues to chase down, so we're going to get moving again now and get this investigation as far as we possibly can. We'll be likely to come back and speak to you again, but in the meantime, if you think of absolutely anything that might be relevant – just give me a call. Any time. Anything. Even if it's so small you're not sure if it might be important, I want to know about it. Deal?"

Precious paused a second, then nodded once. "Alright."

It wasn't quite a promise, but it was enough.

Nate stood, nodding acknowledgement to the cop who had been left to look after the family and then turning to Laura. She murmured a goodbye and a sorry to the family as a whole and followed him out, waiting until the front door of the house closed behind them to speak again.

"So," she said. "To Pete Yalling?"

"To Pete Yalling," Nate confirmed with a grim nod, because both of them knew that when it came to young women, a boyfriend or ex was usually the strongest suspect they would have.

CHAPTER SEVEN

Laura was the one to knock this time, and when the apartment door opened almost immediately, she found her hand twitching towards her gun – but stopping just in time.

The young man who had answered her knock had done a double take when he saw who was at his door, as if he had been expecting someone else. A half-smile dropped from his face entirely when he looked between them, and then he stepped backwards, as if he was going to close the door right in her face.

"Peter Yalling?" Laura asked, raising an eyebrow.

"Yeah," he said, hesitantly, still looking between the two of them. He backed up another step. "I'm not actually interested in buying anything right now, so -"

Laura pulled her badge out of her pocket and held it up, holding back a smirk. She had no idea how he might have mistaken them for traveling salespeople. Jehovah's Witnesses, she could almost see, because of the black suits they wore. But salespeople? No, she felt they had to look at least a little smarter than that.

"Oh," he said, and then stepped back once more, going pale. "Hey, I don't know why you're here, but I haven't done anything."

"Can we come inside?" Laura asked. "My partner and I have a few questions for you in relation to an ongoing case. I think it's probably better if we can all sit down and relax."

The 'relax' part was probably a little bit too far, she had to admit. The way Pete had gone pale, she didn't think he was going to relax at all.

She had to admit, he wasn't what she had been expecting, either. Pete was definitely from a different side of the tracks compared to his ex-girlfriend. Even though he was living in a small apartment, it was well-furnished, and he was well-dressed. For a perennial student who hadn't yet finished his master's degree, it looked very nice indeed. It was nicer than Laura's apartment, actually – and though she'd lost almost everything to her alcoholism, she had begun to bounce back.

That meant that he was possibly working with more than the salary of an FBI agent – something that Laura found hard to believe if he was studying and working only part-time. He had to have inherited money, but then again he'd gone to the same school as Kenya, which didn't make sense if he was wealthy from birth...

Which left something high-income like drug dealing, unfortunately. Laura scanned the airy, bright living room as they sat down, Pete on the couch and Laura and Nate both taking armchairs. It was set up for at least four people, but he lived alone. Frequent gatherings?

"What's this about?" Pete asked, sitting on the edge of his seat, bouncing one of his legs up and down. He was nervous about something. But was it something he'd done, or just the normal kind of nerves some people felt when coming into contact with law enforcement?

"You have an ex-girlfriend," Nate began, but he didn't even get the chance to finish.

"Kee?" Pete said immediately. Laura saw him mentally correct himself, realizing that a pair of strangers wouldn't necessarily know her by her nickname. "Kenya Lankenua?"

"Yes," Laura said, watching him closely. "The two of you broke it off recently, didn't you?"

Pete frowned slightly, staring at her. "Yeah... we did, but... I'm sorry, what is this about? You want to know why I broke up with my girlfriend? What has that got to do with the FBI?"

Laura exchanged a quick glance with Nate, which only seemed to make Pete all the more nervous. He clearly didn't know. No one had told him. If they had any luck, he was going to spill what it was he had done wrong – although Laura was already getting the impression it had nothing to do with Kenya's death. He seemed truly baffled by their interest in her.

"Where were you last night?" Nate asked, flipping open his notebook to double-check the ballpark times they were looking at. "Between around eight in the evening and one in the morning."

"I was with a few friends, at a bachelor party," Pete said. "We stayed out all night, more or less. I ended up getting back here and crashing at like five this morning – I just got up."

"Were you at one of the bars in town?" Nate asked, ready to write down the name so they could check it out later.

"No, not here," Pete said. "We actually went up to Pittsburgh. Took a good couple of hours to get back here this morning with all the early rush traffic."

Ah. Now, that put a new spin on things. If he had that good of an alibi putting him far enough away that he couldn't have just nipped out from the party, killed Kenya, and got back to it before anyone noticed him gone, then he wasn't a viable suspect.

"Do you know a man named John Wiggins?" Laura asked, just in case he had some kind of connection to the first victim that would help them understand why both he and Kenya had been targeted.

"No," Pete frowned. "Who is that?"

"That doesn't matter at this time," Nate said. "Regarding Kenya, can you think of anyone who might have wanted to hurt her in any way? Someone who was angry with her or felt that she had wronged them somehow?"

Alarm blossomed across his face. He was getting it, now. It often didn't take long before they did. Being asked about where you were on a certain day, then right after about whether someone had a reason to harm your loved one – it did tend to create a mental link that connected all the dots.

"What's happened to her?" he asked, his voice going slightly hoarse. "Is Kee alright?"

"I'm afraid not, Pete," Nate said. His tone had softened. Laura knew he'd probably realized, as she had, that this man couldn't be responsible. "Kenya was found dead last night in an alleyway in the center of town, near a number of late-night bars and clubs. I'm sorry to have to tell you this, but she was murdered."

All of the remaining color drained from Pete's face, just like that. He looked like he was going to be sick. He clutched at the air for support until he found the side of the couch, and Laura found herself reaching out automatically to steady him.

The second her hand touched the bare skin of his arm, the headache pulsed and she knew she was about to see for sure whether or not Pete had anything to do with –

Laura opened her eyes on a murky scene, the edges of it swirling away into darkness, hard to hold onto. Like trying to watch a small quantity of milk swirling into coffee, trying to keep track of it as it dissipated and thinned out, disappearing into the darker liquid.

But she was there, seeing something. She was – yes, she was here, right here in the apartment, in a bedroom she'd half glimpsed through a door that was ajar as they walked down the hall.

She was here, and so was Pete. He was on the bed with someone, over them, leaning his face down to kiss them – to kiss her. He pulled back up and shifted his position, and –

Laura saw her face. Not Kenya. It was only for a glimpse, but she knew it wasn't Kenya. Then it swirled away again and she could only see part of the covers of the bed, part of Pete's torso, wisps of vision moving around and disappearing as if driven by the wind, making her feel dizzy and drunk and –

Laura blinked, pulling her hand away and then remembering to check that Pete was actually fine. Her head barely hurt at all. Not surprising, given that she had barely had a vision.

It was confused, patchy, unfocused. But she knew what she had seen. Pete sleeping with another woman, cheating on Kenya. It had to be a vision from the past – she'd seen his arm and it was blank, clean skin, where now there was a fresh-looking and sharp tattoo of a sports team logo on his forearm. A team who, Laura distantly remembered hearing at some point between the frenetic demands of her cases, had recently won a championship.

This had been a vision from only a few weeks ago, perhaps. When Kenya was still alive and the two of them were still together.

"Is there anything you can tell us about why the two of you broke up?" Laura asked, watching him closely. In the corner of her eye she saw Nate move slightly, but then stop, as if he'd forced himself to keep quiet.

"It was my idea," he said, but then shook his head. "I was stupid."

"Why?"

"Because she was incredible," Pete half-choked out, his hand gripping the side of the couch so tightly that his knuckles were white.

"No, I mean, why did you have the idea?" Laura asked, resisting the urge to roll her eyes at the obvious miscommunication.

"I felt guilty," Pete admitted. He looked up at both of them and then his face crumpled. "Oh, hell. You might as well know. I guess you'd probably find out if you wanted to, anyway. I cheated on Kee. I couldn't stay with her after that, knowing I'd been with someone else. Knowing I enjoyed it more than I did with her. But that was dumb. So dumb. I should've stayed with her – then maybe, last night..."

His face crumpled further into a half-sob, and Laura sat back in her chair. They weren't going to get anything else out of him. But this new piece of information could be useful. If it wasn't Kenya who had been cheating, but Pete, then maybe this could somehow be her connection to the killer.

Or, the other possibility: knowing that she had been cheated on, maybe she went out and sought someone to help her do the same. If so, that would explain what the killer was trying to say with his placement of the body.

"You can't think of any reason why someone might want to do this?" Nate asked. "Kenya didn't tell you of anyone acting odd, anyone mad at her? She didn't meet the girl you cheated with and have some harsh words for her, maybe?"

"No," Pete shook his head miserably. "No. I don't know why anyone would want to hurt her. She never did anything to anybody. She was sweet. She just wanted to get her head down and make some money so she could help out her family. She wouldn't even get into disputes at work because she wanted to keep her job – no one would ever have any reason to hurt her."

"That's all we need to ask you for now," Nate said. "Although, I'd appreciate getting the names of your buddies from the party so we can check your alibi. And please, if you think of anything else that could be significant – even if you're not sure about it – just get in touch with us. Anything could be that vital missing piece which leads us to the killer."

Pete nodded. "I understand," he said. His eyes strayed off to the side, focusing on something else. "God, her family. Her sister! I should do something. Send them flowers, or… I don't know…"

"We'll see ourselves out," Laura said. "Is there anyone you can call to come and stay with you? Or somewhere you can go where you won't be alone?"

Pete looked at her, and then a flash of something else came over his face – panic, she thought.

Not a second later, there was a knock at the door.

Laura remembered how he had reacted when he first saw them outside. How he'd opened the door quickly and then been shocked to see them – as if he was expecting someone else.

"Perfect timing," she said drily, getting up. She had a feeling about what she was going to see when she opened the door, and she didn't think it was going to reflect well on anyone in the situation.

This time, she led the way out of the house, seeing Nate's bemusement as he silently followed her. She opened the door and saw exactly what she had suspected.

The woman from the vision, coming here to visit Pete – probably with the intention of a repeat performance.

"I hope you have some tissues in that bag of yours," Laura quipped, stepping neatly around the young woman and out into the hall, confident now that they would be able to track her down later if there was any need to talk to her.

37

As yet, she couldn't see that there was a real link, and besides – she only knew who the woman was from a psychic vision, which wouldn't exactly hold up as a reason for questioning.

"Are you going to explain what that was about?" Nate muttered as they walked down the hall towards the elevator – and Laura almost physically gulped, knowing that now she was going to have to explain her visions to Nate in a very real and imminent way that was somehow more nerve-wracking than she had expected.

CHAPTER EIGHT

Laura got behind the wheel and then breathed, wishing she'd thought of a better way to put the conversation off than waiting until they had privacy.

Then again, she knew full well it was important that they have the conversation. It was just that the first one was going to be hard – and she hoped that somewhere, distantly down the line, it wouldn't be this awkward or stressful to go against her own nature from the last thirty years of her life and actually explain a vision.

"So?" Nate asked. "Did you see something?"

Laura nodded, starting the engine to give her hands something to do. "When I touched his hand. I told you that's how it triggers, didn't I? Through touch. Sometimes I can try and concentrate and breathe deeply and be in the moment to help it along, but I've always got to touch something meaningful for the vision to come through."

"What was it?"

Laura hesitated, toying with the GPS. "What was the address the Captain gave us for the other victim's family?"

"It's already programmed in there on the list of favorite spots," Nate said, almost in a growl. He was impatient. He knew her well enough to know that she was stalling for time. "What did you see?"

"That girl," Laura said. "The one who answered the door. That's who he was cheating with."

Nate frowned. "But how do you know that? Maybe she's someone he met since."

Laura saw the issue: he was thinking that she'd seen a vision of the future. "No, no, it was a vision of something that happened before," she said. "He didn't have the tattoo on his arm yet. It was from the past. A few weeks ago, maybe a couple of months."

Nate shook his head in confusion. "You saw the past? But I thought…?"

Laura bit her lip. Once again, she was faced with a dilemma that would be hard to solve. How could you explain something to someone if you didn't understand how it worked yourself? And yet, a nice, easy explanation would be the only thing that would really put Nate at ease. It was what he needed, to help him navigate this weird world that she had introduced him to. To make him feel like everything he knew about the universe wasn't being turned on its head.

Laura set the car into motion and pretended for a moment she had to focus on not hitting any other cars as she pulled out, but she knew it wasn't going to give her much time. All too soon, she had to answer him. There was no other way.

"It's a new thing," she said, wishing she could be clearer about it. "It only started recently. I just get these little scenes from the past. This one was pretty hazy, but I saw her face for a second. Long enough to recognize her."

"Anything else you can do that you haven't told me about yet?" Nate asked.

Laura winced.

"I don't..." She took a breath, fighting the urge to be defensive. That wouldn't help right now. She needed to show him she was still the same Laura. Still his friend. Not someone who would snap and yell at him for asking questions. "I'm doing my best to be open. I just didn't want to overwhelm you right at the beginning with all these different things. For most of my life, it's been true to say that I only get visions of the future. And you're only the third person I ever saw an aura of death for."

"Why?" Nate asked.

"I don't know why," she said, wishing yet again she had something else to say. Anything else. But all she had was the truth. "Maybe it's because I care about you. The first person I saw it for was my father. The second was Amy, after we'd already rescued her the first time. I felt a lot of responsibility for her at that moment, a lot of relief that we'd prevented her from dying. Maybe that was strong enough to trigger it. Or maybe, I don't know, I just haven't been around enough people who had that strong of a threat of death hanging over their heads."

Nate snorted. "In this job?"

At least that sounded a little bit more like him. "Well, I don't know," she said. "All I know is, it's a horrible feeling and I don't want to experience it again if possible. Knowing someone you love is going to die, but not how or when, is awful."

There was a pause.

"You love me, huh?" Nate said slyly, looking at her sideways with a half-grin.

Laura took her hand off the wheel for just long enough to hit him on the shoulder. "Shut up."

Nate laughed, and just for a second, everything felt like normal.

"We're not far from the house," Laura said, checking the GPS. "John Wiggins, right?"

"Right." Nate pulled out the file again to double-check what they knew about him. "About ten years older than Kenya. He's married, no children. I guess we're going to the wife."

"Hmm," Laura said. "No, I don't think so. Didn't the message from the Captain say Mr. and Mrs.? Like if it was his parents?"

"Let me check," Nate said, grabbing her phone. Again without looking, Laura stuck her thumb out for a moment, allowing him to unlock the screen. "Yeah, that's what it says. I guess that's our first question."

"Right," Laura agreed, pulling up outside a reasonably nice home. It was a reasonably nice neighborhood, too. Again, a contrast to Kenya's family. What she was seeing was that there were very few things that Kenya had in common with John – with the only real potential link seeming to be Pete, who had an alibi.

Still, it didn't necessarily mean he couldn't be the link.

"So, remind me about the mannequin on this one," Laura said, hesitating before she got out of the car.

Nate pulled out the photo and showed her. The scene was, perhaps, even creepier than the way Kenya had been posed. John was sitting on an upturned crate, propped against the wall of a building to make it look as though he was sitting up on his own. Next to him was the mannequin, posed as if it was sitting on the same crate with one hand on his shoulder. Like they were best friends, one listening to or comforting the other.

It had the eerie effect of looking as though the mannequin was trying to tell the dead man things weren't so bad.

Laura shuddered in spite of herself. "Well, this one has a completely different vibe, doesn't it? More of a friend or listener than a lover."

"Meaning what?" Nate frowned. "If the first one was a reference to the cheating somehow, then what does this reference?"

"Maybe he confessed his problems to someone recently," Laura said, but she had to figure out a way to make it negative. You didn't kill someone for doing something you thought was good or helpful. "Maybe he told a secret he wasn't supposed to tell. I don't know. But we don't even know for sure if the other case *was* about the cheating."

"True," Nate said. "Alright. After you."

Laura nodded and got out of the car, walking up to the house. The door opened before she'd even knocked on it, revealing a little old woman who had a sweet face and walked with a cane. On closer inspection Laura thought that she was perhaps closer to her late sixties or early seventies than an older age, but she obviously had some kind of issue with her hips that had her shuffling into position even as she stood at the door.

"Are you with the police?" she asked, peering up at them inquisitively.

"Yes, ma'am," Laura told her. She instantly felt pain for this woman. She was obviously getting on in years, with mobility problems, and now she was dealing with the death of her son. A death that had happened out of order. No parent should have to bury their child, and yet that was what happened wherever Laura went – even if the death was the cause and she the effect, not the other way around. "We're special agents with the FBI. We're investigating the death of Mr. Wiggins – your son?"

She nodded and slowly moved aside to let them in. "Round the corner," she said, nodding down the hall towards a doorway out of sight. "We've been waiting for you to come and set all this right."

Laura moved obediently through; behind her, she heard Nate insist on offering the woman his arm to help her back to the others. The others turned out to be an old man, older than his wife, sitting crumpled in an armchair that seemed to be fitted to his body with wear, and a woman in her thirties who looked horribly uncomfortable about being there.

"Hello," Laura said, looking around at them. Behind her, Nate was shuffling the mother slowly into the room, going at her pace. "I'm Special Agent Laura Frost, and that's my partner, Special Agent Nathaniel Lavoie."

"Have you found the person who did it?" the nervous-looking woman asked immediately. There was a kind of eagerness in her voice that wasn't hard to interpret, given the context of her body language. She was tightly clasping the strap of her purse, still on her shoulder, as though she was about to leap up at any moment. She clearly wanted to know that the murder had been solved so that she could get out of there.

"No, we've only just arrived in town so we're currently getting up to speed," Laura said, which was a good enough introduction to the fact that they were going to have to ask some questions. "You are…?"

"I'm Sara," she said, then seemed to wilt under the next declaration. "Sara Wiggins."

"John's wife?" Laura asked, beginning to put the pieces together. They were at his parents' house. His wife looked uncomfortable to be there.

They were in the middle of breaking up, weren't they?

"Sort of," Sara said, fidgeting uncomfortably with a glance at the two elderly occupants of the room. Nate was finally getting the woman down onto her seat on the other side of the sofa, taking it slow and easy on the way down so as not to exacerbate whatever problem it was she had with her hip. "We were in the middle of a divorce."

"I see," Laura said, raising her chin a little because this was detective work 101. If there was a dispute with the spouse, then it was fairly often the spouse who had done it. Of course, that normally applied when the woman was dead or the man had been poisoned, because women didn't normally commit violent crimes like bashing someone's skull in with a blunt object – but you never knew. "Can you tell me where you were two nights ago?"

"I was staying over at a – friend's place," Sara replied, telling much more with that tiny pause than with the words she had spoken. She obviously wasn't comfortable with sharing anything about her new love life in front of the parents of her deceased husband, even if things had been over between them.

"Can we get the name of this friend, so we can check you were there?" Laura asked, pulling a notebook and pen out of her pocket. Sara reached for them with a grateful nod, obviously pleased to not have to say a man's name out loud.

There was every possibility, of course, that a lover would lie to protect Sara. They could cross that bridge when they came to it, however. No need to embarrass her right in front of these people she was obviously awkward around – not when Laura didn't get any kind of vibe from her that would make her suspicious.

"Now," Laura said, turning to include the two parents in the conversation as well. "It's a horrible thing to think about, but do you know if there was anyone who wished to do John harm? Someone he'd fallen out with, perhaps?"

"We already told the other cops everything," the old man spoke up, at last. "They asked all of that. No, no one comes to mind. There wasn't anyone he had a problem with. Or if he did, he never told us. Not except for Sara."

Sara shifted uncomfortably again, looking as though she would have rather been anywhere in the world but there. Laura wondered if she was there out of a sense of obligation to the old couple, or whether the police had implied she had to stay so it was easier to question her.

"What was the reason behind your divorce?" Laura asked, looking at her again. There could be something there. A new boyfriend, maybe. Jealousy. Control. Something like that.

"We fell out of love," Sara said, tucking a hair behind her ear self-consciously. "I guess that's all it was. John had some hard times lately."

"He was depressed, and you abandoned him when he needed you," the father muttered.

Mrs. Wiggins made a small sound at the back of her throat, something like disapproval, but she said nothing. That told Laura a lot. Even though the older woman didn't want to argue or talk badly about anyone in front of the FBI, she clearly didn't disagree with the statement.

He'd been depressed. That put Laura in mind of a thought. She looked up at Nate, saw him having it at the same time. Someone who was depressed needed a friend, needed someone to listen to them. Was that what the mannequin had been? Exactly what John Wiggins needed – a friendly ear?

"Was your son seeing a therapist at all?" Laura asked.

"Oh, yes," Mrs. Wiggins said, making an airy, quick movement with her hand in the air. "Not one that he saw in person, a lot of the time. They had a few sessions, but mostly it was kind of on-call, I think. He phoned him when he needed help. And they had call sessions, too, over the – you know, the video thingy."

"Video call?" Laura asked, just to confirm she was interpreting that right. At the woman's nod, she continued. "Do you have the name of his therapist? They might be able to give us some insight into John's mind recently and whether he had expressed any fears or worries."

"Yes, I think we have it somewhere," she said, casting around. "It was someone I know who gave us the referral, said he was the best in the local area… oh, over there, on top of the mantle."

Laura made to move, but Nate had already beaten her to it, scouting the various bits of paper and knickknacks along the mantlepiece until he lifted one up. "Is this it?" he asked. "Dr. Usipov?"

"Yes, that's him," the woman nodded. "He did John a world of good and helped him through so much. We really thought he was starting to turn a corner."

"Sorry," Laura said, shifting and glancing around a bit. It was clear this had once been a family home, from the framed photographs on the walls and the battered seating in the room – too many seats for just the two of them. "Was your son living here more recently?"

"Yes. Well, he had to, didn't he?" the father said, bitterly.

"I'm living in our marital home," Sara said, her voice strangely ghostlike. It was as though she had withdrawn from the situation entirely and couldn't quite believe where she was any longer. "My lawyer said it was the best way to ensure I got something in the divorce. That if I was the one to move out, I might lose my right to it."

Laura clamped her mouth firmly shut. She had her own experience with divorce. She knew what it could be like – how nasty it could get. She'd been left with almost nothing when she lost Marcus. Not even the right to see her own daughter. Whatever Sara could do to claw something out of the marriage, that was her prerogative. Laura knew enough not to judge.

But she also knew what it felt like to be on the losing side, and John Wiggins must have been in a terrible place mentally before he died.

"I'm sure you've told the other police officers who spoke to you as much as you can, but just in case there's something missed in the handover – can you tell us anything more that might help us to identify John's killer, or trace his movements on the day he died?" Laura asked.

There was a general shaking of heads in the room.

"We hadn't spoken for months," Sara said.

"Even though he was back here, he was living his own life," the mother added. "We didn't keep tabs on him. He was a grown man. It was hard enough for him to be back here, without us asking him what he was doing every few minutes. He spent a lot of time out, at work or doing whatever it was he did."

Whatever it was he did. That was vague enough to be completely unhelpful.

"Well, if you do think of something," Laura said, standing up slowly and placing a couple of business cards on the table, "please do call us and let us know, any time. Day or night."

At least they had something to go with. Something that might prove instrumental – because a therapist would have to be the person with the best chance of knowing what that reassuring, friendly pose was all about.

Or, perhaps the best chance of being a suspect.

She and Nate made their slow exit, Nate having to fight off Mrs. Wiggins's offers of a small slice of cake or a cup of tea to keep him going on the road as thanks for his help in getting her to her seat. Laura eventually moved outside without him, grabbing her phone and dialing the number that Captain Ortega had given them to call the local precinct's team on the case.

"Hello, this is Detective Thorson. How can I help?"

"Detective Thorson," Laura replied. "This is Special Agent Laura Frost. I trust Captain Ortega has briefed you on our involvement?"

"Yes, he told us to expect a call from you," the detective said. Laura thought she could hear something in her voice, almost like she was sitting up straighter.

"I'm looking to check something," Laura said. "Do you have the call logs for John Wiggins from his service provider yet?"

"Yes, we do." There was the sound of some shuffling, perhaps of papers.

"Okay, look up the number for a therapist for me and check it against the logs," Laura said. "Dr. Usipov."

There was a long pause. Laura heard a little muttering down the line as the detective read numbers from the screen to herself, and then repeated them while scanning down the log.

"Yes, there's a match," she said, a moment later. "I've got quite a few matches, actually. Looks like a regular call on Thursdays, and then some other calls at different times as well."

Laura thought for a moment. How had her family described Kenya? Happy, quiet, keeping her head down.

Repressing everything that might possibly cause any controversy, including her own emotions.

That kind of thing could drive a person to therapy, couldn't it?

"Can you check the same number against Kenya Lankenua's logs?"

"I don't think we have them yet," Detective Thorson said. She sounded like she moved away from the phone receiver for a minute, her voice going faint and coming back. "Oh, wait a minute! Yes, I've got them here. They've just come through. Let me see… oh, God, yes! Yes, there's a match. Regular Wednesday calls, I think. Although not every week."

"Great," Laura said, nodding to Nate as he finally emerged from the house. "Thanks for that, Thorson. Send me the address for the office, if you can, and I'll call back again if we need anything else."

"Of course," Thorson said, and Laura couldn't quite work out from her tone whether she was thrilled by the prospect or just trying to fake it.

"Hey, sorry," Nate said, opening the passenger side door. "Let's get going."

"Absolutely," Laura grinned. "And don't worry about the delay. Because I may have just solved this whole case while you were gone – and that therapist has some big questions to answer."

CHAPTER NINE

Laura strode side by side with Nate as they walked into the office building, ignoring the front desk entirely. The building was the kind with a lot of different small businesses all under one roof, and they didn't want to give Dr. Usipov too much warning that they were on the way.

Not when he was their new prime suspect.

The bored girl behind the desk didn't even look up from whatever game she was playing on her cell phone as they walked by, heading straight for the elevators. It was a trick Laura had used time and time again in situations where a little more stealth was needed: act like you knew exactly where you were going and you were supposed to be there, and people generally didn't question you. Especially not when you were smartly dressed enough to look like you belonged, and they weren't paid enough to care.

They walked right into the elevator and Laura pushed the number three button, waiting for the elevator to whir into life. She'd clocked the list of business names on the wall behind the desk as they approached, from behind convenient sunglasses which she now took off and stuck in her pocket. The therapist was set up on the third floor, so that was where they were going.

"Ready?" Nate asked.

Laura nodded smartly. They knew the drill since they'd run similar things together so many times over the years. They had to get in, use the element of surprise to gauge genuine reactions from the therapist, and see what they could find out. It wasn't going to be easy. With someone who knew the human mind well, understood what reactions they should be giving, there was a high potential for faking it. But she and Nate were just going to have to be better at spotting fakes than the therapist was at giving them.

When the elevator dinged and the doors swung open, Laura and Nate stepped out in unison. They moved only a short distance down the hall to a door which was marked with the therapist's name on the glass, and rather than knocking, they went straight in.

The office had been subdivided, a new division made between the exterior – a small waiting room – and the interior office where sessions presumably took place. One of which, it seemed, was happening right now.

There was no one sitting at the desk, but there was a small sign asking anyone who was waiting for their session to please sit down quietly and wait for their turn. Next to it, a leaflet holder marked 'for new patients' held inquiry forms with instructions on what to do with them. Laura swept her gaze over the rest of the room – bland white chairs set slightly apart from one another, a potted plant with wide green leaves swaying slightly, a window that was set open to the smallest possible amount with a lock to keep it from going further.

Nothing of use. That meant they were going right in – right into the room to get the therapist now without giving him time to realize someone was waiting for him.

Laura and Nate nodded to each other just once, and then he strode forward and opened the door with one smooth motion.

"And I really think -" someone was saying – Dr. Usipov, Laura quickly guessed. He was sitting in a chair with a notebook tilted up on his knee, while the other man in the room was reclining slightly on a couch, in a comfortable position.

There was a moment of shock as both men looked around for the source of the intrusion, neither of them quite sure what was going on.

"Hello?" Dr. Usipov said, looking like he was struggling to take stock of the situation and needed the extra data before he could figure out what to do. His initial reaction, though, Laura saw with interest, was definitely on the angry side of things. His dark brows had lowered down over his eyes, his Roman nose had flared nostrils, and his wide mouth had become a straight, thin line.

"Dr. Vincent Usipov," Laura said, not a question but a statement. "We're going to need to speak with you privately. I'm Special Agent Laura Frost with the FBI."

"Special Agent Nathaniel Lavoie," Nate added, holding up his badge.

There was a whimper, and then all three other sets of eyes in the room swung to look at the patient on the couch.

He was a middle-aged white man, and he immediately shrunk into himself, his receding hairline flattened against the back of the couch cushions as intense full-body shaking made his jowly chin and his beer gut wobble.

"Get out," Dr. Usipov hissed. "Right now."

"I'm afraid that's not going to be possible," Nate said, his low rumble of a voice a clear enough threat. There was no mistaking the power in his voice – the implication that he had muscles enough to deal with both of the men in the room if he needed to, even without Laura's help.

Dr. Usipov swung around to look at him with a glare that should have been able to melt icecaps. "Get out of this room immediately," he demanded, his own voice rising with authoritarian power. He was not a man who was used to being disobeyed; Laura could see that immediately. "This patient is working through an intense phobia of law enforcement coupled with violent tendencies. You have made a huge mistake by barging in here, and I'm not leaving this room until I've fixed the trauma you've caused. Now, get out!"

Nate stood his ground, folding his arms over his chest.

Behind him, though, Laura took a step back. She'd looked over at the patient instead of at Usipov, and what she saw there was not a good sign.

His eyes had gone wide and then somehow kind of sharpened, like he was directing his gaze at Nate with an intense deliberateness. His face was slowly moving from red to purple, and his hands were clenched into fists.

A moment later, before Laura could react or say anything or even simply push Nate out of the way, she watched with horror as the patient somehow sprang from a reclined position on the couch into a full-on attack against Nate.

"Stanley!" Usipov shouted, as Nate put his arm up in instinctive defense, managing to just about block the patient's fists from flying into his face.

What followed was pure chaos. Stanley didn't waste a moment in recovering from the block but instead continued to attempt to attack Nate, scratching and clawing towards his face, shouting something incomprehensible as his open mouth sprayed spittle everywhere. Dr. Usipov was also shouting, rising up out of his chair to try to help physically restrain Stanley, and Laura stepped in herself to try to push the patient away. It was so loud she could barely understand what anyone was saying, with Nate under it all yelling and trying to get the man off him, giving growls and yelps of pain whenever a blow landed successfully.

Finally, it was a joint effort: Laura and Nate managed to shove at the man at the same time, and he fell back onto the couch, at which point Dr. Usipov sprang into the space between them and held out his arms to block Stanley's view.

"Stanley whatever your name is," Nate growled, his hand going to his belt to grab some handcuffs. "I'm arresting you for assault on a -"

"Out," Usipov snapped over his shoulder through gritted teeth. "Right now, if you know what's good for you."

For a moment, Laura thought Nate would argue. She put her hand on his arm, and he released the tension he had been holding, letting go. Without a word he began to back out of the room, closing the door behind them when they were back in the waiting room.

"Shit," Laura breathed out, shaking her head. "Are you alright?"

Nate paused, holding up his arms and looking them over, raising the sleeves of his suit jacket to elbow-height and dropping them down again. "I think so," he said. His voice was gruff, but Laura could tell he was shaken.

"Sit down," she said, gesturing to one of the chairs. "Take a breath. Christ. That was…"

"Unexpected?" Nate said, giving her a wry look.

Was he… making a joke about her psychic powers not working?

Laura gave a startled laugh, then dropped down into the chair next to him. "Seriously, are you alright? Even if you don't think you need medical attention, you can get out of here, go to the precinct and check things out there. But maybe you should get checked out. Just in case."

Nate shook his head no. "I'm fine," he said, almost brusquely. "Let's just do what we came for. We need that therapist. And you saw his reaction when we burst in – that cold anger."

"Right," Laura nodded. She tilted her head, listening. She could hear Usipov's voice now, quiet and soothing, through the door. The place wasn't exactly soundproof. Maybe that was one of the reasons he'd opted for a waiting room inside his office rather than putting chairs out in the hall – to provide a small barrier for the sound – but still, it was possible to hear fairly well through the plasterboard wall. "We should keep it down. If we can hear them, they can hear us."

Nate nodded his understanding. No discussing tactics. They had already lost a huge part of the element of surprise, and they were going to need to hold onto every advantage they had.

Usipov was going to be ready for them.

"Alright, Stanley," Laura heard him say. He was closer to the door now, judging by the sound. "Come on, then. Let's use those coping tactics we've talked about. We're going to walk right by them, and no one's going to arrest you. Alright? Here we go, then."

Laura glanced at Nate – he was bristling with anger at what they'd both just heard. But before they could agree on a plan or speak out against the doctor's assumption, Stanley was being shepherded out of the room past them. Dr. Usipov was very literally shielding Stanley's view of them with his body, holding out his arms on both sides and ushering Stanley straight towards the door.

Laura didn't know whether it was fear of setting him off again, or recognition that they had bigger fish to fry, but Nate said nothing as they went, remaining stoic in his chair.

Dr. Usipov carried on talking to Stanley in a low, reassuring voice all the way to the door, then let him out into the corridor with a few more words and a reminder to take his medication as soon as he arrived home. He closed the door slowly, watching through it all the while, as if waiting to be sure that his patient really was leaving the building.

Then, with the door closed, he turned on Laura and Nate – his previously calm and reassuring demeanor replaced by that of pure rage.

"Do you realize what you've just done?" he fumed, stalking towards them on stiff, straight legs and stopping only when he was right up in front of both of them, leaning down into their faces. "Months of therapy completely undone! He could sue for that, you know – and I know who I'd be suing in return!"

"Why the hell did he attack me like that?" Nate exclaimed. "You said he was scared of cops, not homicidal!"

"His extreme reaction to your presence was to prevent *you* from harming *him*, by any means necessary," Usipov growled. "Like the way an arachnophobe might kill a spider to prevent it from scaring them any further. As far as I'm concerned, you brought that on yourself – and you deserved worse!"

Laura tried to stay calm, unflappable. But the more he went on, the more it was starting to look as though they had a very viable suspect.

There were only three of them in the room. As much as she trusted Nate to have her back, anything could happen in such tight quarters. Usipov could flip, hit one of them over the head before the other could react. He could have a concealed weapon on his person.

There was no telling how dangerous he could be – and Laura knew they needed to tread carefully.

She nudged her foot against Nate's, a tiny little movement that might be interpreted as a shuffle if Usipov even saw it. But for her and Nate, it was a message. A message that said *trust me and wait*.

"We apologize for the intrusion," Laura said, trying hard to sound as if she actually meant it. "We had no idea you were seeing a patient who would have such a violent reaction. Given you don't have a secretary out here to let us know…"

"Oh, my fault, is it?" Usipov sneered. "My fault that you barged into what was very clearly a *confidential* session instead of just sitting and waiting your turn, as the sign clearly instructs?"

Laura held up her hands, palm outward, to appease him. "Alright, I'm sorry," she said. "Look, we're only here because it's urgent. We need any information you can give us about a couple of former patients of yours."

Usipov paused in his rant, squinting at her. "You're expecting me to cooperate with you on an investigation?" he asked, as if unable to believe what he was hearing.

"Yes, we are," Laura said firmly. She didn't want to spook him, but she wasn't able to bend, either. She needed him to come with them peacefully so that they could avoid any danger. Right now, the situation was still pretty far away from being defused. "I'm afraid that both of your patients have died. We're here looking into an active murder investigation, and your cooperation could mean that we get the answers that their families so desperately need."

She hoped that appealing to his better nature would work – because she didn't have a whole lot of other ideas.

To her dismay, Usipov simply scoffed. "From the way this has gone so far, I'm going to go ahead and assume that you're going to expect me to break doctor-patient confidentiality in order to answer your questions. Well, you've wasted your own time and everyone else's. Although you clearly don't feel the same way, I value the privacy and the mental health of every patient who steps through those doors – and I'm not going to violate that for a couple of morons who think they can just barge in anywhere with no consequences! Now, give me the name of your superior. I'm filing a formal complaint against you."

Laura sighed. This was getting nowhere. Usipov's hands were still balled into fists at his sides – but at least he wasn't clenching a weapon.

"Sir," she said, trying one last time. "We really do need your cooperation on this. What if more of your patients could be in danger from the same killer? Would you be willing to come and talk with us in that case?"

"Killer?" he said, and there was a note of what seemed like genuine surprise in his voice. Laura didn't read too much into that, however. It could have been innocence – or it could have been surprise that he'd already been caught. He quickly recovered, either way. "I don't care what kind of inducement you might try to make, there is no chance I am going anywhere with you two goons!"

53

Nate stood slowly, rising to his full height. He stood at around the same level as Usipov, but it was very clear that Nate was the more muscular of the two. He flexed slightly, letting his biceps bulge through the sleeves of his custom-made suit.

"I would actually put the chance at being very high," Nate said. "I would advise you to call a lawyer, because they'll tell you that cooperation is absolutely what you should be doing right now."

Usipov looked for a moment as though he was going to back down, but then he did something else.

He burst out laughing.

"You think you intimidate me?" he asked. "I know Krav Maga, asshole. So, come on. Try me. I'll take you on any day. And as for lawyers – you'll be hearing from mine, but not about *your* investigation."

Laura took a breath and stood up quickly, before the two of them turned this into more than just a measuring contest. "I was afraid you would make us do this, but now it seems we really have no choice," she said, pulling a pair of handcuffs out of her belt and grabbing his wrist before he had a chance to pull away. "Dr. Vincent Usipov, I'm arresting you on suspicion of murder."

"What?!" he yelped, but it was too late. Laura snapped the second cuff around his other wrist and handed him to Nate, so they could get him down to the car and then to the precinct.

Whatever he was hiding, they were going to find it out – attitude or no attitude.

CHAPTER TEN

He looked at himself in the mirror, smoothing a hand back over his hair to neaten it. He wanted to look perfect. He wanted to be more than himself: polished to a shine, smart but fashionable, ready for the social event he had been looking forward to so much.

It wasn't a party or a big night out or any other kind of event. No, that wasn't really his style. Maybe he would go to a party with all of his friends later in the year – or maybe they would get together on New Year's Eve, which, after all, was only a few weeks away. Yes, perhaps they would do that. It would be a lot of fun, and he was sure they would all rather spend time with him and each other than with their families. Oh, that would be a lot of fun for everyone.

But focus: now was the time to think about right now. He had an important visit to make tonight, even though other people might not think it was so important. Dropping in to see your best friend and spend time with them – what could be more natural and casual than that?

But see, that was the thing. That was what he knew set him apart, made him a better friend than most. The fact that he valued every single moment with his friends so much. That he treated every time they went out together or saw one another as a special occasion.

He had so much to talk about with his best friend. They didn't have enough chances to talk. They never had. That was the way of life, always something or someone getting in the way.

Well, tonight, nothing was going to get in the way. He had made a whole plan to make sure of that.

Tonight they would be able to talk as much as they wanted. And every night after this, too. They would never be interrupted again. That was the beauty of his plan.

Because when you had a best friend, someone who was really important to you, you had to make sure that you had all the opportunities in the world to appreciate and value them as much as you could. Life was too short to spend it without the people you loved.

He'd only decided that recently, although he knew how true it was as soon as the thought settled in his mind. You had to spend time with the people you loved, and if there were barriers in the way that would stop that from happening, you simply had to do all you could to remove them.

He'd done it twice before. He would do it again.

He would do anything for his best friend.

Even if that best friend was never really going to know all that he had done, all that he had sacrificed. It wasn't about that. You didn't do things for people in order to receive their thanks. You did it because you loved them and you knew they deserved it.

He straightened his tie in the mirror. Yes, tonight he was going to make sure that he and his best friend had the time of their lives – and that the party would never stop again.

He took one last look, finally satisfied that he looked good enough to call on his best friend, and then gathered his tools. He stepped out the front door and locked it behind him, glancing around the neighborhood. No one was going to notice him. He wasn't afraid of that.

No one ever did.

CHAPTER ELEVEN

Laura stared at Dr. Vincent Usipov, sitting across from her in the precinct's interview room, and mentally dared him to say it again.

"Where were you yesterday evening, after you finished your sessions for the day?"

"No comment."

Laura felt her teeth grinding together against her will. The therapist was outwardly cool and calm, even though she could sense the undercurrent of furious anger rolling off him like a storm cloud.

Suspects like him were hard to break. They knew all the tricks. Not only that, but they could read Laura and Nate, sitting beside her, just as easily as they could read one of their patients. It was hard to bluff, trick, or phase them. It was hard to make them blurt out something they didn't want to say.

Something he had proven over what felt like a day of interrogation, but had really been more like thirty minutes. Usipov was so coolly confident he hadn't even asked for a lawyer again.

That didn't mean she wasn't going to try her damn hardest to get him to confess what he'd done, though.

"We have your patient log," Laura said, picking up a tablet wrapped in protective plastic and waving it at him. "We know your last appointment was at five in the evening. Where did you go after that?"

"No comment."

Laura tried not to let anything show on her face. She sighed as if she was bored and leaned back in her chair. "You know there's CCTV outside your office building, don't you?" she asked, almost casually. "And you know that we can use that to see when you got into your car, and then follow camera footage across the road network to see where you drove. You might as well tell us now."

"No comment."

Laura pinched the bridge of her nose, sighed again in spite of herself, and decided on a different tack. "Look. I get that you're not our biggest fans right now. But this isn't about us, or about you, or even about Stanley. This is about two of your patients who have lost their lives. Been murdered. Now, you can continue acting like a suspect, or you can act like a therapist who cares for his patients and actually talk to us. Which is it going to be?"

Usipov hesitated. She saw it in his face: she'd got to him a little bit. Just a little bit. But that was a start.

"You said former patients, before," he said, surprising her by not repeating his usual words. "How do you know they were my patients, if it was ages ago?"

"I didn't say anything about how much time had passed," Laura replied. "I called them former patients because they're dead. They aren't anyone's patients now. We know they were both working with you because they both have your number as a frequent repeated fixture in their call logs, over the last few months."

Dr. Usipov sat up straight. Beside Laura, Nate flinched as if he was about to physically intervene. When Usipov didn't try anything further, Nate relaxed. "You mean they're current patients?" he asked, his face going into a very different expression from the calm mask he'd been wearing. He actually looked concerned – worried. "Who?"

"Kenya Lankenua," Laura said, watching his face carefully for his reaction. He seemed to crumple a little. "And John Wiggins."

There: complete shock and sorrow. The doctor was good, but Laura didn't think he was faking it. Either he'd had no idea those patients of his were dead, or he was a much better actor than she had him pegged for.

"Oh, God," he muttered, staring down at the table, his eyes moving from side to side as he processed the information. "Oh, no. John was doing so well. We'd just turned a corner. And Kenya – oh, God. She had her whole life ahead of her."

"Are you going to answer our questions, now?" Laura asked.

Dr. Usipov shifted in his seat, looking up. His whole demeanor had changed, his face dropping open, his shoulders drooping. "Last night I went to stay with a friend of mine. A female friend, if you catch my drift. It's a new thing – we've only spent a few nights together. I can give you her name and number, and the roads I drove along to get there, if that will help speed up the process."

"Thank you, yes," Laura said, spinning her notebook around and pushing it towards him, open on a blank page. She'd pass the information on to the local police via Captain Ortega as soon as they were done with the interview, get it checked out. Just because he was acting like he was cooperating now, didn't mean he wasn't lying through his teeth. "Can you tell me if there was any link between the two victims, anything they might have disclosed that would put them together in any way."

Usipov thought for a moment, tapping his lip. "Well, yes," he said, opening his eyes wide in alarm. "They're both linked to me. You don't think any more of my patients are in danger, do you?"

"What makes you ask that?" Nate said.

"Well, it can't be a coincidence, can it?" Usipov asked. "They're both my patients. And no, there wasn't anything else they had in common. They had totally different lives, totally different issues. John was depressed, but Kenya was struggling with self-confidence and shyness. Two very different afflictions."

"There wasn't any other resource or service that you would normally refer your patients to, for example?" Laura asked. It was always worth asking. "Perhaps you sent them to get medication from the same pharmacy, or referred them to a massage therapist to work out physical tension, or sent them to a GP...?"

"No, not at all," Usipov shook his head. "I wouldn't. There's no connection between the issues they were dealing with, so the same solution wouldn't fit both of them. Besides, the only 'cure' I believe in is the talking cure – therapy. And that's what I provide for them. Look, do you think my other patients could be in danger? Don't I have a duty to warn them?"

Normally, Laura wasn't against telling people to stay on their toes – but what would it achieve in this case? They had no idea if the killer was exclusively going after his patients, and if they were, they didn't know what criteria he was using. They still hadn't fully established, until his alibi was checked out, that Usipov himself wasn't the murderer. And even if the third victim turned out to be one of his patients, too, Laura didn't know what kind of precautions to tell them to take. They hadn't worked out where the killer attacked his victims, how he attacked them, whether he got them in the alley or brought them there afterwards somehow.

"I wouldn't jump the gun on that just yet," Laura said. "First, let's talk about these victims. John, first."

"Alright. What do you need to know?"

"Anything you can tell us about him," Laura said. "You said he was suffering from depression."

"Yes, it had plagued him for a good few years before he made the decision to come to me," Usipov said. "He told me that when his wife announced she wanted a divorce, it took away the one thing he wanted to live for. He was suicidal for a while. He would call me whenever he was at a particularly low point, and we had our phone sessions as well."

"What about when he came into the office?" Nate asked.

Usipov looked up at him in surprise. "No, he never came in."

Laura blinked. "You never met him face to face?"

Usipov shook his head. "Some people can't," he said. "Either through social anxiety, or because they can't get out of the house, or because their lives are just too busy. John was working two jobs to try to make ends meet. He'd lost his former position around the time of the divorce being initiated, and he was worried he wouldn't be able to afford a lawyer. But, he said, the need for therapy to keep him alive was greater than that. I gave him a discounted rate so we could continue talking over the phone, rather than charging full price."

That shed a new light on things.

If Usipov had never even met his patient in person, then Laura believed more and more strongly that he wasn't the man they were looking for. Of course, he could be lying once again – but it was too easy to check, with the CCTV and his patient records all available to them.

"And Kenya?"

"I never met her, either," Usipov said. "She was also very busy, and then there was the shyness. Sometimes I would struggle to hear what she was saying over the phone. We exclusively called and always exactly at the time of her appointment. She was very punctual and respectful. Never made a mistake. Actually, that was one of the things we were working on – trying to get her to see that it was alright to be a little messy sometimes."

Laura thought for a moment. She reached into her file, tilting it up so Usipov couldn't see, and then glanced at Nate with a raised eyebrow. He quirked his eyebrow back at her, which she took to mean *well, might as well try it*. Permission granted, she pulled the photographs she'd been touching out of the file and placed them onto the table, facing towards Usipov.

The two crime scene shots: Kenya and John, both posed with their mannequins. "What can you tell us about this?"

Usipov blinked, and his face went a funny shade of gray as he looked down at the photographs. He clearly had never seen anything like this before – not just the strange poses, but the fact that the people in the shots were dead. People he had known. Laura supposed it must have been a shock, if you weren't used to it.

"That's…" He seemed to gather himself, giving his head a small shake and then frowning at the photographs again. "This kind of scene – I take it that's not very usual in murders."

"Not at all," Laura said. "This is clearly a very deliberate staging. What do you think the killer might be trying to say?"

Usipov mulled over the pictures for a moment. "It's disturbing," he said. "But the way John's posed – the mannequin almost makes me think of… well, *me*. A listener, someone who is there in a professional capacity to try to make him feel better."

"What about Kenya?" Laura pressed.

"I didn't have any kind of relationship with her that would prompt this kind of staging," Usipov said right away. Laura had to resist the urge to roll her eyes. He wasn't much of a psychologist if the only thing he could see was how the world related back to himself, rather than being able to put himself in someone else's shoes. "I don't really know what it means. Maybe it's about being in a relationship with Kenya. Have you looked into her boyfriend?"

"Yes," Laura said, resisting the urge to snap *of course* at the end. "Do you think it could relate to the fact that he cheated on her?"

Usipov stared at her for a moment. "He cheated?"

It was Laura's turn to be surprised. "She didn't talk about that in your sessions?"

"No," Usipov said. "I knew they had broken up recently. Actually, our recent sessions focused on that a lot. She wanted to understand why he had broken it off with her. According to her, it came out of the blue. She said she'd done everything right – this was part of her issue, you see. She had the feeling she had to do everything exactly correctly, and when she didn't get what she perceived as an appropriate reward, she would obsess over any small mistake she had made. This would then fuel again her perception of just rewards, and support her perfectionism, to the point of it being neurotic."

Something clicked in Laura's head. The boyfriend, Pete, had been so remorseful and upset about Kenya's death and his cheating prior to it. He would now never be able to confess the truth to her or explain why he had wanted to break it off. That was why he was so guilty. Not just because he'd ended the relationship, but because he'd done it with a lie.

Still, neither Pete Yalling nor Vincent Usipov remained as suspects – which meant that they were running out of leads faster than they were finding them.

Laura sighed.

"We're going to access your patient list," she said. "With your permission, I think it is best that we warn as many of them as we can, after all. We'll have some detectives from the local PD call each of them individually and let them know about the potential threat, just in case these murders are connected to your practice in some way."

A drawn, harrowed look passed over Usipov's face. "I hope I don't lose any patients," he said. A moment later, the look turned to one of horror. "I mean, or that anyone else dies, of course! I just – well, this is my livelihood, you know."

"Of course," Nate drawled, with complete deadpan seriousness. He shifted, and Laura did the same, gathering up the photos and her file. "You're free to go home, Dr. Usipov. But please don't go far. Remember, the same precautions should also apply to yourself. My advice would be to take all of your sessions over the phone from home until this case is solved – and keep your door locked."

Usipov nodded grimly, his face pale. As she stood to leave, Laura was already putting him out of her mind, dismissing him now that he was no longer useful to the case. He clearly couldn't even help by psychoanalyzing the killer any further than the basic observations she'd already been able to make, herself.

And there were far more serious things to focus on than whether he was going to lose his business as a result of the panic.

Because if Usipov wasn't the killer, then the killer had to still be out there somewhere – and Laura had a growing uneasy feeling that it wouldn't be too long before they were looking at another body posed next to a mannequin.

CHAPTER TWELVE

Nate blew out a breath in the safety of the corridor, where no one could hear them. He and Laura were walking back through the precinct – but they'd come to a halt, realizing they had nowhere in mind to go. They hadn't yet set up an office or desk space with the locals, and they hadn't made a plan for what to do next.

"Well?" he said, turning to look at her. "What do you think, next? Morgue? I don't know if we'll learn anything new from the bodies, but it could be worth a shot, even just to get a feel for the killer."

"No," Laura said decisively. "I want to see the mannequins."

There was a moment of confusion – what could the mannequins tell them beyond what they could already see in the photographs? – but then the penny dropped.

She'd told him, hadn't she? She needed to touch something connected to the killer or the forthcoming events in order to get a vision. She needed something that was physically connected to the case. And these mannequins were clearly central.

Nate's heart was thumping wildly, even though all they were doing was standing still in a corridor. It was stupid, but so far he hadn't really had to be confronted with these visions of hers. Even when she'd used one to save his life, he hadn't been there when she had the actual vision.

"I'll come with you," he said, his tongue feeling thick in his throat. Even if he was nervous – no, afraid – to really witness her psychic ability in action, he had to. This wasn't like seeing her blank out for a second and then carry on. This would be watching her turn it on deliberately, trying to make it happen. And when she did, there would be no way for his rational mind to hold on any longer to the thought that maybe, just maybe, all of this was made up.

Seeing it happen in real time, from start to finish, and having it affect the outcome of a case – that was going to be hard to take.

All the same, he knew that if he was ever going to be as comfortable around her as he used to be, he was going to need it.

"Alright," Laura nodded. A hundred things passed between them in a glance, as they always did. She knew what he was saying: that he wanted to see it happen. And he knew that she was accepting that. In many ways, he guessed it was going to be just as weird for her to let him in on the process as it would be for him to see it.

"I guess they'll be in the evidence room," Nate said. He had a feeling of wanting to take charge, to lead the way, so that at least he was in control of something. Underneath it all was a certain protectiveness, too. He'd always felt that, as the physically stronger of the two of them, it was his job to protect Laura from things that might try to harm her. Being law enforcement, unfortunately, getting put in the way of harm was sort of an occupational hazard. He couldn't shield her from this. It was all inside her own head. The only thing he could really do would be to make sure there was nothing in her way.

"I'm pretty sure it will be down in the basement," Laura said. He had been thinking the same. There were kind of blueprints for these types of buildings, and most cities stuck to them. There wasn't a lot of variation, and once you'd been to as many different towns as they had – always seeing the same thing over and over – you began to get to a place where you could pretty safely make assumptions.

"Let's go down, try and find it," Nate suggested. "Probably easier than finding the Captain, anyhow."

Laura nodded in agreement and they started to walk again, everything feeling suddenly more tentative than it had been before. It was like he sometimes forgot about everything that had happened, everything he'd learned about her – and then it would come crashing back, just as things were starting to feel normal between them again.

Did it say something about the pair of them that things only felt 'normal' when they lost themselves in investigating a case?

He didn't have enough time to riddle that out in his head before they were getting off the elevator and walking to a door marked 'EVIDENCE' in block capitals printed on the glass, mentally high-fiving themselves for the victory.

"Alright," Laura said, taking a breath. She squared her shoulders and walked ahead, and Nate remembered her saying something about headaches. About the constant headaches she always suffered, caused by the visions. He tried to imagine willfully putting himself through pain again and again just to solve a case. Would he have been mentally strong enough to do it?

There was a sleepy-looking evidence sergeant on the other side of the door, leaning on a desk with his head propped up on one elbow. Laura flashed her badge at him as Nate did the same, and they didn't even have to speak.

"You're here to see the mannequins," he stated with confidence. As if they couldn't have been there for any other reason. Nate supposed he was right. What other evidence was there, in the only case the FBI were investigating here?

"Lead on," Nate said, gesturing ahead.

The sergeant lead them into the room with a set of keys from his belt, unlocking a metal cage-style door and leading them right to the back of the storage space. It was packed with all kinds of evidence from the various cases that were being processed through the precinct, which was apparently quite a large amount. But unmistakable at the back, wrapped in plastic to protect them from dust, contaminants, and fingerprints, were the mannequins.

"I'll leave you to it," the sergeant said. "I'm sure you guys know what you're doing."

"Right, thanks," Laura said, a little distantly. Nate wasn't sure if the sergeant noticed, but he turned to go back to his desk either way.

What they were going to do was probably going to be against regulations. After all, you weren't supposed to touch evidence. That was one of the key rules you learned very early on in law enforcement. If you touched it, you might end up obscuring another fingerprint or contaminating the evidence. It could end up upsetting the whole case at trial.

But Laura knew what she was doing – he had been right about that. If she thought that touching one of these mannequins would help her to get a lead, then it was worth it.

"Are you going to do it now?" Nate asked in a low voice, as soon as the sergeant was out of earshot.

"Yeah," Laura said, glancing up at him. "Look, it's not... just remember I've done this in front of you hundreds of times. Maybe thousands. You just never knew before. It's not that big a deal."

Who was she trying to convince – him, or herself?

"Right," Nate said, fully aware that his own voice was also none too convincing. "Totally normal."

Laura smirked a little at that, as if realizing the stupidity of the situation, and then looked at the mannequins with a shudder. "Creepy, aren't they?"

Nate looked at them again. They were pretty creepy, actually. They had painted faces, though they still weren't even close to looking like real people. Maybe if you squinted in a dark room.

Or a dark alley.

Now, that thought made him feel a little chill.

Then he thought about how Laura was going to touch them, as if they were real people and she was touching their flesh, and how they would tell her a story even without animation. *That* was even creepier.

He took a step back and gestured, ostensibly to give her room to work but actually because he now wanted to get out of this creepy storage room away from the creepy murder-witness mannequins.

Laura reached out quickly, grabbed the fastenings at one end of one of the evidence bags, and opened them with a jerk. She slipped her hand inside and pressed just the very side of one of her fingers against the mannequin, pausing for a moment in anticipation.

And then she frowned.

"What?" Nate asked, immediately. Had he missed it? He'd been trying to see that moment when she would space out, disappear, but he hadn't seen anything.

"Nothing," Laura said, sighing. She drew her hand away and refastened the evidence bag. Her sigh had a sharp edge to it, like she was frustrated. Angry, even. "I didn't see anything."

"What, like you couldn't work out what you were looking at?" Nate asked.

"No, like I didn't have a vision," Laura said.

Nate frowned. "But, I thought you said if you touched them…"

"Usually, I would get something," Laura said, then seemed to amend herself, her blue eyes half-disappearing into a squint as she thought. "Well, maybe not 'usually.' Often. But it's not an exact science. I mean, I guess it's not science at all. I don't know what it is."

Nate bit his lip for a moment, wanting to ask a hundred thousand questions. What was it, if not science? When did she usually get it triggered? What usually worked? What didn't work? Why hadn't it worked this time? Would she be able to try again? Was there something blocking the visions, like they were a signal or something? Could he do anything? Could she do anything?

Instead, he cleared his throat. "Well, I guess it's not so bad," he said. "We're no worse off than we were."

That was his attempt to make her feel better.

Even as he said it, he felt the words falling flat.

"Yeah," Laura said, clearly not convinced either. "I guess we go back to the drawing board."

Nate opened his mouth to ask something again, but shut it. No, he couldn't ask. He'd already messed up big time by assuming it would always work no matter what, and making her feel bad about not being able to do it. All he was going to do if he spoke again was put his foot in his mouth. Besides, if she wanted him to know something about it, she'd probably tell him. What was it she'd said earlier, when he found out about her visions of the past? That she didn't want to overwhelm him?

Given the way he'd overreacted when she first told him about all this, he figured that was totally fair. In fact, it was generous that she'd decided to carry on keeping him in the loop at all.

No, he wouldn't push his luck. She could tell him everything in her own time. He was just going to have to be a good detective: listen, observe, pick things up on his own.

"What's on that drawing board, exactly?" he asked, leaning against one of the racks of evidence, careful not to actually brush against any of the exhibits – even if they were all wrapped up.

"I don't know," Laura sighed, rubbing a hand over her eyes. She smudged her mascara slightly, leaving a trail of small black dots near the corner of her eye. "I don't know if there's anything on it at all. We're out of leads, aren't we?"

"For now," Nate said. "I'm sure if we look closer, go back over everything, we'll find something new to chase down. We've only just started."

"Yeah," Laura agreed, but she looked so tired even as she said it that Nate couldn't help but take pity on her.

Did the ability leave her that drained, even when she hadn't used it?

Or was it just that she was already tired anyway?

"It's late now, anyway. Let's go to our hotel, get some rest," he suggested. "Tomorrow's a new day. There hasn't been another body yet. Maybe there won't be. Maybe we have all the time in the world to solve this."

"Except you know as well as I do the trail gets pretty cold after forty-eight hours," Laura said reproachfully, then sighed. "I guess you're right. We can take a short break. Get up around dawn and get right back to it."

"At dawn," Nate promised, privately hoping she would forget to set an alarm or fall asleep again after turning it off so she would get some proper sleep.

And knowing, at the same time, that she would be knocking on his door at dawn, ready to go.

CHAPTER THIRTEEN

He pulled up outside his best friend's house and carefully parked the van, rolling to a gentle stop and applying the handbrake. No squeal of tires or brakes, no drama. He didn't want any of the neighbors to notice him, after all.

Not that they likely would even if he held a one-man parade down the middle of the street.

Well, it was always nice to visit, anyway. That was the great thing about having a best friend. Sometimes you didn't even have to talk or do anything together. You could just sit together in silence, and that was enough.

It was that way with all kinds of relationships, really, once you got close enough to someone. That was how you knew that you really had a great relationship. Just being able to be together, not even having to acknowledge it.

He glanced into the back of the van, using the light from the streetlights positioned a few cars away in either direction to guide him. There was no point in putting on the interior light – no, that could be disruptive for his friend, and he didn't want that. He wasn't the type to be intrusive. He liked it best when everyone could do their own thing, without someone getting in their way. It was more comfortable like that, wasn't it?

He checked everything was where it should be in the back of the van. Yes, everything was present and correct. Nothing had moved while he was driving, which was because he was a very careful driver. You had to take good care of your things. Keep them clean and tidy, keep everything in its place, make sure that you didn't ruin or damage anything. Unless you had to. Unless that was the only way to keep it safe in the long run, in the ways that really mattered.

He reached out a gloved hand and ran it over the arm of the mannequin tenderly, lovingly. It was all ready. That was going to be the best possible gift for his best friend. He'd prepared it so well. All he had to do now was wait for an opportunity to present it to him. It wasn't the kind of gift you could just give on the fly, after all. It had to be the right moment. The kind of moment that would make it all the more special.

He looked up through the window, right into the house opposite. The house where his best friend was. Ah, and there he was! Sitting on the sofa, just waiting for him! He allowed himself to relax in his seat, shifting his legs and laying his hand down on the side of the seat to adopt the same pose. That was what people did when they felt a deep mental connection – they moved in the same ways.

His best friend laughed, soundlessly through this distance, his eyes fixed on the screen.

He sat up straighter in his seat in the van, frowning. He was laughing at something on the television. He hadn't started the movie without his best friend, had he?

It looked like he had.

He wound down his window and frowned, pausing, straining his ears. The front window of the house was open just a tiny amount, letting in some fresh air. And…

Yes! He was watching the movie already! He'd started before his best friend arrived!

Wasn't that rude?

But best friends should forgive each other – right?

He wrestled with the dilemma, unsure what to do, with no one to guide him.

***

Xavier Perez reached over for his beer and took a sip, still shaking his head and chuckling about the last scene. Man, what a doozie. This was a great film. He'd made a good choice.

It was nice to really take the weight off – not just his feet, but his mind. It had been another long day at work in a string of long days at work, and coming home to an empty house with no hope of a visitor really sucked. He was used to it, but it still sucked. The key was just distracting yourself with enough entertainment that you stopped noticing how alone you were.

He put the beer down and chuckled again, appreciating another of the jokes. Yeah, there was nothing like a good comedy to put you at ease, help you relax from all the tension of the day. You could forget about that stupid, entitled customer, or that coworker who just wouldn't let anything go, no matter how petty. And Xavi had a stinker of a day to forget. It was good to kick back with a beer.

He thought briefly about dinner. What was he going to make? But, no, he was too tired to cook. And it was always a drag, cooking for one.

It felt like way too much effort. What was he going to do except eat it and leave no trace or evidence it had ever existed, no matter how delicious or well-plated it was? A waste of time. He could just grab one of those TV dinners out of the freezer and heat it up and have done with. Maybe they didn't taste as good as the real thing, but at least they were easy.

He reached for the volume control and turned it up a little more, making it more comfortable for his ears. He could swear he was starting to go deaf. It seemed like every month he needed to turn the TV speakers up a little louder. Or maybe it was just the kind of content. He'd read something at some time about how a lot of movies were produced with optimization for the theater, not the home, and that could make the sound kind of muddy. Maybe it was just producers not doing their jobs properly, not making it easy for people like him who didn't have anybody to go to the theater with.

Ah, whatever. He took another drink of his beer. There was a sound somewhere in the house, but he'd lived on his own for long enough to know that houses made weird noises sometimes. You just had to ignore it. He hit the volume control on the TV one more time – if he was still hearing house creaks, then maybe he hadn't turned it up as high as he thought.

"Ah, man!" he exclaimed out loud, grinning at one of the scenes. What an awkward moment. Oh, he could feel the cringe. How awful it would be to be in that kind of situation! He found himself chuckling out loud again, focused on the screen and the action, ignoring the annoying pull of a creak of the floorboards right behind where he was sitting, the kind of noise that the house always made and there was never anyone there when he turned to –

An explosion of pain hit the back of his head, so unexpected and fast that he had no idea what was happening, only that his head hurt and it hadn't hurt a second ago, that he wasn't looking at the movie anymore. Hadn't there been a movie? But now there was no movie, and he didn't understand how someone could have moved the screen of his TV so fast without him noticing – and then he realized, no, no, it wasn't the TV that moved, it was him.

He was on the floor. Yeah, the floor – he could feel the carpet under his hand, and the ceiling was up above him. He had moved somehow – his brain started to connect – the pain in the back of his head must have moved him – some kind of force – some kind of hit...

Something hit him over the back of the head.

Xavi blinked his eyes, the only thing he could figure out how to move, slowly starting to gain some consciousness about what was happening around him. A blow to the back of the head. The creaking. There must be someone else in the house. Someone –

Someone who wanted to hurt him again?

There was another sound, or at least a kind of sense of movement, somewhere to the side. Xavi tried to look towards it and managed only to flop his head to the side, letting any remaining tension go from his neck. The movement made his brain thud inside his skull, leaving him with a pulsing pain that only seemed to continue and grow. He could see something. Someone.

No, not someone. What the hell was that? Not a person, but person-shaped.

A mannequin. Faceless and blank, though almost staring down at him from where it was propped up against the wall nearby. The wall of his own home. It shouldn't have been there.

He couldn't make sense of it. A mannequin with no eyes could not come to life and attack him. And yet…

Fumbling to the side, Xavi managed to move his arms but not his legs, finding them heavy and unresponsive. He tried to make a sound, a kind of scream really, but all that came out was a mumble he could not control. A sound with no words, no purpose. Something hot and wet slid across the back of his head as he used his arms to push himself a little, away from the mannequin. Away from that blank face. Away from the threat that maybe, maybe, this *had* been the thing that attacked him.

It took all his strength to push himself backwards on his fingertips, but he looked at the mannequin and saw that it looked like it was just as close as it had been before.

Xavi tried to make a noise again, to shout for help, but only that mumble came out, that broken noise that made no sense.

Something blocked his light; he blinked to bring it into focus, trying to fight against the overwhelming sound of the television, the brightness of the lights, the heat of whatever it was on the back of his head spreading down his shoulders and back against his cold skin. A face. This time with no body.

A mannequin with no face, a face with no body.

Some kind of pair.

But no, the face was attached to a body after all, to an arm holding something, something he blinked at to try and see, but it was moving too fast, moving towards his face –

Xavi saw nothing, and his last thought escaped him like a sigh, gone on the wind before he could finish grasping hold of it.

CHAPTER FOURTEEN

Laura sat up on the lumpy, flat mattress the motel had provided, sighing. She'd been trying to sleep for twenty minutes, but all she'd gained was more and more frustration.

This wasn't right. None of it was. It felt like her whole world had tilted on its axis, leaving her unbalanced and without the footing she was used to.

Nate knew about her ability. Some weird stranger had turned up having claimed to have seen a vision of her, and neither of them knew why. She'd had to hide that, and keep lying about her visions, to Chris, even if it was only the lie of omission that she was used to using on everyone else in her life. It was just that suddenly, now that one person did get the honest truth, she had an itchy feeling that she was being awful to everyone else she should have been able to trust.

And then there was this ongoing problem with her visions, which she still wasn't any closer to solving.

It was stupid – she normally avoided touching things in public places as much as possible – but she got up and started running her hand along every surface in the room, hoping for some kind of sign that her ability wasn't broken.

Nothing came, of course. Why would it? Everything here was over-saturated, touched by too many people, and most of them only old echoes. There wasn't anything special here. Nothing she could focus on.

Laura turned and got back into bed with a sigh, closing her eyes, but instead of darkness she was looking at images from the case in the back of her eyelids. The mannequins posed with both of the victims. The positioning. The bodies. What had they missed? It wasn't like her and Nate to stall when they were only this far into an investigation. There was another lead out there, another clue they hadn't been able to explore yet. All they had to do was find it.

She traced over it all in her mind. The connection with the therapist. The office and that weird waiting room. Dr. Usipov's manner – barely controlled rage. The patient with a thing about law enforcement officers going for Nate. What was really connected, and what was just a red herring? It felt almost impossible to tell.

And those mannequins. God! Why did it have to be now? Why did it have to be right after she had told Nate everything, right when he was waiting to be blown away by how efficient and useful her visions were, that they failed her?

There was still time, obviously. Sometimes the visions did take a while to come in a case. But the utter lack of anything coming up with the mannequins, combined with how shadowy and hard to see her vision of Kenya's ex-boyfriend had been, was worrying her.

Was it performance anxiety? The fact that she knew Nate was watching and their whole relationship could rest on whether he did or did not accept the way she did things?

It was terrifying, in many ways, to have to reveal herself like this. To bare something she had spent her whole life hiding. But that couldn't be the only thing. She'd been scared or nervous before. For most of her childhood and teenage years, she'd dreaded the visions, wished they would go away. She'd tried to suppress them. Still, they had remained strong, as if to spite her.

It would be just like those spiteful visions to fail now when she was finally able to embrace them more fully.

Laura tossed the covers aside again, frustration making her movements sharp and snappy. She couldn't sleep like this. Not when she was still unsure what was going on. It was just going to keep going around and around in her head until she figured it out.

And right now, there was one person who might actually be able to help her – someone she'd never had a chance to ask for help before.

Laura took a long, deep breath and then grabbed up her cell phone, trying not to give herself enough time to think and talk herself out of it.

There was a ringing tone twice, then a faint crackle, and then he spoke. "Hello?"

"Hi," Laura said, hesitating. Did he even realize who she was. "Zach. This is Laura Frost."

"I know," he said, with a hint of a smile in his voice. "I do have caller ID. I know I look like I belong to the last century, but I do have a few modern touches here and there."

Laura felt a moment of panic that subsided under his soft tone. Joking. He was just joking. He wasn't really mad at her.

"Sorry for calling so late," she said. "I'm just out on a case, and I couldn't sleep, and -"

"Nonsense," Zach said, cutting off her excuses. "You can call me at any time of day or night. I thought I made that clear. You don't have to have a reason. What's an old man like me going to be doing that's so important I can't take your call?"

"Sleeping, for one thing," Laura said, but she sensed they were getting off-topic. "Look, I just needed to ask you something. About your visions, you know, the experiences you've had."

"Shoot," Zach suggested.

Laura took another breath, trying to figure out how to put it. "Have you ever felt – I don't know – blocked? I'm having a lot of trouble with getting the visions to come right now. When I do, they're murky – hard to see. Like I'm in a dark room trying to see with the beam of a single light."

"Hmm." Zach paused, and Laura got the sense of him moving – maybe pacing the floor or rubbing a hand over his chin thoughtfully. "Blocked. That's an interesting way to put it. Well, I never tried to force the visions like you do – I was more often than not hopeful of avoiding them, not encouraging them. But, sure. I've had times when they didn't come for a while, and the ones that did were unclear. I suppose that sounds like what you're experiencing now."

Laura breathed for a moment. Normal. It was normal for this to happen. That's what he was saying, right? Nothing was wrong with her. It was just a block. Something that could come on from time to time. She only hadn't been trying to force her visions, as he put it, for long enough to come across one of these blocks yet.

"What did you do to make them go away?" she asked, but even as she did, she feared she knew what the answer was going to be.

"I didn't do anything," Zach said, crushing all of her hopes. "Like I said, I was happy they were gone. When they came back, sometimes it would feel like a curse coming back over me all over again. But they did always come back, I'll tell you that. Whether I wanted them or not, time would pass and there they would be. Sometimes after days, sometimes weeks, sometimes months. I guess I don't know the rules or the whys and wherefores, but my experience was they always came back."

Laura nodded slowly even though he couldn't see her. "So, I just have to wait," she said, and sighed. "I feel like I would be a lot more patient if I wasn't sitting here waiting for a clue in a case that feels unsolvable so far."

"You'll get there," Zach said encouragingly. "Just keep at it?"

"How do you know that?" Laura asked. "Did you see it in another vision of me?"

"No," Zach said with a chuckle. "I just know from what I've seen of you already that you're a good agent. You'll get to the bottom of this."

Laura took another breath for what felt like the fifteenth time she'd had to, telling herself to calm down. She wasn't good to anyone like this. She was just panicking, going from one thing to another. She had to slow down. Rest. Keep her brain in good shape.

That was the only way she was going to get to the bottom of this – and he was right. She was a good enough detective in her own right. She didn't need the visions. She and Nate could do this the old-fashioned way.

"Thanks," she said. "Sorry again for calling."

"Don't be sorry," Zach said, his voice taking on a slightly more authoritative tone – Laura remembered he'd been a teacher. "You must call me whenever you have questions like these. I'd be more upset if you didn't call, no matter what you interrupt."

Laura nodded, rubbing a hand over her head. "Thanks," she said again. "Bye, then."

"Goodnight, Laura," Zach said, and she ended the call, throwing her cell phone back onto the bedside table where it belonged.

She let her head hit the pillow next, trying to let go of everything that had been keeping her up. If she could just move past all of this, accept that it might not work this time, she would be able to stop worrying about the visions and instead focus on the case.

With the intention of doing exactly that as soon as the sun rose, she closed her eyes, letting herself drift away at last.

She was in a dark space, unable to see anything at first, simply staring out into the blackness. She had this feeling, though, that she wasn't staring out into a void or an empty space: there was something out there, an impression of boundaries, something with walls and a ceiling.

Even if those walls and ceiling were so vast she couldn't see the sides at all.

It wasn't completely dark. It was like the thought she'd had before: standing in the darkness with only a small light. It wasn't a light that was helping her see, though, but a kind of soft glow, like from the moon on a quiet night without clouds but when the moon wasn't full. Enough light to begin to see the vague shapes of things.

Not enough light to really see the details or understand what was going on around you.

Laura strained her eyes, trying to figure out what she was looking at. There was a vague paleness in front of her, a smooth shape, something just out of sight and out of reach...

Her breath caught in her throat when she realized what she was looking at.

A person.

Someone standing right in front of her, so close she felt like she could reach out and touch them. Or they could reach out and touch her. *But instead of moving towards her, looking at her, or speaking, this person stayed stock still. Expressionless and unmoving, staring right ahead as though Laura wasn't even there.*

As Laura's initial fear began to subside, replaced with a different, chilling kind of feeling about the way she was being ignored, she glanced behind the figure in front of her. That was when she realized they were not alone.

The person in front of her was not the only one standing there, staring straight ahead, as though they were all waiting for something. Like soldiers waiting for a speech from a general, all of them in neat formation, all of them standing the same way and staring in the same direction.

The further her eyes allowed her to see, the more Laura's heart began to race.

There had to be hundreds of them. Maybe even more. Her view of the back of the room was blocked by those in front, and she had no idea about where the space ended. It could stretch on as far as the moon, for all she knew.

Hundreds of them. All standing there silently, waiting for something to happen. Ignoring her.

But all of them facing in her direction, all of them pitted against her – and there were so many that she knew she would be overpowered in a second if they decided to take her down.

She kept staring ahead, up and up and across the hall, all of these bodies just standing there in every direction, making her heart beat so loud in her ears that she thought all of them must be able to hear it, making her sweat, her breath coming faster and faster.

And as she looked down one of the rows of people –

One of them was not in line with the others.

He was not facing forward, without expression, towards some unseen thing behind her.

He was not standing neatly in his row.

He was staring right at her, and as she watched, he stepped out of the line – and then took a step towards her, purposefully, angrily.

Laura's heart exploded with fear at the sound of a loud ringing, an alarm which he must have sounded somehow, a signal to the others to seize her, to stop her –

Laura shot upright in the bed and grabbed her phone, shutting off the alarm with a practiced movement that relied on muscle memory rather than her still-sleeping eyes. But the sound didn't stop. The alarm was still going off.

Looking down, Laura realized it was a phone call, not her alarm, even though the pale glow of dawn was just starting to edge through the thin motel curtains, replacing the yellow aura of the streetlights.

She answered the call, pushing her hair out of her eyes with a frustrated movement. What had that been? A nightmare? A vision? Her hair stuck to her forehead with sweat. "Special Agent Laura Frost?"

"Agent Frost," a man said. She thought she could place him, but for a moment was unsure from where. "I thought you'd want to be notified right away. My officers have just been called to a crime scene downtown. There's been another one."

"Posed with a mannequin?" Laura asked, her brain sorting through the murk to identify the caller as Captain Ortega.

"Exactly the same as the others," Ortega replied. "I'll send a patrol car to guide you to the scene. He'll be there in about ten minutes. Is that good for you?"

"We'll be ready," Laura promised, already getting out of bed ready to bang on the dividing wall between their rooms and wake Nate.

CHAPTER FIFTEEN

Laura glanced around as she waited for Nate to follow her out of the car, placing her hands on her hips. They'd been awake and sitting in their car waiting for the cop to lead them by the time he arrived. The extra couple of minutes she'd had on Nate had made a difference, as had the fact that she'd woken up from a nightmare and into full awareness while he still had to fight through the grogginess. She'd managed to jump into the shower for less than five minutes to make herself feel fresh, get dressed, and point a dryer at her hair for a minute before deciding it was done enough and just tying it back. Nate, on the other hand, seemed to still be catching up.

"What are we looking at?" he asked, rubbing his eyes as if he still needed to clear the sleep out of them.

"Over there," Laura said, nodding at the view through a window into the house, where Captain Ortega was standing with his hands on his hips, his position slightly slouched, looking down at something a few feet away from him. Laura couldn't see what it was because of the wall blocking their view, but she could guess.

A body.

Nate followed her as she led the way to the Captain, nodding a greeting at him as he glanced through the glass. The scene was strangely quiet, given the fact that it was swarming with law enforcement. The darkness of the night seemed to have instilled a hush in everyone, together with the fact that this was yet another murder in a string that had to be shocking to the locals. The suburban location was another factor – no one wanted to wake the neighbors, even though it was abundantly clear that every house in the vicinity was full of people who were already wide awake and watching through their curtains.

People spoke in hushed tones – two crime scene forensics officers who walked by in white suits were whispering to one another as Laura and Nate passed by them. The red and blue lights from the ambulance and police cars were flickering across everything, bathing everyone in the two alternating shades again and again. Laura shivered, and it was not because of the cold dawn air.

She stepped across the threshold and into the home, though the temperature barely changed – the door had clearly been open for some time, letting the cold air into the house. Round one corner and through another open doorway, and there it was – the thing they had been afraid they would find. Another victim, marked so very clearly with the hallmark of this killer.

Nate made a low whistle under his breath, which just about seemed to sum up the situation for everyone else, too. There was general nodding and murmurs of agreement from the Captain, the two other detectives in the room, and even Laura herself.

It was a strange, eerie sight. The body of a man, his head clearly smashed open with a blunt object just as the other two had been, propped on a sofa as if he was just casually sitting there at the end of a long day. While the first two victims had one neat blow to the back of the skull, this one had two visible injuries – one to the back and one on top of the head.

He was sitting next to a mannequin, as they had been forewarned. The mannequin was posed in a similar fashion, with a seated-style body that was already posed correctly to look as though it was just joining him on the sofa for a movie night. Between them was what had to be the most macabre detail of all, though Laura couldn't put into words exactly why it sent a shiver of dread down her spine: a bowl of popcorn, popped and ready to eat, set on the cushions between them so that they could lean over and take a piece whenever they got hungry.

Laura turned from the sight and caught more motion out of the corner of her eye: the television was on, set to a movie channel and playing one of their early morning screenings. The black and white film flickered darker and brighter lights over the carpet and the large bloodstain that had been left on it – the part of the floor that the Captain and his detective were meticulously avoiding.

This was not the same as the other cases, where he'd obviously had to rush to avoid being caught. There, he'd had to prop up the victim, set the mannequin next to them, and then run. This time he'd clearly attacked the victim right here, and Laura could see each of the two blows as distinct events: one that had him dropping to the floor and then rolling slightly, trying to move himself perhaps away from the killer, and then the second creating a deeper pool and splatter that ended the victim's life. She didn't need a pathologist to tell her that.

Afterwards, he'd had all the time in the world to create his scene. This one wasn't just about the mannequin and the body. This time, he'd brought *props*. Spent time in the house arranging it when the victim was there, dead, his body slowly cooling, approaching rigor mortis.

"The sound was off?" Laura asked, gesturing towards the TV.

"No, we turned it down when we came in," Captain Ortega replied. "We didn't want the noise to be a distraction."

"What about the curtains?" Laura asked.

Captain Ortega shook his head. "Those haven't been touched. They were left open. That's how the crime was reported to us – a neighbor heading out to an early shift at work spotted him through the window."

Laura bit her lip, glancing at Nate. She could see the same concern in his own eyes. "He's putting them on display," she said.

"Egocentric," Nate replied, a basic criminal psychology analysis. "He wants us to see what he's done. Wants the bodies to be found. Maybe he's trying to send us a message."

Laura shrugged thoughtfully. "Or trying to make these scenes into some kind of entertainment or show," she said. "I don't know. Maybe it's just because of the window in this one. It reminds me of the Christmas windows in stores, you know? How you see everything set up in this representation of a perfect little winter wonderland or a family enjoying the festivities. In all three, it's like this idealized state. Spooning with a lover. Having a friend to listen to you. Sitting to watch a movie."

Nate nodded, with Captain Ortega watching them both work silently. "Question is," Nate said darkly. "Did he do all of this with the windows open, or did he open them up once he was done?"

"We're dusting for prints, but there's nothing yet," Captain Ortega offered. "Looks like he was probably wearing gloves, like in the other two scenes."

Laura looked out of the window onto the street, trying to picture it. Trying to put herself into the killer's shoes. She desperately wanted to touch something to try to get a vision, but with Captain Ortega watching closely, it was too much of a risk. People didn't usually take kindly to the soiling of evidence.

But she could do what Zach had suggested. She could use her years of experience, her knowhow as an investigator, the things she had seen before.

"I think he did it with the curtains open," Laura said, thinking out loud, seized by sudden conviction. "He wasn't afraid of acting in public before – the two alleys were places where anyone could have stumbled across him. He wouldn't be afraid now. He's efficient, quick. Maybe he came with the popcorn already made, the mannequin ready. He knew what he was going to do. Why else would he bring a mannequin that was already in a seated position?"

"This was planned and then executed with precision," Nate agreed. "It looks like the victim was taken by surprise, and the first blow didn't kill him, which is different from what we've seen before. Maybe he got a little second of warning or something. Do we know who the victim is yet?"

Captain Ortega nodded. "The homeowner. Xavier Perez. He lived here alone."

"So, the killer knew he wouldn't be disturbed by a wife or housemate," Laura suggested. "Maybe that's why he took the risk of attacking him here in his home. Think about it – John Wiggins lived with his parents, and Kenya was in an apartment building. He couldn't do it where they worked as other people would be around there, too. It had to be out somewhere else. But with Mr. Perez here, he had the opportunity to take his time and do it right."

"Who was he to the killer?" Nate asked, throwing up another thought. Laura liked it when they could bounce off one another like this, getting into the zone of the investigation, feeling things out quickly. This was how they worked best. "A friend? A family member? It looks like the message is one of closeness."

"Could be," Laura said. But then she made a face, shaking her head. "But if he's like the other two, we're going to have to work hard to figure out who the connection is here. Someone who joins all of them. If we didn't find the link yet, I have a feeling that this third variable is going to make it harder, not easier."

"Surely it will be easier to narrow down the field of people who could have come into contact with all three," Captain Ortega argued.

"Maybe," Laura replied. "But to get there we need to sift through all his friends, his family, his coworkers, everyone he came into contact with. It's like searching a haystack for a needle while more hay keeps getting poured on top all the while. We've already ruled out the therapist that linked the first two. We can check just in case, but we know he's not the killer, so I don't even know how much a connection there would help."

"And this is going to keep being a problem," Nate said, his voice a low rumble. "Because if he's already set up three scenes for us to find, he's not going to feel like he's done and he can stop. He's going to keep on killing until we stop him."

Laura nodded. She had been thinking the same thing.

This was a relentless killer, the kind who could carry on racking up a huge body count if he wasn't stopped. They couldn't let that happen.

"I guess we'd better speak to this neighbor who found the body," she said grimly, wanting to get on with this case as quickly as they could.

CHAPTER SIXTEEN

Laura spotted the neighbor in question immediately when they walked outside. He stuck out like a sore thumb: dressed in a cheap and ill-fitting suit, very obviously not law enforcement from how uncomfortable he looked, hugging his arms against himself and glancing at the house with a distressed expression then away, as If trying to stop himself from remembering or thinking about it.

He was standing with a police officer who stepped aside as Laura and Nate approached, as if letting them take the floor.

"Hi," Laura said, injecting her voice with a little lightness but still keeping it low and quiet, trying to reassure him without being gauchely cheerful. She thought of her partner on the last case, the inimitable and indefatigable Agent Bee Moore, and fought down the urge to smile at the image of how sunny and bright she would have been right now. "I understand you're the neighbor who found the body?"

"Yes," he said, his voice shaken and stuttered. "I'm Owen. I live over there." He pointed a few houses down, making it clear that his route must have had him walk along the sidewalk past Perez's home on the way out.

"Can you tell me what you saw?" Laura asked. "Start from the beginning and describe everything, if you can."

Owen glanced nervously at the cop who had been standing with him.

"We know you've probably been asked this already," Nate said sympathetically. "It's just standard procedure. We need to get the information from you so we can carry on with the investigation – you'll make a more formal statement later. We just want to hit the ground running."

Owen swallowed and bobbed his head in a quick nod, his eyes going down to the ground and tracing invisible patterns there. "I was walking to work," he said. "I saw this glow coming out of the window of Xavi's house, which was weird because it's so early. Everyone's usually asleep when I head to work. And if they aren't, they would have their curtains closed. Xavi usually goes out to work before I do, so his curtains are usually closed and his truck is usually gone, but the truck was still in the driveway."

That was one confirmation, at least. Xavier Perez would have closed his curtains when he went to bed. Either the killer left them open because they hadn't been closed yet, or he opened them on purpose. "Was there anyone else around?" Laura asked. "Before or after you saw the glow?"

"No, it was quiet like usual," Owen said. He shivered slightly, glancing towards the house involuntarily. "As I got closer, I saw that it was kind of flickering and I realized it must have been the TV I was seeing. I thought I'd glance in and give Xavi a wave if he was awake. Or maybe knock on the door if he'd fallen asleep on the couch or something, you know. I thought maybe he'd slept in and didn't know he was late for work. So I looked in."

"What did you see?" Nate asked, when he seemed reluctant to continue.

"Xavi was on the couch," Owen said, his eyes going unfocused as he stared at the ground. "His head – there was blood on his head. And his eyes... I could see he was gone. And there was that creepy mannequin. I turned away and called 911 right away."

"You did the right thing," Laura assured him. "Was there anything else you noticed that stood out?"

Owen looked at her. "Other than the fact that my friend is dead?"

Laura picked up on that immediately. "So, you weren't just neighbors?"

"No," Owen said, and shrugged. "Well, yes. I guess that's just how Xavi was. He saw it as neighborly to help people out. He wasn't like how some people can be, all cold and only interested in themselves. He was nice to everyone."

"What kind of things did he do to help out?" Laura asked, curious.

"He was just helpful all the time. Helping people carry stuff, or move furniture around. He would always offer if he saw you struggling with something. If anyone in the neighborhood had bad news he would cook them a big dish of something. He even gave me advice sometimes about work stuff when I wasn't sure what to do."

"He was a big part of the community here, then?" Nate asked.

"Yeah, totally," Owen nodded. "I mean, if you can call it a community. Not a lot of people around here get involved with one another. We don't have, like, cookouts or parties or whatever. But Xavi was different and he was always open for a chat with anyone."

"What about his work?" Nate asked. "What did he do? You said he was usually up even before you were."

"He was a third-party freight driver," Owen said, sounding as though he was reciting something that Perez had once told him. "I don't know what that means exactly, but I guess he drove a lot of trucks and took goods all over town. Out of town, too. Like a courier, I think, but with really big loads instead of just someone's lunch or whatever. He worked for this company, I think it was like... Mariesville Freight or something obvious like that?"

Laura nodded. "I think we get the idea," she said. That was an interesting lead they could possibly follow up. If his work took him all over town, then it was possible he had connections in lots of different areas. That could make it easier to find a link between him and the two others. Or maybe he *was* the link. "Have you seen anything unusual around the neighborhood over the last few days or weeks? Maybe a strange vehicle, or someone you didn't recognize who was hanging around?"

Owen shook his head slowly. "I don't think so," he said. "But, you know, I'm out for most of the day, so if there was someone hanging around I probably missed it. But wait, you think he was targeted?"

The phrasing struck Laura as odd. "Targeted?"

"Yeah, I mean, we've all seen the reports about the bodies on the local news," Owen replied. "This mannequin thing – it's, like, a theme or whatever, isn't it? It keeps happening? So, I guess I just figured this is some crazy serial killer or something. Don't they usually go after strangers, not people they know?"

Laura blinked.

"Sometimes," Nate hedged. "Anyway, we're following up all avenues right now to make sure we don't miss anything. There's nothing else you can think of to tell us?"

"I don't think so," Owen said again. He looked down sadly. "Man. I just can't believe that this guy took out Xavi like that. He was such a good guy. And this means there's a killer around here somewhere, right? At least, he was here. Right in the same neighborhood as me. Any of us could have ended up victims!"

"Don't worry," Laura said, trying to put him at ease so they could get away. It didn't seem like there was anything else of value he would be able to give them. "We're going to do our best to catch this killer. In the meantime, it's worth thinking about carpooling to work so you don't have to walk on your own – and keeping all of your doors and windows locked when you're home. I'm sure he won't strike here again, but it doesn't hurt to take precautions."

"Right," Owen nodded, looking even more worried and afraid than he had when she'd started speaking.

"Thanks," Nate said, effectively breaking the conversation off. "We'll be back in touch if we need to ask you anything else, but for now, please follow the instructions of the local police officers. I'm sure they'll want you to head down to the station and give a statement."

They walked away a bit, into the quiet of the street. Laura indicated their car with her head and they crossed the road together, heading to stand against the car instead of getting into it right away. The sun was up properly now, illuminating the whole road. It was strange to see everyone bleary-eyed, still feeling the effects of the night before, even as the sun brought the new day into full force.

"What now?" Nate asked. "Apart from coffee, which I'm going to have to insist we stop off somewhere for. I don't feel human yet, and there's no way I'm relying on the precinct coffee."

"I don't know," Laura said, tapping her fingers on the top of the car as she touched the door handle with her other hand, contemplating getting in. "Do we follow up his cargo schedule, see where he's been and what he's been delivering? It could take hours. A lot of hours."

"We should let the locals handle that," Nate said. "Give it to some of their junior detectives to get the work done and bring us the results. It's too much of a waste of our time."

"Well, then, what do we look into?" Laura asked. "No family. A completely different job and neighborhood than the others. Where is the overlap?"

"I don't know," Nate admitted, and Laura felt a flash of fear running through her.

Fear that they weren't going to get any leads to follow at all – and without her visions coming to the rescue, they were groping along in the dark, all the while letting the killer get further and further ahead of them on the path to his fourth victim.

CHAPTER SEVENTEEN

Laura sat down next to Nate at the desk, grateful that they at least had a private area to work in at this precinct. It felt a bit like a storage room, and there was only one desk with two chairs, but at least they had somewhere. It often felt like there was too much attention on them when they had to sit out in the bullpen. Here, they could focus on getting the job done.

"We've got to work through this the logical way," Nate said. "They'll tell us if they find anything with the freight. Meanwhile, we've got to try and see where we can make links."

"What about the therapist?" Laura asked. It was the first thing she'd thought of. If the first two were his patients, then surely the third had to be as well. They had the complete list of everyone he'd ever seen, emailed over to Nate at their request yesterday evening. He opened up the file and quickly searched it, looking for Xavier Perez.

"No match," Nate said, his voice heavy and tired.

Laura heaved a sigh. Despite a night of sleep, she felt the same way he did. "It's social media time, isn't it?"

Nate chuckled at her reaction. "Sorry, but yes."

"Alright. You find John Wiggins, I'll work on Kenya Lankenua. First person to finish gets Xavier Perez."

"How lucky for them," Nate smirked. They both knew it wasn't exactly a prize. It was a punishment for being too good, almost.

Checking social media profiles was boring and often unrewarding work. First, they took the usernames that the locals had searched up for them on every social media network possible – a job that they sometimes had to outsource to their own FBI techs if the local police were limited, but thankfully here it had already been done.

Laura and Nate then navigated to the profiles of their chosen victims, and searched one by one through all of their follower or following counts. On some networks there was a search function, which made it easier – but on others, it was a case of literally scanning manually down a list of what could be thousands of names.

Whether or not there was a match, the next step was even less thrilling. They would scroll through posts and photos, looking for something that linked the victims together. It could be a comment or like from one of the other victims. It could be a photograph which happened to have all three of them in it – perhaps in the background of one another. It could even just be that they had all mentioned going to a certain bar or a yoga class or whatever other interests they might have had.

But as Laura scrolled down through page after page of data from Kenya Lankenua, she started to have a sinking feeling that they weren't going to get anywhere at all.

There didn't seem to be one single connection. Laura kept writing down the names of places Kenya had visited, checking them against Nate's list, but there was no concurrence between them.

All three of these people seemed to have lived, worked, and loved in completely different spheres than one another, now that the link of Dr. Usipov was ruled out.

And if there was no link between them…

"We could be looking at crimes of opportunity," Laura said, with rising horror. Crimes of opportunity were the worst. You had nothing to go on as to who the next victim might be. There was no way to predict it. You had to go after the killer alone, and when he was leaving so little evidence, that would be a huge challenge. There was no doubt in her mind that if they were dealing with an opportunity killer, there would be more bodies stacking up before they got anywhere close to catching him.

"It's so deliberately arranged, though," Nate argued, making a face. "I don't know. It feels like he knows these people. Like he's trying to send a message."

"What if the message is about him?" Laura asked. "Not about the people. What if they're just like – like mannequins to him. Once they're dead, they can be posed and arranged however he likes."

Nate nodded. "Alright, that does make a little more sense. You think maybe if he was able to kill two people in one place, he wouldn't need the mannequin?"

"Yeah, could be," Laura said. She didn't know. Neither of them did. Without the visions, she felt like she was lost, trying to find some kind of direction without the knowledge to do so. Orienteering without a compass.

"Well, then, we should be focusing on the mannequins," Nate said. Laura could see that he was working something through in his head, having an idea out loud. "Where does he get them from? I know we haven't seen any identifying markings, but where could they come from?"

"I guess he could buy them," Laura said. "I don't know how many you can get in one batch, whether it's wholesale only or you can buy them one at a time."

"They don't necessarily look new," Nate replied. "If he's buying them second-hand, it could be hard to trace them down. But you'd want a single source, wouldn't you? To make it easier to find the ones you needed when you needed them. You'd want to know you could reliably get more."

"Then you'd go to a wholesaler or dealer," Laura said. "We might be able to trace the purchases through."

"We could do that," Nate said thoughtfully. He was tapping a pen against the side of his wrist, an almost hypnotic and rhythmic movement. "But I think we should ask Captain Ortega to put someone on it and look in a different direction ourselves."

"What direction?" Laura asked, fighting back the urge to laugh at him for being melodramatic with the reveal.

"Thefts," Nate said. "If I was picking up a bulk load of something that I needed for my crimes, and I knew it was going to stand out as a signature, I would steal them instead of buying them. There would be no paper trail. And since I'm already committing murders, I probably wouldn't consider theft to be so huge of a crime, especially if I was already in a position where it would be easy for me to steal them."

"Where would that be?" Laura asked with a frown. "An easy position, I mean."

"I guess somewhere like a retail store," Nate said. "A big one or one that changed the style of mannequins they used, so they have a lot in storage. If they don't check on them often, that would be totally ideal, but then I guess it would also be a case of opportunity. He might take them wherever he can get them. Maybe even getting each one from a different place if he really has to."

Laura nodded. "Then let's look into thefts," she said. She nodded towards the computer they'd been loaned by Captain Ortega, which was situated on Nate's side of the desk.

He fired it up as Laura picked up her cell phone. She dialed Ortega's number, then waited for him to answer.

"Captain Ortega."

"Captain, can you direct one of your team to start looking into purchases of mannequins in the local area?" Laura asked.

The Captain grunted. "You don't think that would have been one of the first things I tried?"

Laura bit back a retort at his prickly tone. "And?"

"And, no dice. If this killer is buying them, it must be online. We haven't been able to find any local sellers at all."

"Thank you," Laura said. "What about thefts?"

There was a long pause. "I'm not sure."

"Never mind," Laura said, seeing Nate's gestures at the screen. "I think we've got the reports up now anyway. I'll let you know if we need anything else."

She ended the call as Nate tapped the screen excitedly, shaking his head. "I don't know if this is it, but there's a report of theft at a local department store that has been logged but not followed up," he said. "I guess Ortega has reassigned almost everyone to the murders, and there aren't enough bodies to follow up. The report says good stolen from the back room, but not what the goods were. Want to go check it out?"

Laura gestured to the stuffy, small box room and their utter lack of leads and results. "Is the Pope a Catholic?"

Nate laughed, standing up and grabbing his coat from the back of the chair. He swung the FBI-branded windbreaker over his shoulders as he moved around the table. "Race you to the car," he joked, but Laura didn't need to be challenged twice. She shot forward, beating him out of the door and speed-walking all the way down the hall.

***

Laura bobbed on her feet impatiently, straining her neck to try to see over the crowds of shoppers for a sign of the oncoming manager. She couldn't catch sight of anyone in uniform, and she was starting to grow impatient – when a sound from behind the customer service desk drew her attention, and she turned to see an unfamiliar man standing there.

"Hello," he said politely, using the respectful yet firm customer service voice that retail workers always seemed to develop eventually. "I'm the manager here. I'm told you're here to follow up on the theft report we filed yesterday?"

"That's right," Laura said, showing him her badge just the same way she had shown it to one of his subordinates at the desk a few moments ago. Nate did the same. She was worried by that word – yesterday – because if there hadn't been any theft before then, it wouldn't be possible to connect them to all of their murders.

"I didn't expect to have the FBI respond," he said, blinking from behind round eyeglasses that made him look about ten years older than he probably was. His brown hair was very neatly combed and parted, as if he'd taken inspiration for his look from Victorian-era shopkeepers in England.

"Well, we're actually investigating another case, but we're checking out some local cases while we're here," Laura explained. "Is there somewhere we can go to discuss your report?"

"Yes, of course," he said, gesturing towards a door behind him. That must have been where he had emerged from to surprise her. Laura followed Nate around the side of the counter and through the door, experiencing a moment of that strange feeling of entering an area that was normally reserved only for staff. As an agent, she went into private places all the time – but not usually while customers were still walking around, given that it was often part of a murder scene.

The door turned out to lead into a slightly grimy staff room, with a small coffee table surrounded by a battered sofa and several armchairs as well as a row of lockers against the wall. It was currently empty, a fact which allowed the manager to sit down at the coffee table and gesture for Nate and Laura to take the sofa.

"I didn't think much of it, at first," the manager said. "You must be taking it seriously, then? You think there's a link?"

Laura blinked. "A link between what?" she asked. The question sounded blunt once she'd said it, but she was confused as to what he was talking about – he clearly already thought she should know, but they hadn't even mentioned the murders yet.

"Oh," he said, his turn to be a little taken aback. "I'm sorry – you said you'd seen the report?"

"We saw a report that you've had a theft from your back room, but those are all the details we have," Nate said, spreading his hands wide to follow the explanation. "We came down here to find out more from the horse's mouth – so to speak."

"Oh, right!" the manager said, wide-eyed. "Well, it's a good job you did, then. We've had four mannequins stolen."

Nate and Laura blinked at one another. There was a slight tightening of a muscle in his jaw, which Laura thought she recognized as a quickly-stifled urge to grin. He'd been right. Without any psychic ability, too. She couldn't imagine he wasn't going to brag about this later.

"When did this happen?" Laura asked. She was going to need some serious answers about why this hadn't been flagged before. Surely, it should have been of the highest possible priority.

"Over the last few days," the manager said. "I went into the stockroom a few days ago and I noticed the mannequins looked different than normal. I couldn't put my finger on it, but then I checked our stock list and I saw we were missing two of them. I can't say for sure when they disappeared, but that's when I noticed it."

"But you said four were missing?"

The manager nodded. "I didn't think much of it at first, really. They're just a bunch of old mannequins that we don't use anymore. You've seen the mannequins in the front of the store?"

Laura nodded. Of course, she had. It was one of the first things she'd noticed when they walked in. In fact, she was seeing them everywhere – in every store window they passed. But the mannequins on display here were a different kind than those used by the killer. They had sculpted faces and hair, a modern style that was somehow less creepy because it was a little more realistic, even though that didn't make much sense to her.

But the killer had used a different kind of mannequin – faceless and featureless, with no hint of an expression. The heads were essentially a smooth white oval, the minimum effort required to make the mannequin the right shape.

"Well," the manager continued. "We replaced them all a few years ago, and since then the old ones have just been sitting there in the corner of the storeroom, not doing anything. I thought someone had probably taken them for an art project or something – we have a lot of students who end up doing part-time work here. Then a couple of days ago I went down there and saw that another was gone. That sort of annoyed me, until I heard about the murders on the news and how they were both posed with a mannequin. That flagged a bit of an alarm bell for me and I called the police to report the theft right away."

Laura almost ground her teeth, managing to loosen her jaw only with the fact that she was facing a member of the public and had to remain professional. Whatever halfwit had been working the desk on the day this was called in had reported it only as a theft, not flagging it as connected to the murders at all. They could have been a day further along in their investigation. They could possibly have saved Xavier Perez's life with this knowledge.

"And the fourth one?" Nate prompted.

"That disappeared just this morning," the manager said. He paused, then corrected himself. "When I say this morning – I mean last night, really. I checked the storeroom right before closing up the store last night. When I came in to open up this morning, one of them was gone. It was there before. I know that for a fact."

"Then the question we have to ask is, who has access to the storeroom after hours?" Laura asked.

The manager nodded somberly and pulled a piece of paper out of his inside jacket pocket. "I'm ahead of you there," he said. "I've already been thinking about who it could possibly be. It has to be someone with a key or who comes in every night. We do have a security guard who can let people in, though I do think he would notice if someone came out with a mannequin, and he told me he hasn't."

"Is the name of the security guard on that list?" Laura asked, taking it from his outstretched hand.

"Yes," the manager said. "And myself, of course. Just for the sake of elimination from your inquiries."

"Alright," Laura nodded. "So, where were you last night after you left the store?"

"I went home," the manager replied. "I live in a shared apartment, and I ate dinner with my roommates before watching a film. Then we all went to bed separately, of course. But I'm sure they would be able to testify that none of them heard the sound of the door opening and closing in the night. Oh, and two nights ago, I was staying at my girlfriend's house – she will be able to tell you for certain that I was there all night."

Laura nodded. It wasn't a bulletproof alibi, but it was good enough. If he was the killer, there was no way he would have been bold enough to actually tip them off to the theft. And even if this was all some kind of strange double-bluff, she could always investigate him and see about those alibis if the rest of the list came up with no results.

"This is a short enough list," she said, scanning it and then showing it to Nate. Seven names. The manager, a security guard, and five others who occupied various roles within the store. Only seven. It wouldn't take long to get through them. Laura felt a burst of mad hope.

"No one else can get access to the storeroom at all?" she asked. "Not even your other employees?"

"No, I can verify that," he said. "Once inside, it might be possible to go out through one of the emergency fire exits without being seen by security – but otherwise, you'd have to walk right past him, and he swears he hasn't seen anyone with a mannequin."

"Alright. Thank you," Laura said, standing up. Nate joined her as she put the list into her pocket. They would probably have to come back here within a short period of time to interview some of the employees, but for now, they could explore the list back at the precinct to avoid raising the alarm. "Don't tell anyone you've spoken with us or

94

that we have this list. Your employee out there who fetched you for us – you'll need to ask her to keep quiet, too."

"Of course," the manager nodded enthusiastically. "Anything I can do to help."

"Alright," Laura said, nodding at Nate. "Let's go."

For the first time, as she strode out of the staff room and through the store, she actually felt like they were about to get somewhere with this case – even as the fear that he was about to take his fourth victim solidified into something much more real.

CHAPTER EIGHTEEN

Laura typed the last name into the computer and scanned the results that came up, shaking her head. "Nothing on this one," she said.

"Still, that's promising," Nate replied. "One employee with a criminal record – that's all we need, after all."

Laura looked over the list again. It was true – just one of the people on the list was previously known to the local police. A woman who had been cautioned over a small theft when she was a teenager. That was over a decade ago, but then it didn't necessarily matter. It only meant she hadn't been caught again, not that she had stopped stealing or committing other crimes. Maybe she'd just become better at it.

"We made up our minds fairly certainly that this was the work of a male killer," Laura mused, looking at the names again. Tanya Hamilton. Could she really have the strength to hit someone over the back of the head hard enough to kill them? Perez had needed two hits, but he was the first one. The others had died on impact. That required significant upper body strength.

"Maybe she steals the mannequins on behalf of the killer," Nate suggested. "It wouldn't be the first time that a woman got caught up in helping a lover commit his crimes. Myra Hindley and Ian Brady, Karla Homolka and Paul Bernardo, Charlene and Gerald Gallego."

"Maybe," Laura agreed. That situation was a little more plausible. And maybe the staging of the bodies pointed at that kind of complex situation – it would be a lot easier to explain the weirdness of it all if there were two people involved. "We should pay her a visit, see what she has to say when she has no warning we're coming. Maybe we'll get lucky and find a mannequin right there in her home."

"Then let's head out," Nate said, already starting towards the door.

Laura followed him to the car, getting into the passenger side while he drove. The GPS showed that they weren't far from their potential suspect's home, which was a plus. Five or ten minutes and they'd be there. "What about the others?" she asked. "If this doesn't work out, we'll have to work our way down the list."

"I agree," Nate said. "The one I'm most suspicious about, other than Hamilton, would be the security guard."

"Really?" Laura asked. "The manager didn't seem to have any concerns about him."

"He didn't express particular concerns about any of them, but one of them has to be guilty," Nate pointed out.

"You're right, as always," Laura said, her eyes drifting to the view out of the window as she thought. It would help a lot if she had something to touch right now. She realized she'd started to subconsciously avoid anything that might help trigger a vision, out of the fear that it wouldn't come. But it was selfish, that fear. It could be keeping the killer free, allowing him – or possibly, now, her – to go after another victim. She needed to push it, try to find something.

But what?

"So, you haven't seen anything for a while," Nate said, as if he was reading her mind. His tone was a forced casual, clearly faked. "I mean, you've seen things. Just not – *seen things*. Uh, you know."

"I haven't had any visions," Laura said wearily, helping him to translate what he actually meant. "Yes, I know. I'm working on it."

"Okay." Nate glanced at her sideways briefly. "Anything I should be doing to help?"

"I've managed it fine for thirty-three years without your help," Laura said, and regretted it immediately. "Damnit. Sorry. I'm just – I'm aware I haven't been very helpful on this case. I do want to see something, it's just – not coming right now."

"We're managing fine," Nate said, which she thought was extremely generous on his part given that they still hadn't arrested anyone. "Don't stress out about it."

"Easier said than done," Laura sighed, putting her head against the backrest, and trying to think.

Maybe she would get lucky. If they were about to pull up outside the house of someone who really was involved with the case, maybe just touching the door or shaking hands with her would be enough. She would make an effort here. She had to.

"This is it," Nate said, pulling up alongside a small, thin house squeezed between two others. Laura took a breath. She had to do this. She had to.

They got out of the car and Laura hung back for just a moment, trying to gather her courage. She needed to face this head-on. Why was it so terrifying now to think that she might fail? She'd spent a long time wishing she had no visions at all, and now here she was scared that she'd touch something and not get one?

She shook her hands out to her sides in an effort to clear the mental block and then stalked after Nate, who was already on his way to the door.

He knocked, and they both waited in silence, the tension building. They were both keenly aware that this could be their suspect – even if it was a female who had stolen the items, that didn't mean she lived alone or that the actual killer wasn't going to answer the door. No matter what happened here, it was likely to lead them to the killer either directly or indirectly – unless they were wrong, which was something Laura didn't even want to contemplate.

The woman who answered the door was clearly not expecting to see them. She blinked as she took them in, looking them up and down. "Hello?" she said.

"Hello," Laura replied, pleasantly enough. "Are you Tanya Hamilton?"

"Yes," she said, then looked between them again more doubtfully. Laura always liked to imagine what was going through someone's mind at this point. Did she think they were here to sell her something? To deliver a subpoena? Maybe as debt collectors?

"Excellent," Laura said, whipping out her badge, watching for the moment Tanya's face would change. "I'm Special Agent Laura Frost. Could we come in and talk?"

Tanya's face did change – into utter surprise and then horror. "What is this about?" she asked nervously, glancing up and down the street behind them."

"We're investigating a recent theft from the department store you work at," Laura said. "Can we come in? It would be great to talk with a little more privacy."

Tanya nodded, the color all drained from her face, and stepped back inside the house. Laura and Nate followed her inside the small, cramped space, and Laura glanced over her shoulder to stifle a laugh at how cramped-up Nate looked walking down the entrance corridor between a shelf at his head height and a low-hanging light fixture. Laura trailed a fingertip along the wall, slid her hand along to the door handle of the next room, but no headache sparked inside her skull.

Inside a tiny, rectangular sitting room, Tanya turned to face them, crossing her arms over her chest. She was small – wiry. Maybe not strong enough for the murders, but she looked strong enough for the theft. "I haven't stolen anything," she said, immediately. "I know I have a record, but I didn't do anything this time. I honestly don't know anything about any theft."

"It wasn't such a serious crime," Laura said, trying to trip her up by making it seem like it was nothing. "You probably thought no one was going to miss them, right? After all, they haven't been used in so long. They were just sitting in the storage room, gathering dust."

"What? No, I don't – I have no idea what's been taken," Tanya said. "I literally don't. I mean, you can look around if you want. You won't find anything here."

"That's very kind of you," Nate said, nodding and then disappearing back into the hall. Laura couldn't imagine it would take him long to look.

"Was it someone you know who asked you to get them?" Laura asked, thinking she would do best to press on. She was deliberately not using the words – not saying exactly what it was that had gone missing. She wanted Tanya to slip up and say it. To deny taking the mannequins, at which point Laura would have to ask her how she had known they were here about the mannequins, and then the arrest would be clear.

"Get what?" Tanya asked, frustration visibly evident on her face. Her features were pinched, her skin tight over her face, as though she'd been struggling to get enough to eat for a long time. That put her in a good demographic for theft, especially if she'd been paid to do the job.

"They're not easy to move," Laura said, turning to glance around at the décor in the sitting room as though she was looking for clues. "Did you have help? Or did you take your time and sneak out the back way?"

"What?" Tanya shook her head, staring off into the distance. "Hard to move – storage room – I don't know, you think I took some big wholesale-size bags of something or whatever? I don't even go into the storage room that often!"

"Your manager told us you're one of the only seven people with access to it after hours," Laura commented, looking at her sideways.

"I'm one of the cleaning staff," Tanya snapped, clearly without any pride. "You think I have time to mess around? I have to clean the entire store. Top to bottom. Most days, I barely manage to get out of there before my shift ends."

"Hmm," Laura nodded faux-sympathetically. "You probably aren't paid enough, either. I suppose that's why you needed to bring in a bit of extra income?"

"No!" Tanya exploded, her hands going up to her head to run through her hair. "This is – I haven't done anything! I swear! It took me long enough to get that job – I don't want to risk it! I wouldn't!"

Nate appeared in the doorway, giving Laura a quick shake of his head. No mannequins.

Laura was on the verge of believing that Tanya had no idea what was going on. She was doing a very convincing acting job if that wasn't true. She seemed scared, but not like she was scared of getting caught.

Like she was scared of being framed and losing her job over something that was out of her control.

"When were your last two shifts?" Laura asked, seizing onto an idea that hadn't occurred to her until now – stupidly, she thought, internally berating herself.

"Last night and three nights before that," Tanya said. "I get two days off a week, though it's not always the weekend, just whenever they can bring in agency cover."

"You weren't working the night before last? Where were you?"

"Night school," Tanya said, lifting her head up defiantly as if to dare Laura to suggest that a woman like her wasn't going to get anything out of going to night school.

Laura sighed internally. They were barking up the wrong tree. Night school would give her witnesses, so the alibi was most likely airtight.

They'd struck out again.

"Alright, Ms. Hamilton," Laura said. "We're sorry for the intrusion. Before we go, do you have any idea who might be stealing from the store?"

"I would guess Will James," she said, folding her arms over her chest. "He's the one who gets the run of the place."

The name sparked a memory of the list they'd been given. "The security guard?" Laura asked.

"Yeah, that's him," Tanya sniffed. "He's a weasel, too. Now, are you going to leave me alone?"

"We are," Laura said, totally understanding her attitude; after all, she was innocent. She looked at Nate. "I guess we'd better go see a security guard.

***

Laura looked at the house, squinting, unconvinced. "I don't know," she said. "It doesn't look like the home of a criminal mastermind."

100

"It's registered in his parents' name, by the looks of things." Nate looked up from his phone, where he'd been conducting a quick search. "He's a young guy. Must still be living at home."

"This doesn't seem right, does it?" Laura asked. "We're in the middle of suburbia, he's a young guy living with his parents and working as a security guard. A steady job that will help him get his own place before long. Our manager clearly trusts him."

"But what Tanya said is right," Nate shrugged. "He's the only person who has access to the storeroom for his whole shift without oversight. Every other person would have to get the mannequins out past him, or leave through the back exit and raise suspicions by never leaving after their shift. It's a good bet that he would be behind it."

Laura nodded. "I hope he is," she said, sighing. "Because if we're wrong, our next step might be poring over hundreds of hours of security footage to see if we can catch a glimpse of someone – who probably knows where the cameras are – sneaking them out."

"Come on," Nate said, getting out of the car and leading her over to the door.

He knocked once, loudly enough, then stepped back. They waited for a long moment, but there was no sound or sign of life from inside the house.

"There's a car still in the driveway," Laura pointed out. "And he's a nighttime security guard. It seems kind of implausible that he would be out at this time of day."

Nate shrugged. "Maybe he's asleep," he said. "If he sleeps during the day, I guess he would possibly need to wear headphones or use a noise machine to cancel out the noise from the street, in which case he might not hear my knock."

"That's true, I guess," Laura said. "Should we take a look?"

Nate nodded and moved towards one of the windows.

The curtains were open, so it was possible to see through the ground-floor windows into the home itself. One of them revealed a dining room with a slightly dusty dining table and a cabinet full of dainty dishware. The other showed them an empty living room with a sofa and TV set, along with framed photographs of the family. There was no sign of anyone moving or even sleeping inside.

"Back windows?" Laura suggested in a low voice. She could see there was a path around the side of the building. It led to a fenced-in yard with a solid wood gate just as tall as the fence, but that wasn't going to be a problem for Nate.

He nodded once, walked over to the gate, and – with the help of a garbage can set out for collection day – pulled himself over it, dropping down to the floor below.

A moment later, the gate creaked open, Nate pushing it from the inside.

Laura joined him in the backyard, a small space without much to define it – there was a small, paved area at the back of the house and some flowerbeds, but no other signs of activity. What there were, however, were two wide windows and a French patio door, giving them excellent visibility into the back of the house.

Laura looked into one of the windows, the one furthest from the gate, strolling past the others and seeing no sign of movement. Her breath caught in her throat when she saw someone inside the room, standing with their back to the window.

No. It wasn't a person.

Laura grabbed Nate's arm silently and pointed.

It was a mannequin.

CHAPTER NINETEEN

Laura pulled her gun out of its holster as Nate did the same, both of them quickly giving their weapons a visual check. Everything was silent, stealthy. They had to retain the element of surprise as much as possible. He couldn't know they were coming.

There were two exits from the house – front door, back door. They couldn't cover both, because both were locked. The only other way to get in would be for Nate to kick in the door, then rush all the way to the other side and let Laura in, potentially turning his back on their suspect and allowing him to get off a shot. No, they had to do this together. Safer.

Nate sized up the back door, nodded with grim determination, and then aimed one solid kick right below the door handle where the lock was holding it firm. The second kick blasted it open, leaving a broken mess in his wake, and Laura surged inside with him right behind as soon as he recovered from the momentum.

The first room was clear, they'd been able to see that from outside. In fact, almost the whole of the lower floor could be ignored. Laura kept her eyes open for extra doors: there was one under the stairs, but throwing it open revealed only a downstairs toilet.

There was a crashing noise from upstairs as if someone had stumbled into something, then a shout. A moment later it came again from the top of the stairs, much clearer.

"Hey! Who's there? Get out of my house!"

"William James!" Nate thundered. "Get down on the ground with your hands where we can see them! This is the FBI!"

"Wh-what…?"

Laura could see him now as she circled around to the foot of the stairs, looking up at him and seeing no sign of a weapon. He was dressed in a pair of pajama pants and nothing else, his brown hair mussed up with sleep and his eyes wide open but his mouth hanging slack. He looked like someone who had been wrenched out of sleep and then put on high alert, in short, and his hands were hesitating halfway into the air at his sides.

"On the ground with your hands where we can see them," Laura repeated, clearer and more calmly. "Now."

James's mouth opened and closed but then he complied, mumbling something as he lowered himself swiftly to the ground, putting his hands far out to either side of his body. Laura slowly advanced up the stairs, knowing Nate had his gun trained on the security guard's head just in case he tried anything rash.

At the top of the stairs, Laura stopped, eyeing him. He would be pretty cold out there if they took him like this. Then again, he was a killer.

But then – again – if he wasn't…

Laura glanced into the bedroom, the room he had quite clearly just come out of, and spotted a shirt lying haphazardly across the back of a chair. It looked like it matched the pajama bottoms he was wearing, probably part of a set. Laura moved past him, grabbed it, and threw it down on the floor in front of him.

"Put that on and then lay down again with your hands behind your back," she said.

He swallowed and then slowly moved, as if he didn't want to make any sudden movements that would startle her into shooting him. Laura dropped the muzzle of her gun to point at the floor. He was complying. There was no need to risk an incident with a twitch of her finger.

He slowly began to put the shirt on, pulling it over first one arm and then the other. He made a kind of shrugging movement to flip it up onto his shoulders, and then –

It happened far too fast. One moment he was there, slowly and calmly dressing, the next he was running. Laura only had the chance to dodge to the side out of instinct as he ran right at her, all of her weapons' training becoming useless in the small space and the heat of the moment.

He whooshed past her with a wind that stirred her clothes, and then he was running back into his own bedroom, shirt flapping behind him like a cape as he jumped up onto the bed. Laura saw with horror that he was heading towards the window, probably about to enact some long-perfected escape from his childhood window, ready to run from them –

As his feet tangled in the messy duvet he had left on the bed, he flailed his arms in the air, and he went down flat on his face.

Laura surged forward, training her gun on him again. Nate was already there, having shot up the stairs when he saw their suspect rush past her, and he dove headlong into the room to tackle the young man. Laura started forward, trying to provide tactical support but not having any chance of a clear shot as they grappled on top of the bed, the security guard still trying to fight his way clear. They rolled off the bed with a heavy *whoomph*, and Laura rushed forward, gun trained on the floor until she could see them –

Nate was sitting on top of their suspect, grabbing a pair of handcuffs from his belt to cuff his hands behind his back, panting for breath but grinning with victory.

"Alright," Nate said, grimacing as he clicked the final cuff into place and sat back on his heels. "William James, I'm arresting you on suspicion of murder."

Laura tuned him out as he read James his rights, turning to look around the room and take in what she could. It looked like a normal young man's bedroom, in all honesty – an awkward combination between a teenager's bedroom and the man that now inhabited it, old toys and figurines jumbled next to aftershave on the dresser and a selection of blue silk ties hanging from the side of the mirror.

"We'll need backup to secure the scene before we go," Laura said, trying to ignore how fast her heart was still pounding now that the adrenaline was starting to wear off. "His parents could come back and tamper with the evidence."

Nate nodded, getting up and hauling James to his feet. "We'll put him in the car," he suggested. "You call Ortega now."

Laura did as she was told, not because he was giving the orders but because it was a reasonable division of labor. She walked behind him as he took their suspect to the car, keeping her eyes open and focused, in case he tried to make a break for it again. She requested the backup and then they both leaned against the side of the car, with James silent and surly locked inside of it.

"We've got him," Nate said. He didn't quite lean over for a high five, but the gleam in his eye expressed the same message. "We did it."

"Yeah," Laura said, although she couldn't help but glance over her shoulder and into the car. At this kid. Because he was just a kid, really. And, yes, she knew two obvious facts: one, that the older she got, the people she saw as kids encompassed a wider and wider age range; and two, the majority of serial killers did turn out to be young white males in their twenties when they started.

But still. He *looked* like a kid. Still living at home. Sleeping in his childhood bedroom. She could see how a psychologist might point out that this environment could make him feel like a failure, make him want to prove he was a man. But that wasn't the vibe she got from these murders.

Not only that, but she hadn't had a single vision the whole time they'd been in there. Was it really that her visions were so bad now that she wasn't going to trigger anything even by touching the killer? Or was it that there were no visions to come because he was caught, now?

Or the third option – that there could be no visions about the killings if he wasn't the killer...

"It was almost too easy," she said, thinking out loud, keeping her voice quiet enough that the kid in the car would only hear a murmur and not know what she was saying.

"Easy?" Nate shot her a look. "Speak for yourself."

Laura smirked at him and shook her head. "In terms of the investigation, I mean," she said. She looked at the house, shaking her head and muttering. "He just left it out in the open, right there..."

"Here's backup," Nate said, nodding up the road at a patrol car approaching rapidly.

Laura shaded her eyes to watch them come, mentally preparing for the interview they would conduct when they got William James back to the precinct.

If they didn't get it right – and he was the killer – he could still walk away.

She wasn't going to let that happen, doubts or no doubts.

***

Laura leaned back in her chair, happy to let Nate take the lead on this one. They'd already come to blows, after all. The kid was likely to be far more intimidated by him than he was by Laura, given that all she'd managed to do was let him run past her.

"I didn't know the FBI were going to get involved," he was saying, his words coming out like a ten-car pileup on the highway, all on top of one another and running over. He was stuttering, gesturing wildly, sweating in his pajamas. "It was just supposed to be a quick buck, that's all! I don't know anything about any murders!"

"A quick buck?" Nate repeated. "How's that? You thought you could get some notoriety for those sick little scenes you set up, is that it?" He was laying it on thick, playing bad cop. Leaning forward across the table so James had nowhere further back to go, making aggressive and accusatory statements with each question, making sure to scowl at him as much as possible in between. He was doing a very convincing job of being the guy who wanted to make this guy's life miserable in revenge for the fight they'd had.

"No!" James exclaimed, his eyes wide and his face a shade of gray. "I don't even know what – what scenes you're talking about!"

106

Nate scoffed, rolling his eyes, and turning his head to the wall momentarily as if to find someone to agree with him on the other side of the one-way glass. Laura knew there was no one there, but the kid didn't. "Come on. You expect me to believe you haven't heard about the local murders over the past few days? The news channels around here have practically been showing nothing else. Not to mention all that water cooler talk."

"I work nights, alone," the security guard pointed out. "I have no idea what you're talking about. The first time I heard about any murders was when you said you were arresting me for them!"

"Alright," Nate said, shaking his head with a disbelieving smile as if he was just allowing him to lie for now. "So, why did you steal the mannequins?"

James clamped his mouth shut for a moment and looked at his lawyer, who until now had been sitting so silently that Laura had almost forgotten he was in the room. Only almost, because you knew as an agent that if you took your eye off a lawyer, they would start poking holes in your case.

He brief leaned in to whisper something in James's ear; he turned and whispered something back, and then they exchanged a quick nod.

"I did take the mannequins," James said, his face pale as he confessed. "I've been selling them to art students at the college for a couple hundred bucks each. It's still cheaper than what they would pay for them online or from the manufacturer, so there's been a bit of demand. The first one was for my girlfriend and the orders have kept coming in since then."

"Can you give us the names of the students you sold them to?" Laura asked. Inwardly, she felt a flash of despair. It was a good story. Good enough to be the truth. "We're going to need to check that your story is true."

James nodded wearily, reaching out for the pen and paper in the middle of the table. It was supposed to be for the start of recording his statement, but this would do just as well.

"In the meantime, you can tell us where you were after your shift last night, and before your shift the night before," Nate said, his voice flat and still clearly not buying the idea that James was innocent. Of the murders, if not the theft.

"I just went home," James said, his voice almost a squeak. "I was at home before and then I came home after. That's it."

"And can anyone other than your obviously biased mother and father verify that?" Nate snapped.

"My client has been very open and honest with you," the lawyer interrupted, folding his hands on top of the table. "I suggest that you look into the sale of the mannequins as has been described to you before you ask any more accusatory questions. He's been very forthcoming and cooperative so far."

"Once we got into this room," Nate grunted through gritted teeth. "He was a bit less cooperative in the house."

Laura had the feeling she was about to have to step in and prevent another fistfight, but the door to the interview room cracked open a second after a rapid knock and all of the heads in the room swiveled to look at it. Laura glimpsed one of the detectives working under Ortega through the gap, and got up to hear what they had to say.

"What is it?" she asked, keeping her voice low as she stepped out into the hall and held the door all but shut behind her.

"It's the mannequins," the detective said, somewhat nervously. Laura took that as a very bad sign. "Captain Ortega said we should notify you right away."

"What about them?" Laura asked, bracing herself for the bad news she already, in her gut, knew was coming.

"The one we retrieved from the suspect's home has a stamp on it marking it as property of the department store," the detective explained. "We hurried over to the store to check out the storeroom, and all the others do, too. But the ones found at the crime scenes didn't have any identifying marks. There's no way to remove the stamp – the porous material kind of sucks it up, so you'd have to scrape off part of the mannequin to get it off. There's no sign of any tampering like that."

Laura gritted her teeth against an oncoming headache. Not the kind that usually precipitated a vision. No, this was a regular old frustration headache.

"Alright. Thank you," she said, before walking back into the interview room and shooting Nate a look of hopelessness.

"Mr. James," she said, leaning heavily on the back of her chair. "Thank you for your cooperation. We'll be speaking with your manager about whether he wants to press charges on the theft. For the moment, you're free to go."

She turned towards the wall rather than watch the look of victory on the smug lawyer's face, or see William James realize he was no longer in danger of being put away for something he didn't do. It wouldn't make her feel any better.

And somewhere out there, the killer was still ready to make his next move.

CHAPTER TWENTY

Laura shook her head when Nate took a step towards her, holding up a hand. "Don't," she said. It was just the two of them in the interview room now, but she didn't feel ready to leave. "I can't believe we got it wrong again."

"This is normal," Nate reminded her. "We always have to fight through the different leads until we find the one that works. If there was an obvious culprit, they wouldn't need to call in the FBI. You've just forgotten that because you're frustrated about your – you know."

Visions. He didn't even want to say the word. "Yeah, well. We'd be a lot further along right now if they were working."

"Maybe, maybe not," Nate said. He was probably just trying to be kind, but the failure burned into her like a brand against her skin. She hated herself for a moment, hated that she couldn't get the visions to work, hated that she wasn't a good enough detective to solve the case without them. Hated that she was wasting time on thinking these things instead of going out there and finding the next lead.

Her phone buzzed in her pocket, and she snatched it out as if it was on fire, hoping for a new clue. But her heart only skipped a single beat when she saw it was Chris on the caller ID – and then she hated herself for being apprehensive instead of excited to speak to him, too.

"It's Chris," she said, shortly. "My, um." She didn't really know what to call him. Boyfriend? That felt too juvenile, but they were definitely dating.

"Right," Nate said quickly, gesturing towards the door as he stepped in that direction. "I'll give you some privacy."

He was gone before she'd hit the answer call button, taking a breath before speaking to try to stop her voice from sounding so short. "Hi, it's Laura."

"Hey!" Chris's voice was far too upbeat, making her wince. "How's it going with your case?"

"You know I can't tell you any details," Laura said, which wasn't fair. She knew that he only meant to ask if it was going well or not. It was just that she couldn't bear to tell him that they were getting nowhere.

"Oh, right," Chris said, sounding a little taken aback before he rebounded. "Well, I was just wondering about this weekend. I wanted to book something, but obviously if you'll still be out there, there's no point. What do you think? Will you be back in time?"

"I don't know," Laura sighed. "It's like asking me how long a piece of string is. The case is over when it's over."

"Right, I get that," Chris said. "I was just wondering if you had, I don't know, a gut feeling or something. If you think you're close to solving it or if it's going to be a long and difficult one."

"I don't know, Chris," Laura said, gritting her teeth. "I never know. I've told you that before!"

Her voice came out so much harsher than she intended it to. "Got it," Chris said, his previous exuberance all but gone. "I'll, um. Hold off. Let me know if you do get it figured out, and if there's still time I can always book something at the last minute."

"Chris," Laura said, sighing, knowing she needed to apologize. "I'm sorry. You've caught me at a really bad time. I'm just – I'm stressed out."

"Good luck with it," Chris said, brushing over her. "The case, I mean. I'll see you when you get back."

"See you," Laura began, but he'd already put down the phone.

Damnit. She'd messed up again. Chris was an understanding kind of guy, but how much patience did he have before he would get tired of her being snappy and unappreciative? At least she didn't worry anymore about him turning out to be violent like his brother, but that didn't mean she wasn't going to lose him.

And if she lost him, she lost access to Amy – lost the chance to make sure she was alright.

God, it was all falling apart. Laura held onto the back of the chair with one hand and sunk her head into the other, wishing it wasn't so hard. They'd reached a dead end in the investigation and all she'd been able to muster so far was a vision of someone cheating and a creepy nightmare. She wanted a drink. She really wanted a drink. If she snuck out without Nate seeing –

The door opened and she sensed more than saw Nate enter the room, knowing him by his presence, by the sound of his footsteps. She didn't need a drink. She would be fine without a drink. She had to stay strong.

"Everything alright?" Nate asked, coming to a stop beside her.

Laura dropped her hand from her head and looked up with a dull nod, letting her hand settle on the back of the chair next to the other one. "Just wish we were getting somewhere," she said.

"We will," Nate assured her. "Trust me. This killer isn't going to get away with it for long. We'll get him."

"It's how long he gets away with it that worries me," Laura said, taking a deep and slow breath. She just needed to calm down and focus. She needed –

A spike of pain went through her temple and she stopped thinking, waiting for the vision to suck her down into it and show her what she needed –

There was a man, walking along, his back to her. All she could see was the back of his head. Short-cropped black hair. A blue collar – a collared shirt, so something smart. She tried to take in every detail that she could, anything that might identify him. If this was their killer – or even his next victim – she needed to remember. She needed to know.

It was so dark, so hard to see. Even the edges of his head were fuzzy, like they were threatening to spiral off into the darkness all around him. There was no sense of time or place, no sense of motion. No – she thought maybe he was walking. But to where, where from? She had no answers.

The vision pulled out slightly, and she thought – this was it – she was going to see him, see his face. All he had to do was turn. Even to the side – even to give her a profile would be enough. She just needed more data. Was his nose long? Did he have a moustache or beard? What color were his eyes? Anything – anything to help her track him down...

He stopped moving, she thought, and then there was some sound, muffled as if from underwater and far away. She couldn't make out what he was saying. Then there was some kind of grunt, a curse – something going wrong? What was she seeing? What was going wrong for him?

The vision pulled out further, started to solidify a little more around the edges, getting brighter. Laura tried to take in as much as she could, tried to understand what she was seeing. A dim room, maybe – a gray room – the blue shirt in more detail, with epaulettes on either shoulder, with a badge just visible further down on the sleeve –

Laura came back to herself furious and aching, her head pounding for no good reason. Who cared what was going to happen in this interview room to another police officer sitting in this chair? Why would she need to see a vision about that? Even if it *had* related to their case, she couldn't see the officer's face or make out anything about what was happening! It had probably been a case of him stubbing his toe on a doorframe, and she couldn't even warn him about being careful!

She stood straight and turned to the door, only to find Nate standing in the way with a troubled look on his face.

"What did you see?" he asked. His eyes were wide, his mouth open like he was ready to cheer with excitement. Like he thought she was about to give him the answer to the whole case and they could go wrap it up right now.

Oh, how utterly bizarre it was now that he knew about the visions. How strange to have him asking her what she'd seen, when for so long she had been trying to hide that she had seen anything at all. Sometimes Laura didn't think she liked this new reality. It had been easier to stomach these kinds of useless distractions when she was the only one who knew about them.

Laura shook her head. She didn't want to go into it. "It was nothing," she said. What was she supposed to do – admit to him that she had failed yet again?

"Wait," Nate said, moving to block her exit as she tried to leave the room. He held out his hands, his voice still fast and excited. "It wasn't nothing. You had a vision, didn't you?"

Laura wanted to lie so badly. She wanted to pretend she'd just been spaced out thinking about going on a date with Chris over the weekend, but it was the stupid kind of lie that would create more questions than it answered.

"I did," she said. "But it was nothing. I have those sometimes. It didn't help."

Nate sighed heavily, dropping his arms back down by his sides. "Damnit, Laura, you're not supposed to be keeping this stuff from me anymore," he said. "You can tell me now. It's not like I don't know what's going on."

"I'm serious," she said. "It was nothing you need to know about."

"Need to know about?" Nate repeated incredulously. He shook his head. "Wasn't the whole point of the dance we've been doing over the past couple of months that you were going to be honest with me from now on? Why did you even tell me about your visions if you're just going to keep shutting me out and hiding them?"

Laura looked at his face and almost balked. He was angry with her. Again. All those frustrations from the last few months, all the times he had repeated that he couldn't work with her anymore if she wasn't open and honest. It was all bubbling right back to the surface now that the issue had come up again. He was furious with her, not just for avoiding his questions this time but for all the other times as well.

And in that moment, something inside Laura cowered away rather than facing up to it. Something inside her was kneeling in front of Marcus, begging him not to take Lacey away from her, even though she was so drunk she could barely say her own daughter's name right. Something inside her was sitting alone in her car, having received the news that Nate had put in a transfer and was never going to work with her again. Something inside of her was seeing the look on her mother's face when she realized that Laura had seen her father's death ahead of time and never said a word about it.

She brushed past Nate and out into the corridor, her mouth clamped firmly shut, and half-walked, half-ran out of the precinct into the cold air and the escape that their hired car offered.

CHAPTER TWENTY ONE

He sat and looked at the mannequin, admiring it as he put the rag to the side. He'd done everything he could to make it as clean and shiny as possible, going over every single millimeter of it until he was absolutely sure he had erased every trace of whatever life it might have had before.

It was clean, but he did not take off his gloves. No, there was no point in risking getting it dirty and having to start all over again. And like this, he could be free to run his finger along the curves and smoothness of it, admiring what he had done. Knowing that everything was ready.

Tonight, he would be able to put his final mannequin in place, and everything would be complete.

Ah, everything had gone so well. Better than he ever could have hoped. No one had even been by to ask about the missing mannequins yet – because no one had noticed they were gone. He had calculated everything well. It was true that no one would notice what he was doing. It was true that no one would notice the missing bodies. And now here he was, standing on the precipice of completing his work.

To think, that all this would soon be done. That he would have finished. And, being uncaught so far, he had to assume that he would remain uncaught. That had been one of his worries, that someone would misinterpret what he was doing and try to get him into trouble. If they didn't see the beauty in it, the magic, they might think that he needed to go away somewhere – and then he wouldn't be able to finish. But he no longer had that worry.

No, now he was just quietly happy, ready for the final stage. Tonight he would be going to see his cousin! Wasn't it incredible? To have spent so long without any family at all, and then to find out that you had a cousin all along!

It had been an incredible discovery. He'd thought that he had no family left at all. He only dimly remembered the concept, now – a home full of smiles and laughter when he was very young, so long ago that it felt almost like someone else's memory. Something he had seen in a film, maybe.

He'd given up hope.

But then he'd found out about the fact he still had a relative left – and better than that, they even worked in the same place! What an incredible coincidence that was, so amazing he could barely believe it. To go your whole life looking for something, and then to find out it was right on your doorstep all along!

Well, tonight was going to be something special, and make no mistake. Tonight, he was going to have such a good time. He and his cousin were going to spend the evening together, just hanging out and getting to know one another. What a happy day it was going to be!

He was so blessed lately. Finding a cousin, such close friends, and even a lover all at once. What a lucky life. Maybe things had been hard before, but he'd really stumbled upon some luck in recent times.

He turned, catching sight of his own reflection in the windowpane, and stopped.

He looked tired. Worn down. And behind him was a mannequin – faceless, expressionless. Just a mannequin.

He was alone with a mannequin, because no one else would be around him.

He stared at his own reflection for a while, unmoving. It all flooded in on him then. It wasn't true – none of it was. And he knew it. He was all alone here, was always all alone. He had been alone for such a long time, and no one was going to start noticing him now. Not in the way he wanted, and not before it was far too late.

He had no family. He had no friends. That was the truth of it. He was all alone.

It struck him dumb and froze him to the spot, the crushing weight of it all. Alone for his whole life with no possible end in sight. No hope of finding a special person to spend his life with – not even a friend. Because no one ever noticed him, and when they did, they turned away.

He was never going to find a person who wanted to be around him as much as he wanted to be around them. Not even one-half or one-fifth. That was what hurt the most, more than anything else he had been through. Being alone.

He looked away from his own eyes and stared at the floor, ashamed to even meet his own gaze anymore. What did he deserve to be looked at for?

Without the image to hold him in place, his hands relaxed, fists unfurling, and his shoulders slowly dropped. He turned and looked at the mannequin, still pristine and waiting. Yes. Waiting for him. That was right. He had an important thing to do tonight.

Everything was going to be amazing.

All he had to do was put the finishing touches into place now. Yes, that was right. He was going to make sure that everything was set up just perfectly for his cousin, because that was what you did for the people who were important to you in your life. He was sure his cousin would do the same for him!

He touched the mannequin one last time and then turned, avoiding his reflection this time, to start gathering his things for the truck.

CHAPTER TWENTY TWO

Laura sat in the passenger seat of the hired car, slumped down, not even sure what she was doing. What a stupid, juvenile thing to do – literally running away from Nate with no actual destination in mind.

But she was under so much pressure. The only thing she really wanted to do right now was go for a drink. That was why she'd made herself get into the passenger side and not behind the wheel – if she was there, it would be too easy to just turn the engine on and drive to a bar.

In fact, right now, she could slide over the central console and climb into place –

No, no, she couldn't do that. Laura pressed her hands against her face and let out a muffled, frustrated scream, then flipped open the overhead mirror to examine her own face. She looked tired. Older than she remembered. There were fine lines around her blue eyes that just seemed to get deeper every time she checked, and she was only glad that the light-blonde tone of her natural hair hid the grays she was sure were absolutely peppered throughout it now. She felt old before her time. But then, years of alcohol abuse would do that to you.

Laura leaned back and sighed. She had to do something. She couldn't just sit here. She needed to figure this case out.

She got back out of the car and walked into the precinct, tense the whole time at the thought of running into Nate. She wasn't quite sure what she would do if she saw him. Run away again? Scowl and ignore him and give him the silent treatment? Apologize?

She passed through the corridor safely, to her relief, and then headed down the stairs into the basement, retracing their steps from last night. The same officer was behind the desk at the entrance to the evidence locker, and he nodded at her quickly as she grabbed the sign-in sheet and scrawled her name down. She flashed him a smile, hoping that he would think the obvious insincerity of it was down to the pressures of the case and not the fact she was experiencing a low she didn't know how to get out of.

She walked right to the back of the room, feeling her way unerringly past all of the other exhibits and to the mannequins, crowded in together in the corner, three of them now instead of just two. The plastic wrapping on them made them look even more grotesque, somehow. Like they were prizes from a carnival. Wrapped up in plastic and just missing the big gaudy ribbon to mark them out as a gift, a human-sized mannequin instead of a goldfish.

She had tried with them before, and nothing had happened. She wasn't going to strain herself and risk having that be the case again. She didn't think she was mentally ready for that failure. Not a second time. But trying with something else… well, if she touched something else and it didn't work, then she could tell herself that the item she'd chosen didn't have a strong enough connection to the killer. It wouldn't have to be that she had failed. It could be pure chance.

Even though she'd had visions in the past that were strong enough to come through when she touched the vibrations of a speaker that was playing a recording of the killer's breath –

No. No, she couldn't let herself think that way. She was going to make this work. She had to.

She had to.

Laura turned her attention to the other items sitting in the locker, all of them carefully wrapped to avoid contamination. One of them, looking so incongruous right there, was the bowl of popcorn. Wrapped or not, it wouldn't be long before the popcorn itself went bad and any evidentiary value it had would be lost. And the killer had prepared it himself – he must have stood there and listened to all those pops in the microwave, waiting for them to slow down, pulling it out at just the right time so it didn't end up burning. There was a strong connection in that.

Laura glanced over at the door to make sure that no one was watching her or coming into the locker, and then she quickly unzipped the evidence bag and thrust her hand into the middle of the bowl of popcorn.

For a moment there was nothing – only the slightly gross feeling of the day-old popcorn against her hand. And then –

She was standing in a big space – maybe a warehouse. It was dark, so dark she could barely see anything. There was, at first, only a sense of the vastness of the space and nothing else. She couldn't see anything. She couldn't hear anything.

Then, like before, her gaze traveled down and she seemed to adjust to the darkness, slowly looking at the picture as it emerged before her. First, a face, emerging from the dim shadows only to the extent that she could make out the briefest shape of the features, not enough to see the details of the face. Then, once the initial shock of that subsided – and it was still a shock, even though she'd seen it before – there was another, close by the first and also staring right ahead, also unmoving.

Her breath caught in her throat once again as the full scale of the situation became clear to her. All of these men, standing and staring right at her or ahead, all of them standing perfectly in rank and file. And then...

Just like before, one of them broke rank and moved and looked right at her. She couldn't see his face – not in the gloom of the huge space. But she could feel his intention. And when he started to move right towards her –

Laura opened her eyes with a small gasp, pulling her hand right out of the popcorn as quickly as she could. She hastily grabbed a few errant pieces that had escaped as she moved, shoving them back inside the evidence bag and then zipping it shut. She paused then for a moment, leaning on the shelving, breathing hard.

It hadn't been a nightmare, last night.

She had dreamed a vision.

And this time, there had been no headache. What did that mean? Did it mean she was seeing the past? A future that was so distant the headache was all but unnoticeable?

A new quirk to her visions, coming at a time when she already had no understanding at all about how the rest of them worked?

She pressed the heel of her hand against her temple for a moment with her eyes squeezed shut, almost wishing that she had a headache after all. At least that would be something to focus on. Some real, tangible evidence that she'd had a vision at all.

She hadn't just... fallen asleep standing up, or something, had she?

No – she was sure of one thing, and that was that she had been in a vision. It had all the hallmarks except the headache: the weird viewpoint that she had no control over, the length, the dark shadows swirling off into nothing at the sides of the vision. This was what she had been waiting for. Now, she just had to interpret it.

And that was going to be a lot easier if she had two heads instead of one.

Laura rushed out of the evidence locker, pausing only to slam the gate shut behind her, dialing Nate's number on her phone as she went. She was calling him by the time she was halfway up the stairs and had reception again, and to her surprise, he answered within two rings.

"Nate," she said, hoping that he would accept the fact she was calling him again and not demand an apology or something before he would listen to her. "I just saw something. Where are you?"

119

"I was on my way to the evidence – oh." Nate stopped, putting the phone down and waving at her with a kind of sheepish motion. They'd almost run into one another at the top of the stairs. The arrested motion left Laura breathless and restless, feeling like she still needed to hurry somewhere but having nowhere to hurry to. "Hi. Uh. I just... I was going to say, I shouldn't have snapped at you like that."

"It's fine," Laura said, even though it hadn't been – because she cared more about their relationship than about who was in the wrong. "I shouldn't have run off."

"You said you...?" Nate trailed off with a small smile, prompting her to resume what she had been saying on the phone.

"I saw something," she repeated, then glanced around. There was no one in sight, but that didn't mean there wouldn't be. "Let's go to our little office."

Nate nodded and led her there, a rushed and strangely silent journey through the halls and up the stairs of the precinct, both of them holding in everything they needed to say – Laura with her story and Nate, she had to imagine, with questions. As soon as the door shut behind him, Nate whirled around and fixed her with an intense gaze.

"Well?" he asked.

Laura shook her head quickly as if to dismiss what she was about to say even before she said it, well aware that she had more questions than answers from the vision. "Look, I don't know what it means yet," she said. "I was in a big, dark space. I couldn't see anything at all, really. But then as my eyes adjusted, I could make out all of these men – all of them just standing there, staring right ahead towards me. It was like – like standing in front of the Terracotta Army, I guess. That was the kind of vibe I got."

"Like a warehouse full of mannequins?" Nate suggested.

Laura stared at him with wide eyes for a moment.

Of course.

Of course.

She hadn't put two and two together on her own, because of two key differences. First, because the mannequins she had seen hadn't all been still – when one of them moved, it had thrown her off, made her think she was looking at real people. And second...

"It wasn't like the mannequins we found at the crime scenes," she said. "This was different. They were all dressed in clothes – and they had faces painted on. Until you said that, I didn't even think about them being mannequins – I just thought I was looking at people. And another thing – one of them moved. But now that I think about it more clearly – what if that one was the killer, and the others were all mannequins?"

"You would know better than me," Nate shrugged. "You're the one who saw it. Was there anything else?"

Laura shook her head slowly, reaching for any more detail she could give him. "I don't know. The space – it was huge. Like, not just your average storeroom – a warehouse or bigger. There must have been hundreds of them there."

"Who would have access to a space where mannequins are getting dressed up like that?" Nate asked. "I mean, a department store, sure, but we already know only one of them in the local area has reported thefts. And in that one place alone, we had – what was it, seven? - employees to look into. We can't just tackle every single store that has mannequins."

"We need to think about the individuals who actually work with them," Laura suggested. She wasn't sure if that was even right, but it was something that she felt kind of moving through her, an idea that came to the forefront naturally. "Someone who works with a lot of mannequins. Like, I don't know… isn't there a job where you just dress up the mannequins for the windows of stores?"

Nate made a face, a kind of maybe-maybe-not expression. "Yeah, but they only usually work with the fancy stores. And even then, it's mostly at Christmas. Smaller stores or chain stores would normally just ask an employee to do it. And they wouldn't work with that many mannequins – they just have their own in the storeroom, like at the department store."

"So, then, who does work with a large volume of mannequins?" Laura asked. "Someone we haven't thought of before, I guess – someone we've overlooked until now. Not the obvious."

"What about tailors or people who work with clothes? Like designers or whatever?" Nate asked. "Don't they need to have specific mannequins that suit their customers?"

It was Laura's turn to make the face. "I don't know. Don't they just have a single, adjustable mannequin?"

"Not if they're working on a whole collection at once, or if they have lots of customers coming through their business who all have different needs but the work has to be done simultaneously," Nate pointed out. "Can your visions be, I don't know… symbolic? Like maybe you're not seeing an actual scene that will happen, but more like all the mannequins he's ever worked with?"

Laura opened her mouth but then swallowed back the *no*. She wasn't sure, really. The lack of a headache. It was strange, wasn't it? It didn't make any sense that she hadn't had one. Even when she'd seen the past, she'd had a headache.

Something symbolic – or even something that took place in the killer's mind – his own mind palace of all the mannequins he'd ever dressed… was that even possible?

"Maybe," she hedged, not sure if she was being honest or not. "I don't know." She could call Zach, she supposed, but – not in front of Nate, who didn't even know about Zach yet, and she would rather have been solving the case than making yet another call. Even though he'd told her to call any time, she still felt like she was imposing.

"Well, let's look it up," Nate suggested, leaning over the crappy old computer the precinct had loaned them and firing it up. He waited a few minutes for it to load, impatiently moving the mouse when nothing happened, and then started to type as soon as the screen lit up.

He put a few search terms into the computer and nothing was coming up. Laura couldn't even see the screen from where she was standing, but she could read it all easily in his body language: the frustrated sighs, the way he ran his hands back over his close-cropped, kinky hair. He slammed an open hand against the desk when his last effort brought no results, clearly frustrated that they still weren't getting anywhere.

"I don't know," he said, shrugging. There was a knock on the door, brief and almost timid, even as he spoke. "What do we do? Just search for tailors nearby and start visiting all of them?"

The door opened just a tiny crack, as if whoever was on the other side was hesitating.

"Hello?" Laura called out, and the door opened fully. Behind it, a petite female detective with her hair twisted into Bantu knots emerged, looking them both over cautiously as if to check she wasn't interrupting anything.

"Hi – you're the FBI agents, right?" she asked, even though it had to have been obvious that the pair of them were not part of the normal employees of the precinct.

"That's right," Laura replied, trying to be kind. She recognized the woman's voice from somewhere.

"Um, I'm Detective Thorson," she said. "Captain Ortega sent me to give you these results."

Thorson – then it clicked. They'd spoken on the phone before, on their first day on the case. That seemed like it was about five weeks ago, even though it was actually only yesterday. "Oh, yes," Laura replied, getting it now. The detective had been very helpful, before. The way she had answered the phones, her size, and her unusual hairstyle made Laura think that it was very likely she was on desk duties – whether officially or not.

"You asked for someone to look into wholesalers or dealers of mannequins in the local area," Thorson said. "I just finished making calls."

"And?" Nate asked, leaning forward excitedly. Laura could almost hear the thought in his head. Maybe *this* was the lead they had been waiting for.

"There's no reports of theft from any of them, and they all maintain that the only clients purchasing more than two mannequins for the same address have been the kind of businesses you would expect to need them," Thorson reported. "Department stores, clothing manufacturers, that sort of thing. Actually, even though there are a few businesses based locally, the majority of their business is done on a wider scope. Out of county, out of state, even out of the country."

"Right," Laura sighed. "Well, thank you. At least we can rule out that area of investigation."

"Um, I didn't mean to eavesdrop," Detective Thorson said, hesitating in the doorway still instead of leaving. "It's just, as I was coming in, I heard you say something about tailors."

"That's right," Nate confirmed. "Why? Do you know something?"

Detective Thorson nodded. "I handle a lot of – well, a lot of incoming paperwork," she said, all but verifying Laura's assumption. "I've seen a few reports about a tailor who lives locally. He's been reported a few times for odd behavior."

"There aren't any logs in the system," Nate said, frowning.

"No, there wouldn't be," Thorson replied. "Every time, it gets dismissed. I only know about it because I've seen the same name come up a few times. He's kind of a loner, I think. I've driven by his store, but it's just an empty storefront with a couple of mannequins in the window – he works on his own and you have to place an order ahead. When he is there, he often ends up scaring people on the street. That's where the reports come from."

"Where is the store?" Nate asked, getting up from behind the computer already.

"Well, that's the thing," Thorson said. "The business shut down recently. His erratic behavior had been running over onto the work he delivered to his clients. We actually had someone report him for ruining a jacket of theirs by sewing it up all weird. We referred them to file a suit since it wasn't exactly within our remit."

"So," Laura said, making a careful summary of the situation to be sure she was getting it right. "We have a tailor, who works locally and almost certainly with mannequins, who is already known for erratic and increasingly strange behavior, who also recently had a trigger event in the form of losing his business?"

"Yes," Detective Thorson said, and blushed slightly. "I'm sorry, I should have put it together earlier. I just didn't think of him until I heard you mention tailors."

Laura couldn't blame her for not thinking of it. From the way she talked about it, she hadn't had much personal involvement in the case – she'd just handled the paperwork briefly. If she did that for all the cases that came through the precinct, or even just the majority, that would be a lot of cases to try to remember.

"We'd better pay him a visit at home," Laura said decisively. "You know where to find him?"

Thorson brought her hands out from behind her back, revealing a sheaf of paperwork. Some of it evidently related to the searches she'd done on wholesalers, but the paper on top held what Laura could clearly see was a handwritten address. "Yes, ma'am."

Laura considered it for a moment. She usually hated working with new people – especially since it forced her to hide her abilities even deeper and start the usual old lies all over again. But today, at least, she had something of a confidence boost. Maybe it was being with Nate again, having her partner back on her side. Either way, she was feeling generous.

"Would you like to come along with us?" she asked.

Thorson's eyes widened almost comically, and she nodded faster than Laura had seen a person nod before. "Yes, ma'am," she said.

CHAPTER TWENTY THREE

Laura looked up at the dark building, squinting her eyes. "Are you sure this is it?" she asked. "The place looks like it should have been condemned."

Detective Thorson nodded eagerly. "I'm sure," she said. "I'm pretty sure it would have been, if any building inspectors came over. It's definitely not up to code. I guess over the years the revenue from the business dwindled and he hasn't been able to maintain it. I only know rumors, but I think he inherited the place from his parents."

"Is he home?" Nate asked, leaning forward to crane his neck past Laura and look out of the car's window. It was getting dark even though it was still late afternoon, a consequence of the lateness of the year. "There aren't any lights on."

"No car parked outside, either," Laura said.

"There never is," Detective Thorson replied. Laura glanced at her sitting in the backseat, through her rearview mirror. "I pass this way on the way home. I've never seen a light there. I have seen him moving around outside from time to time, though. I remember because the first time I noticed him, it was right after I'd seen him in the precinct for one of his reports."

"Alright," Laura nodded. "Curtains and blinds are closed. I guess you wouldn't bother doing that if no one was home."

"Unless you wanted to stop kids from breaking in and trying to hold a party in the local haunted house," Nate said, making it clear exactly what he thought about the appearance of the place.

"We should take a look, at least," Laura said. She glanced in the rearview again. "You coming in with us, Detective?"

Thorson hesitated. "I'm not really supposed to do active stuff," she said.

"Because of a disciplinary issue?" Laura asked.

Thorson fidgeted in her seat. "No. The Captain says I'm too small to confront suspects."

"Did you pass the entrance physical?"

"Yes."

Laura turned around in her seat so they could lock eyes properly. "Then you're fit enough for duty. If it's an unofficial ruling, then come in with us. We'll cover you if he gets mad. You can tell him we ordered you to come."

Thorson's face broke into a hesitant grin. It was like the sun coming out. No one had believed in her – Laura could see that. But she'd come up with a great lead, and her local knowledge seemed to be second-to-none.

They all got out of the car at the same time, peering up at the building before Laura led the way up to the front door. She wanted to laugh at Nate for hanging back from what he'd called the 'haunted' house, but as she approached, she found a shiver passing over her spine, too.

Something was off, here. She didn't know what, yet, but it wasn't right.

She reached out and knocked on the cracked, peeling wood of the door, which had apparently once been painted a deep shade of red. Now, there was nothing but scraps of the paint left, looking like nothing so much as blood pooling out of the door itself. Another reason to shiver. Laura listened, but there was no response.

"This is weird," she muttered, casting a glance behind her at Detective Thorson. From the hopeful expression on the detective's face, Laura didn't have to ask again whether she was sure if someone still lived there.

Laura reached out again, and on a whim touched the door handle. She didn't even have to turn it – the door had clearly been left just on the latch, and when her fingers brushed over it, it simply slid open.

Laura swallowed. She wasn't superstitious, herself. Even if she had been – she had psychic visions already. The supernatural or weird shouldn't have scared her. She was still wearing the thin bandage on the side of her hand after the last time she'd been too close to a serial killer, a burn that felt so normal now she barely thought about it, almost healed. She shouldn't have been afraid to come up against another, not given the number of times she'd faced killers and come out victorious.

But still, there was another little shiver down her spine, making her glance at Nate for reassurance this time.

He looked even more unnerved than she did.

"Guess we should go in," Laura said, out loud, just to hear someone else agree with her.

Nate nodded firmly. "Could be someone in distress, with the door hanging open like that."

"Right." Still, Laura had to take a deep breath before she forced herself to step forward, willing a vision to come when she touched the wood again, a warning that would tell her what to expect on the inside.

Of course, there was none.

Laura stepped into a dark and dim hall, barely able to see anything. She grabbed her phone and turned on the flashlight, hearing two steps of footsteps move onto the wooden floorboards behind her. She cast the beam around and frowned; the place looked abandoned. There were personal effects everywhere, yes: framed photographs on the walls and on shelves, a few keys on a hook, even a couple of pairs of old men's shoes shuffled under a bench seat near the door. The problem was, all of it was coated in dust and cobwebs.

It didn't look as though anyone had been here in an awfully long time.

Laura glanced back at Nate and Thorson, not wanting to make a sound still, just in case. Nate was right about teenagers seeing this place as an open invitation to come inside. There was no knowing what they were about to walk into. She made a signal with her hands, gesturing to Nate and to the left, then to Thorson and to the right, and finally to herself and straight ahead.

The others nodded.

Laura moved with stealth down the corridor, hearing the others pad off to the sides as quietly as possible. The floorboards creaked as she moved along them, an unfortunate effect she couldn't control. They needed to be stealthy here, but there were some things you couldn't avoid in a building of this age.

The route she had taken led into a long kitchen space, covering the back part of the building. She cast the beam from her phone in a slow arc. There was nothing – no one. No sign of recent life. There were dusty, moldy plates stacked up by the sink, holding the remains of some long-dead meal. She listened, but there was no low buzz from the fridge to indicate it was turned on. She didn't dare open it, imagining the smell of spoiled food that would spill out as soon as she did.

It was creepy, the whole place. Like someone had got up one day and left halfway through their normal daily life, then never come back. As if they'd simply fled some awful incident. A flood, a forest fire, a volcanic eruption, the onset of war. Some kind of evacuation. But the house was undamaged, preserved perfectly as it had been on that one day – just coated with a film of dust over it all.

Satisfied the room was clear, Laura moved back to the corridor. Twin beams of light swept from both the other sides of the hall and convened as she approached – Nate and Thorson had also conducted their searches. Laura raised her phone just slightly to illuminate their faces without blinding them, watching them both shake their heads. Nothing.

Laura was about to suggest the stairs, hoping they would be structurally sound, when a noise made her breath catch in her throat and froze her in place.

A voice?

Was that a voice?

She glanced at Nate. He had heard it to. He nodded to something behind her slowly.

Laura turned and looked. Another door, one she had overlooked. It was difficult in the pitch darkness; she must have swung her beam of light too far to one side and not seen it, sandwiched between two dusty, thin cabinets in the hall. She shivered lightly. There was a faint noise again, something that sounded just like a voice, even if too distant to work out what it was saying.

She reached for her gun at her belt, loosening it. On second thought, she drew it. If their killer was down there, they could be about to walk into a very dangerous situation.

She moved forward hesitantly, shining her light on the door. There were patterns in the dust around the handle and on the floor, as though someone stood here often to open it. This was it. It had to be.

Laura reached out for the door, bracing herself for a vision that did not come, and then slowly and carefully slipped it open.

To her relief, despite the age of the door and the house, there was no creak as it swung out towards her. It must have been regularly oiled, kept in good shape while everything else was falling apart. If this was the only area of the house that was used, it made sense.

To her dismay, but also not to her surprise, it was not another room that awaited them beyond the door.

It was a set of stairs, leading down. Down into a basement.

Laura took a deep breath, trying not to think about the burn on her hand and the fact that she'd been tied up in a basement when it happened, and stepped out onto the top of the stairs.

She held her breath, listening for a creak, but the wood held. That wouldn't be the case further down, she thought, and the other two joining her would put even more pressure on the structure. They wouldn't have the element of surprise here. They would have the benefit of the higher ground, but only in an enclosed space – and they would have to emerge into the basement presumably in full view of anyone who might be below. Her hand flexed on the grip of her gun, her heart in her mouth. This was dangerous. Maybe too dangerous. Maybe they should retreat as silently as possible and call for backup.

Then the voices floated up to her again from the stairwell. Voices, because there were two.

One of them, soft, impossible to make out fully. A little higher, more feminine, although to her ear it still sounded male. Perhaps someone younger, with a higher-pitched voice. Then there was another that answered, loud and booming. It seemed to echo strangely off the room below and up the stairs, creating an echo of itself that bounced around and confused her ear, making it impossible still to figure out what it was saying.

But it didn't sound happy. It sounded angry.

Like someone shouting at a prisoner that was trying to reason with them.

Laura couldn't wait for backup. Not hearing that. She could hear the potential scenario: the killer and his next victim, waiting down there, pleading for his life. There was nothing to say that the victims had to be killed at their own homes or in a public place, after all. Maybe this tailor of theirs had realized that he was close to being caught and decided to lure someone to his own home instead, delaying their discovery.

She couldn't stand by and wait.

Knowing they would not be able to get the jump on him if they tried to creep down slowly and the wood gave them away, Laura made a split-second decision. There was light coming from below, beyond the bottom of the stairs. She put her phone away, gripped her gun in one hand and used the other to steady herself against the wall, and started to jump down the stairs two steps at a time.

She rushed headlong out of the opening into the basement, whipping her head around in all directions. She swung her gun around towards the first human figure she saw –

And froze, frowning, her brain trying to make sense of what she was seeing.

There was a strange scene spread out before her, one that took her a long moment to digest. There was a long table in the center of the basement, set up like a trestle table for a dinner party for a large group: covered in a white sheet and spread with various dishes across the middle, plates and cutlery in front of each chair, waiting for the guests to choose their food.

And it was not an empty table. At each spot around the table but one, someone was sitting, ready to eat. They were all frozen, as if waiting for something to happen before they could pick up their knives and forks.

At the head of the table, standing, there was one more figure. A man dressed in a dusty black suit, the lines of it streaked with gray. No: when Laura looked closer, she realized that the lines on his suit were marks made with tailor's chalk, as if to mark out all of the places where the garment was to be adjusted.

He turned towards her, lured by the sound of her footsteps down the stairs, and she found her gun swinging up towards him. At the same time, she had heightened awareness of everything else: Nate and Thorson tumbling down the stairs behind her, no doubt with their own weapons ready to fire. All of the people around the table, any of whom could have been a potential threat.

But none of them moved. Not a single one of them reacted to her presence at all.

And when Laura spared one more glance away from the man dressed in the tailor-ready jacket, Laura understood why.

They were all mannequins.

Each of them was dressed in a different jaunty outfit – some in suits, others in shorts and t-shirts, female mannequins in dresses and skirts. Their faces were marked with paint in the approximation of faces, some of it faded or chipped, clearly from old-fashioned mannequins that were meant to resemble real people. They wore wigs and hats to cover their plastic hair, and for a moment with a brief glance, the effect was actually convincing enough to fool the eye – but not now that she'd had the time to look again.

The tailor was holding some kind of dinner party down here, as though each of the mannequins was a guest in his home.

"Who were you talking to?" Laura demanded quickly. If there was someone else down here –

Nate moved behind her, and she sensed him passing by as he began to scan the rest of the room, gun out and ready.

The tailor said nothing, but his eyes drifted down to one of the mannequins. It was dressed as female, with vivid red lipstick smeared on top of the original paint job, a blonde wig covering the eyes partially.

It clicked: the tailor had been talking to himself. Providing the voices for his guests. Acting out the scene, not just positioning it for visual effect.

There was no victim. He was alone down here.

Still, it was the closest display Laura could think of to what she had seen the killer perform. The idea of all of these guests set up and ready for a full scene, an eerie tableau waiting for him every time he came back to the house. A fake life, so removed from reality that he no longer spent any time upstairs in the main house.

"Frank Geharty?" Laura asked, to which the tailor nodded silently. He was still frozen in place, looking right at her, one of his arms still outstretched in a gesture towards the woman he had been 'talking' to. The single movement somehow made his pose even more unnerving: the knowledge that he could move if he wished, and yet was choosing to act like the mannequins around him.

"Clear," Nate said quietly behind her.

"We're arresting you on suspicion of murder," Laura said, putting her gun into her belt with the knowledge that Nate had her covered and bringing out a pair of handcuffs. She opened her mouth to give Geharty his rights, but she found herself stopping in surprise as the tailor turned slowly and placed his hands behind his back, clearly offering no argument against his arrest.

All of which left her feeling more unsure and unnerved than if he had put up a fight or tried to run – and gave her another feeling, too. The feeling that this case, resolved as it seemed to be on the surface, was still far from over.

CHAPTER TWENTY FOUR

Laura groaned in frustration, leaning her head against the two-way glass that looked into Frank Geharty's interview room.

"I knew he wasn't going to make it easy for us," she grumbled, feeling the cooling influence of the glass on her forehead, soothing some of the irritation away. "I just had that vibe from him right from the beginning."

Nate chuckled beside her. "Oh, you did, did you?"

"Don't mock me," Laura scowled.

Nate sighed, leaning against the glass as well. Despite his attempt at humor, he was clearly as frustrated and weary as she was. That was the effect silent interviews had: you wore yourself out shouting at a brick wall, expecting it to talk back.

But so far, Frank Geharty hadn't said a single word since the moment they brought him in. Not to confirm his own name at booking. Not to tell them whether he wanted a hot or cold drink. Not to speak up for the interview tape. Not a single word, and every question they asked had gone unanswered.

"He didn't even flinch when we asked him about the murders," Laura said. "I can't work out if it's because he knows he committed them, or because he's so shut down he didn't even hear the question."

"I know." Nate shook his head. "Whatever's going on, there's something seriously wrong with him. He needs help. I just don't know whether that equates to him being the killer or not."

Laura nodded. He was right. As much as she wanted to have the case solved and done with, they couldn't just make any assumptions. Yes, everything seemed to fit. Yes, his refusal to talk was making the tailor look more and more suspicious. But what did that really mean? All they knew for sure was that he had mental health issues, and if they put away the wrong man, it wasn't only his life that would be affected.

The real killer would still be out there.

Not only that, but a court would need more evidence. A jury would probably accept their witness testimony of the scene in the basement, look at the evidence photographs taken there, and convict him easily. A judge, however, might not think the case even had enough evidence to get to trial in the first place. And if he was the killer, they needed to make this arrest stick.

"What do we do?" Laura asked Nate, turning to him with her hands on her hips, ready to think. She wasn't asking him out of desperation. No – her tone was firm, decisive. She was looking for his thoughts to help compose a plan, which would get them moving on the track towards the evidence they needed.

"He has all those mannequins in his basement," Nate said, slowly. "Of course, with them all being slightly different types, there's no way to be sure that they aren't related to the ones left at the crime scenes."

"The ones in the basement had faces, but the ones at the crime scenes did not," Laura pointed out, kind of playing devil's advocate against her own conviction that he was guilty.

"Right, but that could mean that the ones in the basement were special somehow, and the ones he left behind weren't," Nate said. "Or maybe he just got rid of the less recognizable ones from his collection first. The ones in the basement were all dressed up, and when we burst in, it sounded like he was giving them all voices. If they're real characters to him, he wouldn't want to just abandon them in an alley. Maybe he cares about these ones too much to leave them somewhere."

Laura nodded, musing over that idea. "So, it could be very possible that it's still him we're looking for. How do we verify that? The mannequins at the crime scenes had no markings, so we can't trace the manufacturer."

"We go backwards," Nate said. "He bought them, so there must be a record of that somewhere. Let's look over his bank records, see what they say."

Laura nodded. "Good. If we find a supplier, we can call them and ask for his customer record, see how many mannequins he's registered as buying. We'll have to make sure that they carry both the types in the basement and the type found at the crime scenes, otherwise there may be more than one supplier."

"That's a plan," Nate said. "Let's head back to our office and leave him stewing for a bit. I'll check on the computer whether the bank records have come through yet, and if they haven't, we can ask them to hurry it up."

Laura opened the door and walked out into the corridor, feeling better already. She always did when there was a plan in place. It felt less like they were moving aimlessly. Like they were taking control of the situation. That was a good feeling to have.

The walk up the stairs and down the hall was a relatively short one, and once there, Laura was the first to reach the computer and wake up the screen. She scrolled through the recent emails they'd had regarding the case, clicking eagerly on a digital PDF sent by the bank to start going through it.

"Here we are," she said. "We might have to do a bit of detective work on the names of the businesses."

"I can't think of anyone who would be qualified to do that," Nate said with a sly smile.

Laura resisted the urge to hit him playfully and rolled her eyes instead. "Let's start searching."

"No need," Nate said, pointing at the screen. "Look. There's your starter."

Laura's eyes widened as she read the bank records. Right there, next to a recent purchase – no, not so recent, she realized; it was just that Frank Geharty apparently made very few payments, and the contents of the last three months fit entirely on one screen – was the dead giveaway. The name of the business: MANNEQUINS SUPL. LTD.

"Mannequins.... Supply Limited?" Laura guessed, trying to work out the abbreviation that had been used to make the name fit easily on the statement.

"Looks like it," Nate replied. He was already typing something into his phone – presumably the name. "Yep, here we are. It's a local business. Must have been one of the suppliers that Detective Thorson mentioned."

Laura grabbed the paperwork Thorson had left from the table and scanned it. "Yes, here we are. No reports of recent theft."

"Well, there wouldn't have been, if he bought them," Nate said reasonably. "And what was it Thorson said? No reports of sales to customers who *weren't* legitimately using them. If Geharty was known to them as a tailor, it wouldn't have been flagged as unusual for him to be buying them."

"Then let's contact them," Laura said, but Nate had already yanked up the desk phone from in front of him.

He dialed the number from the search results and then waited, looking at her and connecting their eyes with a significant gaze when the call was answered. "Hello, yes. This is Special Agent Nathaniel Lavoie calling from the Mariesville Police Department. We're investigating a series of murders out here, and – yes. Mhmm. Yes, sir, those are the ones. Well... yes, exactly. We need your help. There's a customer of yours who we believe may be our suspect. What we need from you is to let us into his account history so we can see the details of the mannequins he purchased from you."

There was a long pause. Laura was about to ask what the delay was, whether the person on the other side of the phone was arguing or refusing, when Nate started again.

"Yes, I'm ready," he said, cradling the phone between his cheek and his shoulder and then lifting his cell phone up to eye level so he could type on it at the same time as talking. "Okay. And how will we know what model we're looking at? Oh, okay. Right. Yes, go ahead."

He made a number of notes, typing constantly while making the occasional noise to let the person on the other side know that he was listening. Laura waited with bated breath. She got out of her seat and looked over Nate's shoulder at the screen of his phone, trying to read what he was writing. The first line read *look up images online, check placement and shape*. Laura didn't know what the 'placement and shape' referred to, but the rest was a string of model names and numbers. She typed the first one into the computer's search engine, ready to see what they were looking for. With any luck, it would be a faceless mannequin – maybe one in a sitting position to really incriminate their tailor.

"And that's it?" Nate asked, casting his eyes at Laura sharply. She paused as the images loaded, feeling uncertainty seize her. Something was clearly wrong. "No, no. So this goes back over how long…? Fifteen *years*? Christ. You're sure it's just eight?"

Laura's mouth dried up.

Eight?

There had been eight mannequins seated around the dinner table in that basement. The image was emblazoned onto her brain. Even if she hadn't counted them at the time, she would be able to do so again now just from memory.

If he'd only ever bought eight mannequins in the whole course of his business, then all eight were sitting in that basement, fully accounted for.

Nate thanked the person he'd been talking to and put the phone down, then looked up at Laura with a slack look to his eyes. "Did you get that?"

Laura nodded. "We'll have to check the actual mannequins and make sure there isn't any other mention of a company that sells them in his statements. But…"

"But he's registered as having bought eight mannequins, and there were eight in that basement, and that kinda sounds like all his mannequins have been accounted for," Nate said.

There was a knock on the door, and Nate and Laura both swung their heads in unison as it opened.

"Agents," Detective Thorson said. She had a terrible look on her face. A kind of gray hue. "We've just got done speaking with a case worker who was assigned to Frank Geharty. He spent the first three days of this week in a residential facility receiving treatment for delusions. He was there voluntarily, and left yesterday on his own accord without taking his medication with him."

"He has an alibi?" Laura said, not wanting it to be true but knowing in her heart it was. Some part of her had known from the moment they walked into that basement, somehow. Even though all the signs pointed to Frank Geharty, her gut hadn't been in it. He might have been mentally unwell, but that didn't mean he was a murderer.

"He has an alibi," Detective Thorson said, and all three of them shared a collective moment of utter despair. In contempt, Nate took a sheaf of paper from the desk and swept it into a waste paper bin under it.

But then Laura grasped onto one tiny flicker of hope and held it, looking up at the others with a clear idea of what they needed to do next.

"Mannequins Supply Limited," she said, turning to Nate. "Where is their manufacturing base?"

Nate looked up the answer on the listing he'd already opened on his phone browser. "It's outside of town," he said. "Looks like about a forty-five minute drive."

"Grab the keys," Laura said, getting up from her chair immediately. "We don't have any time to lose."

CHAPTER TWENTY FIVE

There was always something creepy about factories. Maybe it was the fact that Laura only ever visited them in the course of investigating a murder – and that so many of them, when they were no longer in use, seemed to end up being the venue for body disposal. Whatever it was, it gave her the chills, and she felt them trailing down her spine now as they looked up at Mannequin Supply Limited's manufacturing site.

"It looks creepy," Detective Thorson piped up from the back seat, and Laura stifled a smile. At least she wasn't the only one. In fact, she was glad in more ways than one to have Thorson with them again – it felt like backup might be needed when they were looking for what had seemed a whole army in her vision. If the space was as big as she'd thought, they couldn't spare one of them to check the employee rosters and one to search. They needed more hands on deck.

"Oh, look," Nate said, gesturing to the front doors of the space – massive double doors which were set open as if to allow a vehicle inside. There was a man just walking out of them, dressed in worn blue coveralls and wearing a hard hat. Laura had to guess, as she knew Nate had, that it was the man they'd been told would meet them.

She got out of the car and went right towards him, Nate and Detective Thorson not far behind her. She lifted her hand in greeting as she got closer. "Hello. Special Agent Frost – are you the foreman?"

"That's right," he nodded. "Head office gave me a call and said you were on the way over here. Something about needing me to show you around the place?"

"That's right," Nate nodded, having caught up. "We'll need you to answer some questions, too. And we need your employee records. Actually, if we could start there, it could save us some time."

"Certainly," the foreman nodded. "We have our roster set up in the office. I can show you all of our staff, past and present."

"That sounds like my cue," Detective Thorson said, glancing at Nate and Laura for their nodded confirmation. "If you could show me to the office and the records, I can start checking through them with my colleagues back in the precinct over the phone while you show the agents around."

The foreman nodded with an expression that suggested it was a fair idea. He turned and yelled something over his shoulder – the words were lost to Laura as they walked inside the large open space, into the cacophony of the factory proper. She noticed that most of the workers were wearing ear defenders, quite possibly a smart move that they should have copied – but then again, she had no time for safety precautions when there was a serial killer out there and the day was coming to a close. Already, she could see people packing up their stations and starting to clock off for the day.

It felt like time was slipping through their fingers. If their killer was one of the workers here, and he left to go home before they realized it, they would be chasing after him. As it was, there may have been a ticking clock hanging over Laura's head with a sword attached to the pendulum, ready to drop on her. Sooner or later they would get a call that another victim had been found, and she would know that they had failed one more person.

At least, she hoped it would only be one.

"Alright," the foreman said, after a brief word with one of his colleagues who then took Detective Thorson over to a set of stairs leading high up above the factory floor. "It's a tour you wanted, then?"

"Yes," Laura said. "We need to understand more about these mannequins than we do now. Firstly, about the types that you make. We've seen a few lately – ones with faces, ones without, standing and sitting ones…"

"Oh, yes," the foreman nodded vigorously. "We make all of those. Different molds for different customers, you see." He gestured over towards an area behind a plastic wall, where a supervisor wearing both ear and eye defenders was keeping close watch on a robotic arm tipping what appeared to be molten plastic into set molds – one for each side of a body. As they watched, the molds went through some kind of drying process and were cast off the other end of a conveyer belt to be collected and moved to another station. There, the two halves were made into one whole, sealed together.

Nate lifted up his cell phone. On the front an image of the mannequins from the crime scenes – removed from the place where they had been found, simply propped up alone as part of the forensic examination. "Do you make ones like these?"

"Yes. That looks like one of ours," the foreman said, furrowing his brow as he considered the photograph seriously. "We make a lot of those. It's our cheaper model. We don't have to spray on the faces like we do with the others." He pointed to one of the other assembly lines,

138

where a crew of workers were bent over examining the results of the work created by another robotic arm – one that appeared to be spraying ink.

"Is it all done by machine?" Nate asked, curiosity in his voice.

"Yes, these days," the foreman said with a sigh. "When I started out here forty years ago, it was different. You had artists to paint the faces. It wasn't well-paid work, still, but it was skilled. And we'd spend hours putting each one together. Now they're made in minutes by the machines. Still, I guess that's progress."

"Was there anyone you remember who worked on painting the faces and then lost their job with the innovations?" Nate asked. "Maybe someone who ended up struggling, or felt like they really lost their vocation?"

Laura's eyebrow lifted, seeing where he was going with it. A former employee who felt like these new, faceless, robot-made mannequins had stolen his livelihood, made his skills useless. That kind of thing was definitely enough to drive someone to the brink. If they already had the kind of personality that was susceptible to violence or psychotic behavior, then it would be easy to see that loss pushing them over.

The foreman shrugged. "A few, sure. You want me to make sure those get added to your list of staff to look into?"

Laura nodded. "That would be fantastic. I think we've seen enough here to get an idea of it all. Except for one thing." She'd been thinking it from the moment they stepped outside: the big, empty space of the factory reminded her of her vision. Clearly, this space was filled with machinery, but she could see what the potential connection might be. "Can we see your storage facility, where the mannequins are kept?"

"Ah, that's off-site," the foreman said over his shoulder, leading them towards the stairs. "We have a separate storage facility where we keep all the mannequins that haven't been pre-sold to customers. We have a certain amount of orders to fulfil on a regular basis – large chain stores, for example, who always need to order new ones and replace old or damaged models. The rest just sit in the storage space until they're sold, so we didn't have room here at the factory site to keep them all."

Laura exchanged a glance over her shoulder at Nate as they began to head upwards.

"How many mannequins are kept there?" she asked.

"Oh, it depends on how quickly sales are going," the foreman said, reaching the top of the stairs and opening a door. "Could be hundreds, could even be as high as thousands. They move in and out as needed."

"Do you have a way to find out the exact number right now?" Laura passed through the door as he held it open for her, catching sight of Detective Thorson at a desk inside the room with a phone cradled against her chin.

"Not right now," the foreman said, scratching the growth of stubble on his chin as they all paused near the doorway. "We don't do a stock take more than every couple of weeks or so. I'd say we're just about due to get a stock count any day now."

Laura's eyes opened wide.

Two weeks since their last stock count. That meant that all of the killings had happened in the time since then. And if they hadn't checked their stock yet, they wouldn't have been able to report any thefts. They wouldn't know about it yet.

She thought of her vision. If she really was seeing the future, then it had to be a future which took place at that storage facility. All of the mannequins set neatly in rows, waiting to be picked up and delivered to their future homes – it made sense. It had to be there.

"Where is this storage facility?" she asked.

"It's back in city limits," the foreman said, nodding towards an imagined horizon beyond the walls of the factory. "It backs onto a converted office unit, so it's pretty cheap even though we're transporting them around all the time. We even have a deal with a local haulage firm to make sure we keep the costs low."

"What firm is that?" Laura asked, feeling a certain heaviness in the pit of her stomach, a certainty that she knew what she was about to hear.

"It's Mariesville Freight," the foreman shrugged. "Pretty much the only firm around here that can do the job."

"Where have I heard that before?" Nate muttered.

"That was the company Xavier Perez worked for," Laura told him in a hushed tone, the magnitude of it now hitting her.

The freight company that Xavier Perez worked for. The storage facility attached to converted offices, which Laura knew in her bones without having to look it up would have to be the site where Dr. Vincent Usipov would have his therapy sessions. The mannequins from the storage facility, taken during a time when there were no stock checks, which had to mean insider knowledge. The killer had to have known about their window for getting away with the theft.

They had to be an employee.

"That's the last one," Detective Thorson said, putting down the phone and looking over at them. "None of the employees here has a criminal record. Also, I don't know how many people this rules out, but – I noticed a schedule on the wall for the last few days."

She nodded towards it, and Laura moved over, drawn to it as though Thorson had attached her to a string. She read the simple color-blocked schedule and groaned inwardly. There was a block clearly marked OVERTIME FOR ORDER CATCHUP – and the times extended into the evening for over a week of days in the past.

"Who worked these shifts?" she demanded, spinning to look at the foreman.

"Oh, everyone," he nodded seriously. "No one gets out of it. We had a mess made by one of the machines, ruined an order. Supervisor wasn't doing his job, and the checkers missed it as well, so everyone was responsible. We split the workforce in half and did alternating days for the overtime."

"You're telling me that every single one of your employees has an alibi for either last night or the night before?" Laura said. It strained belief. It felt like every time they were really getting somewhere with this case, some improbable force came along and pushed them three steps back. How could it be possible that they were so close, and yet still not on the right track?

"That's right," the foreman said. He frowned, sweeping his hat off his head and rubbing a hand over his forehead. "Yep, I can't think of any absences. No one left early. You don't, when you're on the team. The rest of the guys would never let you forget how you abandoned them during overtime."

Laura turned to look at Nate with utter disbelief and despair. So, now they were down again without a single suspect. When was this going to end?

But to her surprise, Nate didn't look that perturbed at all.

"What about at the storage facility?" he asked. "Does your staff roster here include them?"

"No, it doesn't," the foreman said. "They're a separate staff. We're technically two sister companies under one umbrella, because the warehouse gets used for rentals as well from time to time. So, if you want to know about their staff, you have to talk to the manager over there."

Laura looked at Thorson and then Nate. They had to see this through. No matter how devastating each new blow was starting to feel, they had to carry on. Somewhere at the end of all this was the answer.

Somewhere at the end of all this, they had to stop a murderer from having the chance to kill again.

"Call the manager," Laura said, beckoning both her colleagues as she stepped towards the stairwell. "Tell him we're on the way, and he needs to get his records ready. By the time we arrive, we need to know how many mannequins have been stolen since the last stock check."

She swept past the foreman and took the stairs two at a time, cursing herself for not thinking to check out the local businesses near the therapist earlier, even though she knew in her heart there had been no need to at the time.

And filled with hope that at last, they might be about to finish this case off with one last nail in the coffin of it all – and pin down the employee who had set all of this in motion.

CHAPTER TWENTY SIX

Laura tried not to vibrate with pure rage as she got out of the car, slamming the door harder than she needed to just to get rid of some of that negative energy. The warehouse was right ahead according to their GPS – the entrance around the back of the converted office block they had been to so recently to speak to the therapist.

Oh, if only they had known back then. Maybe all of this could have been avoided.

"Where are we going?" Nate asked, his head whipping from side to side as Laura pointed ahead to the side alley she had already seen. There must have been another entrance which allowed larger vehicles to load and unload at the back of the warehouse, but she couldn't see it and there was no way she was going to waste time insisting they park there now.

She led the way down the side alley and past the side of the office building, then around to a more cavernous entrance that clearly led into the warehouse. Instead of knocking, she tried the door. She didn't want to wait. Even the small delay caused by a person walking over to let them in could be crucial at this point. The door opened and she rushed inside, taking only the minimum time required to assess that she wasn't walking directly into danger.

The doorway led them directly into an entrance way, clearly designed for checking in shipments, completing paperwork, and perhaps loading and unloading smaller orders. There was a desk with someone standing behind it – a balding man with a rail-thin build who appeared to be scratching a few marks on some paperwork, who looked up and pushed his glasses up his nose as they entered.

"Hello," he said, glancing them over. "Can I help? Are – are you the agents I'm supposed to meet?"

"That would be us," Laura confirmed, nodding grimly. "We need your staff roster as quickly as possible."

"I heard, and I have it here," he said, quickly lifting up several sheets of paper. "I was just adding a couple of notes next to anyone who was fired in the last couple of years as to what happened to them."

"Fantastic," Laura nodded, turning to look at Thorson. "Detective...?"

"On it already," Thorson said, stepping forward to take the paperwork, her cell phone ready in her hand.

"As for us, we need a tour of your facility," Nate said. "Have you been able to complete a stock check for us?"

The manager paled a little. "I'm sorry," he said. "It takes us a full day to do the stock check. That's with two of us."

"And you're the only one in today?" Nate clarified, as they walked towards a door at the other side of the short entrance area, leaving Detective Thorson behind at the desk.

"No, I'm the only manager," he said. "I've got a couple of employees with me today. They're here for help with loading and unloading, and organizing the goods in the space. They aren't authorized high enough to do the stock take."

"Got it," Nate nodded. "This is, what, the onboarding area?"

"Something like that," the manager nodded. "Typically the drivers come into this area to show us their paperwork, getting everything signed off, and figure out where to unload. Then one of us will go with them, get the truck unloaded at the bay doors, and start transporting everything where it needs to be by forklift."

They moved through the doors, and Laura felt a gasp escape her throat without any way to prevent it. The space they were walking into now was the one she had seen in her vision – she was sure of it. Here, it was brightly lit, and she could make out the back wall of the warehouse to easily define just how large it was. But no matter what the vision had concealed and blurred for her, the details she could remember were all there.

Right in front of them, stretching out into the distance but facing towards the right-hand side of the room, was a veritable army of mannequins.

"Yes, it's a little creepy if you aren't used to it," the manager said, chuckling lightly. "Newcomers often have that reaction."

Laura didn't bother telling him that he was wrong – that she wasn't afraid. No, she was pleased. This meant they were close – closer than they had been for the whole case. They were finally in the right place. She gave Nate a significant look, and he nodded in understanding.

This was it.

A chill traveled up her spine as they moved fully into the huge open space, looking right out across the storage area. Now that she could see it from this angle and in clearer light, she saw that there weren't only the standing mannequins in lines – though they did seem to take up the majority of the occupied space. There were also other kinds of mannequins arranged behind them – seated ones, partial body forms such as disembodied torsos that were probably used to display lingerie, and, if she squinted, what looked like one area of only heads. She shuddered again. It was a good job the killer had chosen to use the full mannequin and not just heads. Somehow, that would have been even creepier.

"This is your full stock?" Laura asked, looking around. She couldn't imagine there was any more. The collection was vast – and now she understood why it would take a full day to do a stock take.

"Yes," the manager said. He had a kind of pleased, satisfied look as he admired the neatly-arranged rows. It had probably been his guidance to set them up this way and not just in a ragtag arrangement. "A lot of them are just here temporarily, waiting to be transported to the stores and boutiques that order them. Some, particularly the mannequins closer to the front, are overstock. We sometimes experience a rush on our services and need to make sure we have some spares around to cover it."

It made sense, of course. Laura found herself drawn to the right, walking down the side of the rows of mannequins and then out in front of them. There was another opening right at the front of the room before all of the mannequins, the place where she knew she had been standing in her vision. She couldn't resist stepping into that exact spot, turning, looking up to see the weight of all the collective mannequins seemingly gazing back at her...

And up ahead, somewhere in the middle of the huge collection, she saw one of them move.

"Over there," she said, turning to the manager who had followed her over. "Is that one of your employees?"

He squinted ahead and then nodded. "Looks like that's Dan. I asked him to take a look at the rows, see if there were any obvious gaps where someone might have taken something. Seems like he's almost done."

Laura felt something in her gut. She had no reason to suspect that this Dan was the person they were after. Not really. After all, he was just a random person she'd spotted among the mannequins.

But he was the one person moving in the field of unmoving bodies, just like she had seen in her vision, and that had to mean something.

"Can we speak to him?" she asked, glancing at the manager. "Just a quick interview, to see if he's spotted anything."

"Sure," the manager nodded. He raised his voice suddenly, lifting his chin as if to physically throw his voice further. "Hey! Dan! FBI here want you!"

There was a pause, and Laura saw the mysterious Dan emerge from behind a column of mannequins and stare right at them.

Before she could fully process the realization that he was going to do it –

He turned and ran.

CHAPTER TWENTY SEVEN

Laura set off immediately without waiting, not needing either permission or guidance as to whether giving chase was the right thing to do. To her left she was aware of Nate also giving chase, his larger frame almost knocking over one of the mannequins as they both entered the thin rows, one line apart.

She raced with her elbows tucked into her sides, trying to pump her arms without knocking into any of the silent guards that seemed bent on slowing down her progress. The employee slipped out of her line of sight but it didn't matter – he was wearing basketball shoes with rubber soles that slapped loudly against the hard floor of the warehouse, echoing off the walls but not enough to conceal the direction the sound came from. Laura carried on straight, sensing from his progress that he was going for an exit somewhere towards the back of the room.

Somewhere to her left, there was a loud clatter as a mannequin fell, and she heard Nate swear just before several other clatters sounded one after another. A domino effect. She didn't let it distract her, but it did send her heartbeat racing up another notch: make one mistake here, and you could get yourself stuck, hemmed in by an avalanche of plastic.

Somewhere up ahead, she heard another clatter, and it was her time to swear – because it sounded as though their suspect had just figured out the same thing.

If he brought down enough of them, they might never catch up to him.

Laura put on another burst of speed, seeing the back of the warehouse in her view at last. If she got out of this tangle of mannequins and props and staging, she could at least get a chance of catching up with him –

An oversized plastic arm caught on her sleeve as her increased pace reduced her control, and she found herself having to dive to the side, only to almost fall onto a crate stacked with unattached legs. She caught herself and kicked off the ground to almost dive out of the last row of mannequins, glancing over her shoulder just once to see that Nate was still fighting his way through, several rows back, then focusing in front again. There was no one in her immediate view, but she could still hear his shoes – off to the right somewhere – she burst around the corner of the last column of the display, and there he was, fighting his own way out of a tangle of what looked like dog-shaped mannequins – some of them small, some of them larger.

He saw her and turned to back away, only to trip over one of the smaller dogs, sending himself flying. Plastic models scattered before him like bowling pins, each knocking over another and another, the sound of it multiplying into a cacophony that echoed back from the walls of the warehouse, drowning out everything else.

Laura didn't let it stop her. Didn't pause or hesitate. He was down, and she had her chance.

She leapt over what looked, in her heightened state of awareness, like a model dalmatian, putting her hands down on its back and vaulting forwards until she was right on top of him. He was scrambling on his stomach, trying to get to his feet, models shifting under him like marbles. Laura reached –

And clamped her hands down on top of his, pushing him back to the ground in a vice grip, determined not to let him go.

"Dan -" she said, panting for breath and stopping for a moment. "Wait, what's your name?"

"Dan Molloy," he said, in strained groan.

"Dan Molloy," she repeated with satisfaction. "You're under arrest on suspicion of murder." She caught her breath as Nate came over, tripping over another two fake hands and almost bringing down what looked like a plastic tree before he made it over to them.

Somewhere at the other end of the warehouse, she imagined the manager looking over his ruined storage with utter dismay, and the adrenaline made her hysterical enough that she actually laughed.

***

"Alright," Laura said, throwing a closed file down on the interview room's table and sitting opposite their warehouse employee. "Dan Molloy."

The suspect in question sneered at her from across the other side of the table, his cuffed hands clinking slightly as he tried to move and found himself unable to. "What do you want, pig?"

Laura glanced at Nate, who rolled his eyes as he took the chair next to her. "How original," she commented drily. "I've never heard that one before."

"It's inaccurate, you know," Nate pointed out. "We're FBI, not police."

"What do I care?" Molloy spat, looking both of them over with a derisive snarl on his face. "Doesn't make any difference what you are."

"Oh, it makes a difference, buddy," Nate said. Just the size of his muscular arms made them vaguely threatening as he leaned on the table and pitched forward slightly. "Because it means we can put you in a whole new world of hurt compared to what the police can. You don't want to provoke us into increasing your charges. Judges listen to us."

Molloy actually scoffed, turning his head towards the ceiling as if he had no need to listen to them.

Laura knew why, and she was almost beside herself with anticipation on how his face was going to look when he found out he was wrong in his assumption.

"You don't think we can do anything to you, do you?" she asked. "You think you're going to get away with this. As soon as you're let out on bail or allowed access to the outside world, you'll be gone into the wind and we'll never find you again. Is that it?"

Molloy turned to stare at her with a hard expression on his face. He said nothing. He was clearly waiting to see where she was going with this before commenting.

"That's not going to happen," Laura said. "Firstly, because multiple murderers like you don't usually get bail – and with a history like yours, I can guarantee you're not going to get it. And second, because you're not going to be charged as Dan Molloy. You're going to be charged as Dan Martin."

His eyes widened in the way she had known they would, panic taking over his formerly cool outlook. He stared at her for a long moment and swallowed hard, then tried to recover. "Whatever. It doesn't matter what you charge me as. I'm not a murderer."

"Hmm." Nate grabbed Laura's file and started flicking through it, as if finding it extremely interesting. "That's odd. Because when we ran checks on every single employee at the warehouse, none of them have criminal records. The company doesn't hire people who have records. But as it turns out, even though Dan Molloy's record is clear, Dan Martin's isn't. Is it?"

"It was a frame job from your bacon-loving friends that got me charged before," Dan snapped, throwing a look of contempt Nate's way.

"For all three of the assaults?" Nate asked, flipping a page pointedly. "Including the one where there was camera footage of it happening?"

"That was a set-up job," Dan fumed, attempting to fold his arms over his chest with a rattle and then settling for staring hotly into the corner behind Laura's head. He obviously had anger issues. Even now, he was having a hard time holding it in.

"Right, right," Nate said, and then closed the file very deliberately, looking their suspect in the face. "And this is a set-up too, is it?"

"What do you expect from a Black cop like you -"

"ALRIGHT," Laura said loudly, mostly because she wasn't about to sit there and listen to Nate be insulted for the color of his skin – but also because she didn't want this to escalate into something that he could use in court. If he provoked one of them, he could claim he was subjected to police brutality, and then they could be looking at a retrial or even a failed conviction. "Let's get this settled, shall we? Why did you change your name?"

Dan looked at her and scoffed as if she was the stupidest person he'd ever met. "Why do you think? You said it yourself already. They don't hire people with criminal records. Nobody does. I had to fake everything just to get this crappy warehouse job."

"How terrible for you," Laura said flatly, with no sympathy whatsoever. She'd read his file in detail. All three of his assaults were committed against women who were left battered, blackened, and bruised. One of them had ended up in hospital for an extended stay. He was a piece of crap, and he deserved anything bad that happened to him. "Where were you the last four nights?"

"I don't know," he shrugged. "At home. Where were you? Out getting some?"

Laura ignored the obvious attempt to provoke her further, even when she saw Nate's fist curl slightly tighter on the table next to her. They needed to stay focused. The guy was just trying to distract them from the point at hand. "You're saying you have no alibi at all for the times in which we know both the thefts and the murders were committed, is that right?"

"I don't need an alibi," he sneered. "I'm innocent. Anyway, if you really want to know where I was, you'd better ask your mom."

Oh, God. He really was scraping the barrel of the most juvenile insults and responses. They weren't particularly getting anywhere, but it didn't matter too much. They had him. They had all the time they needed to talk to him. And they had other tools at their disposal, too.

"As we speak, there are detectives going through your home," Laura said, doing her own intentional provoking this time. "Looking in every room, under every cushion, at every single thing you own. Every

150

private thing you thought you had. And they're going to find something which tells them it was you."

"They're not going to find a damn thing," he scowled, though she could see how uncomfortable he was at the idea. She didn't blame him. It *was* uncomfortable, having someone go through your home. But murderers and assaulters didn't deserve anything less.

"Really?" she asked. "You're absolutely confident in that? Because I know you know how this works. You keep denying it now, and you're going to get the worst possible sentence that judge can throw at you. On the other hand, if you cooperate, things will go a lot easier on you and we can get this done with the minimum amount of trouble. Maybe even make sure that you get put in a nicer facility with a few perks, instead of the worst place they can think to throw you."

"That's great," Dan said, then slammed his hands on the table with a rattle of his cuffs and leaned forward to stare at her. "But I didn't do it!"

Laura shook her head. He wasn't willing to give in; she could see that. But she wasn't willing to give in, either.

They were going to sit here and carry on having this conversation for as long as it took. And in the end, if he didn't break, the evidence would get him. It always did. These days, even the criminals that thought they were good at it were inevitably leaving behind far too much evidence to keep them free for long. There were too many ways for them to test things now.

Confidence and faith in the system. That was what got Laura through when she faced a killer like this, who refused to give anything away.

There was a soft knock at the door. Laura looked up, seeing no need to refuse an interruption since they weren't getting anywhere anyway.

"Enter," she called out, and the door cracked open just a tiny amount to show the face of Detective Thorson wielding a piece of paper.

"For the tape, we're pausing the interview at seven twenty-eight P.M.," Nate said, getting up. "We're not done, Martin. You better think carefully about how you want this to go."

Laura followed him out of the room and into the corridor. With the heavy interview room door shut behind them, she gestured towards the next door. All three of them walked into the room which overlooked the interview, standing behind the one-way glass. They could see Dan Martin, sitting with his head bowed low and one leg twitching up and down, but he couldn't see them.

"He looks furious," Laura commented.

"You're getting to him," Nate replied. "Keeping going, L. We're going to crack him. Or, do we even need to, Detective?"

Detective Thorson gave an apologetic wince. "Sorry. I have the report from the search of his home."

"And?" Laura asked.

"Nothing to connect him with the murders," she said. "The techs haven't found any evidence of a digital connection with him and the victims, either. Of course, he would have come into contact with Perez through his job, and we could argue that he might have seen the other two victims going into the therapist's office, but it's tenuous."

"Any lawyer worth the bar would be able to dismiss that as circumstantial," Laura sighed. "Damnit. I was hoping we would have something to force his hand to confession and we could be getting a plane home tomorrow."

"We did find some illegal narcotics, though," Detective Thorson said. "That's something."

"Yeah, that puts him away for a year or so thanks to the conditions of his previous release," Nate said. "I really hope it doesn't take a year for us to get a confession out of him, but it's something."

Laura sighed, blowing out a long breath. She was getting tired of this case. Tired of trying to work something out. She felt so sure that they had him. He'd been in her vision – the only really useful vision she'd had for the whole case. He was in the right place, and he clearly had violent tendences. He had no alibis. It was so clear to her that they had the right guy.

Now they just needed him to confess – and he wouldn't.

Why couldn't these killers do them the decency of at least trying to make things a bit easier for them?

"You look exhausted, Laura," Nate said.

"Thanks," she said, shooting him an ironic look. It was always great to be told you weren't looking at your best.

He smirked. "I didn't mean it like that. You must not have slept well last night, that's all. And you've, uh. Put a lot into this case." He glanced at Detective Thorson with a side flick back to Laura, so that she would understand what he meant. He was referring to the one vision she had managed to have. He just didn't want to say it in front of someone else.

If he only knew the number of visions she was used to having. She almost wanted to laugh at him.

But…

He was right. She hadn't slept well last night. That late-night call to Zach about the visions, trying to figure out if she was broken. And then the strain she'd been through trying to make one come, coupled with the chase after Dan Martin in the warehouse. It was no wonder she was feeling so frustrated now. She'd worn out too much of her stamina to be able to really put everything into this interview.

"Maybe you're right," she sighed. After all, there was no rush now. Not until Friday, when she would be getting anxious to get home for the weekend. Two more days of interrogation could break him before she had to worry about that. But they had him, and while he was behind bars, he wasn't able to kill anyone else.

She was usually so driven to keep going, to never rest until the killer was stopped. But he was stopped. Maybe it would be okay for her to take a little break. Just this once.

"Go on," he said. "I'll carry on talking to him. Maybe he'll be more intimidated at the idea that the good cop has left the room. Hey, he's obviously racist – maybe Detective Thorson can come in with me and see if that really riles him up."

Laura smiled a little at the mental image.

She wanted to stay. Missing even a moment of the interview made her feel itchy. What if Martin said something important and she wasn't there to hear it? What if something slipped through the cracks?

But she trusted Nate. She knew he would do a good job without her. She had to let him do his thing. Maybe he was right – maybe it would work.

"Alright," she sighed. "Fine. I'll go back to the motel and get a takeout or something."

"Don't stay up late," Nate warned her. "I mean it. Go back and get some rest. We'll tackle him fresh together in the morning."

Laura nodded. She hesitated for an awkward moment – how did you leave a situation like this, where it wasn't appropriate to hug people but felt too formal to shake their hands? – and then she nodded again, stepping out into the hall.

She had a weird feeling as she walked through the precinct and out to the hired car. She hesitated then, considering going back and asking Nate if he needed the car, but she knew he could just ask for a ride from anyone in the precinct.

She had to stop making excuses and get out of there.

Laura got into the car, sat behind the wheel, and sighed, closing her eyes for a moment. She put her hands on the steering wheel and –

She was in a huge open space, so deep and wide she couldn't see the edges of it, all fading off into the darkness. The space was shrouded in gloom, so dark she could barely make out anything. She had the eerie feeling of not even being able to see her own hand.

It was hard to say whether the room was dark or whether it was the vision, but her visibility was almost gone. Then as she continued to stare, she began to see a little more and a little more. First the single figure of a man – a man she now recognized as actually being a mannequin, not a real person – emerged from the gloom. Then, as her eyes adjusted, more around and behind it. Rows and rows of them.

She was in the warehouse again. All of the mannequins were lined up perfectly, as if they had never been knocked over or disturbed. And they were all staring at her as they had been before.

She was here again. Just how it had been last time. But she'd already done this. She'd caught him. So why...?

There was a movement further down the line, a figure stepping out and looking at her. It was gloomy, the vision swirling and obscuring what little sight she did have. She couldn't make out his face, his features. But it didn't matter, did it?

It was him. It was Dan Martin – Dan Molloy. It was him.

She'd already done this.

Why did she have to –

Laura opened her eyes and took a breath, trying to figure out what she'd seen.

What was going on? Why had she returned to that same moment in her head? What was the vision trying to tell her?

How had she even had a vision – when all she was touching was the steering wheel of the hired car? What could possibly have triggered it here?

She had no idea, but she knew in her gut what she had to do if she wanted to get any answers at all.

She gripped the wheel tighter and started the engine – turning the car not in the direction of the motel, but towards where she knew the warehouse was waiting for her.

CHAPTER TWENTY EIGHT

Laura paused a second in the car, looking up at the dark building. Before, even though the sun had already disappeared, there had been lights on inside the space. They had glowed over the sidewalk, leaving it feeling like the place was alive.

Now, though, it was dark. Foreboding. Menacing.

Like it was just waiting for her to step inside so it could spring its trap.

She shivered slightly and shook her head. What was she getting so worked up over? Yes, the mannequins were creepy, and they were going to be even more creepy in the darkness. But she'd been in there before. She knew what they looked like, what to expect. And the killer was already back at the precinct, where there was no chance of him hurting anyone – least of all her.

Plus, she was sure the place wouldn't actually be deserted. There would be a security guard on staff, and that person would let her in and show her around. It would be fine.

She just had to hope that seeing the warehouse this time would give her the answers as to why she was still seeing something she'd thought she had left behind – and why it had only been the one vision over and over again this time, never with any more details or information.

Laura grabbed her cell phone off the passenger seat and dialed Nate's number for the second time, waiting. It rang out, hitting his voicemail. He was probably still in the interview room and wouldn't have his ringtone on. What was she going to do – wait for him to finish and call her back? That could take hours.

She resolved herself and got up, opening the car door and hearing it thud closed far too loud in the stillness of the night. Most people around here were gone, given that it was an industrial area. If there were any residents, they must have been in bed already. The only light came from the streetlights – and wasn't it just her luck that the one right by the warehouse was out, the bulb not responding the same way as its brothers had.

Which was fine. She knew where she was going, and she wasn't afraid.

If she kept repeating that to herself often enough, maybe it would actually be true.

Laura walked into the entrance she had used before, finding it locked and then knocking. She should have called ahead. She hadn't thought. This was all stupid. Maybe she...

There was a sound somewhere further down the alley beside the building and she peered ahead, trying to see. There was no illumination down here at all. She turned on the light on her cell phone and looked, but there was nothing in the alley at all.

Though, it did raise a thought. The other entrance was around there, the one with the loading bay. Maybe she had a better chance of running into a security guard over there. In fact, maybe that was who she'd heard.

She rushed down around the side of the building and round the back, finding it opening out on a wider space as she'd expected. There were clearly marked bays for trucks to reverse into for unloading. There was also an open door – in her head, Laura mentally mapped it out and realized it must be the one facing the mannequins from the front.

Someone stepped out of the door and she almost jumped out of her skin, throwing the beam of light up to illuminate them. In the same split-second, a blinding beam of light was also turned her way, making her flinch and throw up her arm.

"Who's there?" a gruff male voice demanded.

"FBI," Laura said, figuring that being upfront would get her further. "Who are you?"

The beam of light dropped from her face to her body, as if out of consideration of her eyes, and she did the same with her phone. She could make out his uniform now, including a badge holding his name and the logo of the warehouse firm. "Security guard," he said. "Can I see some ID?"

Laura nodded and pulled her badge out of her pocket, showing it to him as she took a few steps closer.

"Great," he said. "Sorry. I just can't be too careful, you know? You could be anyone without a uniform."

Laura smiled. Now that their lights were pointed down, they provided enough illumination to allow them to see one another without making it uncomfortable. "Did anyone tell you about the arrest we made earlier today?"

"Yeah, of course," the security guard said. "They did say there might be some cops or something coming by. Sorry. I was just expecting – you know. The red and blue flashing lights and all that."

Laura laughed. "Sorry, just me this time," she said. "I'm just checking something real quick, then I'll be out of your hair. The official party comes tomorrow, I would think. We're not expecting to find a lot of physical evidence left here, so I wouldn't worry about being ready tonight."

The security guard nodded. "That's kind of a relief," he said. "I don't really feel qualified for all this. It's funny. You spend a long time guarding something and stopping people getting in – being told you might have to let them all in feels weird."

Laura laughed again at that. "I never considered it that way," she said. "I won't be long. I just need to look inside the storage area. You can carry on patrolling if you need to. It's safe now, anyway – we have the killer in custody."

"Thanks," the security guard said, with a look of relief. "I wasn't sure what the protocol is here. I mean, I'm supposed to patrol, but then I have a guest – you know what I mean?"

Laura was starting to think that what he meant was that working the night shift left him without a lot of opportunities to talk to other people, but she only smiled politely. "I'll just head on in, then," she said.

She walked past him as he swept his beam of light across the courtyard a few more times, apparently reassuring himself that there was no one else around. Laura let him go. He wasn't a risk, and she felt like the answer to her vision lay in the warehouse itself. The person in it had already been removed, after all.

Her eyes adjusted to the gloom of the corridor; there was a faint light coming from the warehouse, after all. Another movement up ahead had her tensing up and almost reaching for her gun, but she relaxed again when she saw who it was. A janitor, carrying a couple of heavy-looking garbage bags. He nodded to her as he passed, hefting them a little higher and walking sideways to avoid them hitting her.

It was definitely creepier here at night. Emerging into the warehouse proper, she saw the mannequins standing in their rows. They were back to neatness – at least, they were on this side of the warehouse. She couldn't see all the way to the back past them, to see if there was any debris left from their chase towards the exit. She couldn't imagine that one manager and perhaps the one janitor together had enough time to clear it all up, even in the time they'd spent interviewing Dan Martin. They'd made a lot of mess.

Laura stopped there in the near-darkness, holding her breath. Somehow, she'd though that being here would have been enough alone to trigger something and help her to figure out what was going on. Like the answer would have been beamed down to her from some higher power. But standing here, all she saw was a warehouse full of mannequins. Yes, the same as it had been in her vision. But as much as she strained her eyes and stared, she didn't see a single flash of movement.

Being here was stupid. She wasn't going to see anything new. All she'd discovered was a janitor and a security guard, and they would have been included in the employee checks Detective Thorson carried out. They didn't add anything.

Laura was about to turn and leave when she froze, thinking.

They would have been checked, wouldn't they?

The security guard, his uniform had the logo of the company. He was clearly an employee, and he would have been on the roster.

But the janitor... he was wearing a uniform, too, and there was a logo sewn on the breast pocket. She was sure she'd seen it. But it wasn't the same logo as the one the security guard wore. It had been totally different – two interlocked initials, she thought, one in blue and one in red. MV, she thought, or something like that.

A contractor.

A contractor wouldn't have been included in the employee checks.

Not that it mattered, did it? Because they had the killer behind bars in the precinct. He wasn't going anywhere.

A killer that kept insisting he was innocent, and on whom they had so far not been able to collect any physical evidence.

No, that didn't matter. She'd seen him in her vision. Here, in this room.

Only –

Only this room had been dark like it was now in her vision.

And her brain supplied one more thing to her, one last detail it had been holding onto: the fact that when the janitor passed her, he'd been holding the garbage bags in two hands. Both of them covered by latex gloves for hygiene.

The janitor hadn't been checked to see if he had a criminal record. He had access to the mannequins at a time of night when no one else would have noticed him taking them. One security guard for this whole warehouse - there was no chance that he would have been able to cover the whole ground at once. Anyone could have taken whole crates of merchandise out of there without being spotted.

And he wore latex gloves, meaning he didn't leave fingerprints behind.

Things were starting to click in Laura's mind. The mannequins had been meticulously cleaned before they were placed, ensuring there wasn't a shred of evidence left behind – the kind of professional job you might expect from someone who cleaned for a living. Even the evidence at the scenes had been tidied up. They never had worked out where the blood from the initial blow had gone, and maybe being a janitor had given him a unique perspective on how to resolve that issue.

And his job was lonely. Overlooked, ignored. Even Laura hadn't bothered to speak with him, despite having a reasonably lengthy conversation with the security guard. A guard who had seem starved for attention. How much worse would that starvation have been if you were never even noticed, performing a thankless task every shift.

How you might start to imagine the mannequins were real people. Might start to imagine how your life could be.

And a contractor... they might also be contracted to clean the adjoining office building now that it had been converted, mightn't they?

They might just have the chance to overhear snippets of therapy sessions while tidying the waiting room and emptying the garbage...

Laura had made a terrible mistake.

A strangled scream cut the air and she whirled around, looking back towards the reception area she had entered through on their first visit, the place where the sound was coming from.

CHAPTER TWENTY NINE

The janitor hefted the trash bags a little higher at the sound of someone in the hall, thinking he was going to have to shuffle past the security guard with them, make room for him to come through. No one liked to have to squeeze by loaded trash bags, but in this smaller space, there wasn't a lot of choice. He was almost done with his work for the night, now that all the mannequins were back where they should be. All but one of them, anyway.

The janitor looked up to meet the security guard's eyes and almost flinched, so unexpected was the change. It wasn't the guard at all, but a woman. A beautiful one, with blonde hair in a ponytail swishing behind her as she walked. She looked a little pale, a little tired, but that didn't dim her beauty. If anything, it made her fragile and therefore more wonderful, like a hothouse rose that could wilt at any second. She was dressed in a sharp black suit like what the FBI wore on TV, but she was far too pretty and soft for that.

"Hi," he said, just to break the ice. "Looks like you've had a long day."

She gave a startled little half-laugh, pressing her hands against the top part of her cheeks as if to hide the bags under her eyes. "Oh, God, do I look that bad?"

He laughed and looked down a moment, abashed, before meeting her eyes again. "No, not at all. It's just I don't usually see a lot of people down here this late at night, and you look like you're working. So it must have been a long day."

"Yeah," she said, shrugging her shoulders and smiling. She paused in the corridor just before she had to pass him, as if enjoying the conversation too much to continue on. "And it's not over yet. I have some work to do over there, in the warehouse."

"Oh, don't let me stop you," he said, smiling pleasantly. "You ought to hurry on so you can get back home to your family."

"I live alone," she said, with a sweet smile, before she started to move again. "But you're right. I should get on with things."

The janitor turned his head to watch as she walked away, and she glanced back over her shoulder too, blushing and giving a quick giggle before she disappeared through the door at the end of the hall.

The janitor walked on hurriedly, putting the trash into the containers outside just as the security guard looped around the other side of the building, the beam of his flashlight disappearing. The janitor's shoulders slumped a little. Too slow. He'd wanted to talk to him.

He turned and went back inside the hall, pausing a moment as his eyes adjusted to the light again. Then she stepped back into the hall, walking towards him rapidly with a smile, and his heart swelled a little inside his chest.

"Done already?" he asked.

"Yeah, I just needed one quick thing," she said. "Now I'm *finally* done. What a relief!"

"That's a shame," he said, with a sly little smile, ready for her to react so he could drop his next line.

"What do you mean?" she asked, almost a little shocked but not quite, still dazzled and pleased by the way their flirtatious conversation was going.

"Well, I was going to ask if you wanted to head out for a drink or dinner to celebrate finally getting done, but I've still got a few things left to do here." He let the words drop into the air, leaving them open for her to respond, making sure to add an open and friendly smile alongside them.

"Well," she said, toying with the end of a piece of her blonde hair. "Like I said, there's no one waiting for me at home. I could wait around a little while until you're done."

"Then I better hurry up," he said, grinning. "Why don't you decide where I'm taking you while I finish up? Whatever you're in the mood for, I don't mind. My treat, of course."

"Alright," she giggled, and she stepped outside with her cell phone, already searching for restaurants in the local area that were still open.

He smiled, knowing how this was going to go already. Dinner and conversation, getting to know one another better and finding out they had so much in common. She would see past his job, know it was just a way to make a living. She would see him. He'd change into something smarter on the way and she'd see him for who he really was, the way that few people ever did. And she'd fall for him, the way he had fallen for her. By the end of the night, their first kiss…

The janitor shook himself mentally, telling himself to stop. This wasn't the time. Not right now.

For just a moment he knew: she hadn't flirted with him. And he hadn't had the courage to flirt with her. They hadn't even exchanged a

161

word – only a nod. That was all he had managed. There was no point distracting himself with fantasies when –

But of course, that wasn't real either, and –

He shook himself again, trying to fall back into the way things should be.

She was pretty, but he already had a goal for tonight. He had decided he was going to see his cousin. The security guard. They were going to spend some real quality time together in a way they'd never had the chance to before. They were going to hang out. He'd promised that. He couldn't go back on his word now. Not even for a pretty girl.

He had to focus on one goal at a time.

He dumped the last of the trash in the massive garbage containers outside in the loading bay and then turned, dusting off his gloves. That was all taken care of. Now he could go and see his cousin and connect with him for the first time, explain to him about how they were related and neither of them had known about it for so long. He could finally have that real family connection that he had been craving for so long.

He walked around the side of the building, following the last place he had seen that beam of light go, ready to loop around through the warehouse again until he found him.

CHAPTER THIRTY

Laura drew her gun and began to move, heading in the direction of the scream. Someone over there needed her. Needed help.

And she knew in her gut that it had to be connected to the janitor. Those gloves…

She'd missed all of the signs, misread them, misunderstood them. She'd imagined that she had found the scene of her vision and that was enough, as though she'd forgotten completely how her own visions worked. When she saw something, it wasn't a scene that could be repeated a different way or in a different time or place. It was exact.

The killer hiding among the mannequins in the darkness.

It still hadn't happened yet.

The thought made her heart pound wildly as she left the warehouse storage area and moved cautiously through the door, pausing to point her gun in the general direction of the desk and then sweeping across, checking the whole space for signs of anyone else there. She saw a man slumped on the floor but checked one more time before she was confident enough to run over to his side, believing now that they were alone. How long for, she didn't know. The janitor was nowhere in sight.

"Hey," she whispered urgently, then a little louder when he didn't respond. It was the security guard, she realized, recognizing the back of his uniform. He was face down, not moving. "Hey. Are you alright?"

Maybe it was a stupid question. He was on the floor. He obviously wasn't okay.

Laura checked his pulse and found it beating. "Alright," she said, her voice low. "Alright, I'm going to get you some help. Don't worry. Just focus on staying with me, okay? Everything's going to be fine." She could see blood pooling on the floor near his head, dark as tar in the dimness, illuminated only by the moonlight streaming in through the open door to the outside.

The door the killer must have gone out through.

Laura stepped back, her heart pounding. She had to do three things. Call for backup and an ambulance. Keep the security guard alive.

Find out where the killer was.

A movement and a sound outside made her draw back into the shadows behind the desk. She slipped downwards into a crouching position and then moved back as soundlessly as she could, out of sight. She could see the security guard on the floor but nothing else. She found her cell phone in her pocket and turned on the screen by feel alone, a move she'd practiced, to make sure she could always call for backup in an emergency without giving herself away by the light.

Someone stepped into the pale sliver of light around the security guard.

Laura worked hard to not audibly let her breath catch, trying to calm her racing heartbeat so she wouldn't give herself away. In her pocket, she found the bottom corner of her phone case and then navigated up about the length of the first joint of her index finger, then tapped. If she'd got it right, she'd opened her quick dial options from the widget.

He was standing over the security guard, standing and looking around as if he was straining to see or hear something. Looking for her, maybe, Laura realized. He had to have known that the scream could have brought someone over. He was trying to see if his cover had been blown.

She tapped her finger on the same spot again, without moving it. The spot where she had saved Nate's icon in the menu. Without wasting a single second she transferred her grip to press down hard and long on the volume control at the side of the phone, reducing it all the way to silent –

But not quickly enough to stop that first dial tone still being audible, even if so quietly it was almost totally muffled by her pocket.

But still, the janitor's head whipped in her direction, his eyes searching as if to sniff her out of the darkness.

Laura's heart was in her mouth as he leaned his weight forward, about to take a step in her direction –

And the security guard made a strained noise from the floor, a heartbreaking noise, a garbled cry that sounded like it came from a brain that no longer had enough capacity to understand where the pain was coming from.

The janitor looked down at him as if remembering he was there. He was holding something in his hand, something large and club-like. It took Laura a second, but then she placed it. A mannequin part – an arm, disjointed from the rest of the body. From the way he wielded it, it was also weighted – maybe supposed to be part of a display for jewelry or gloves.

And he raised it over his head, ready to bring it down on the security guard one more time and finish him.

No, she thought. She couldn't let this happen. Not even to guarantee her own safety. And it wasn't guaranteed, because he would come after her next as soon as the deed was done.

Laura shot upright behind the counter, lifting her gun as she did so and raising it to arm's length, aiming at his head. "Freeze!" she shouted, the one single word she knew to be the most effective in any situation, the way her training had told her to those years ago.

And he froze.

It was just a moment, the two of them staring at each other, for such a short time that she wasn't even sure their eyes had really connected in the darkness. She couldn't make out his face properly, only the vague impression of something – just like the expressionless mannequins. He was shaking just slightly and then it stopped; he stilled, as if he was one of the things he obviously felt such a deep connection to.

But then the spell broke, and the janitor turned and ran. Laura fired her gun, recoil bouncing up her arm and rattling her, but she knew even before she saw him fly through the open doorway that she'd missed. She hadn't had time to aim when he moved.

Laura snatched the cell out of her pocket, only glancing at the screen long enough to see that it was connected with Nate's number, not turning up the volume to hear him because it would take far too long. "I'm at the warehouse!" she shouted, the only thing she could do at the same time as starting to run after the janitor. "Man down, ambulance required! The killer is here – the janitor! It was the janitor!"

Then she shoved the cell phone back in her pocket and simply ran, right out of the door and then up the side of the building after the figure she saw racing away from her in the darkness.

He was too far ahead to catch now. She cursed in her head as he turned the corner far ahead of her, needing to conserve her breath too much to do it out loud. She put on as much of a burst of speed as she could while still keeping hold of her gun in one hand, slowing down to be more cautious just as she went around the corner, just in time to see him racing back inside the warehouse via the back door.

And she knew, in her gut, exactly how this was going to play out.

She knew what she was about to see before she saw it.

Somehow, for a moment, the fear dropped away completely. She was only walking into a vision, that was all. Walking into something she had already seen. She knew where he would be. She knew where she had to stand. Everything was all preordained. Why be scared about that?

But she stepped into the large warehouse space one more time and looked up to see the whole army of mannequins facing her, and *there* was the fear. So many of them. Arranged perfectly in their neat rows, unmoving, unchanging. And they were his creatures – his tools. He knew everything about them. How to position and move them, how to clean them right down to the inside of every single possible joint or crack, how to remove every trace of where they had come from.

How to kill with them.

She knew, now, that she'd been wrong before. It hadn't been Dan she'd seen in her vision. It had been a man emerging from the darkness in the rows of mannequins. Not running from her.

Running at her.

Time seemed to slow to a crawl as Laura took her place, standing there in front of the mannequins, waiting for it to happen. Waiting for her eyes to adjust. Waiting for him to make his move.

But this wasn't a vision. She wasn't trapped here. She had full autonomy. She could make her own choices to change the way all of this was going to turn out.

She pointed her gun at the place where she knew he would emerge, and called out. "You must have been so lonely," she said, and there was no response.

In her view, no response was good. No response meant he was frozen there still, standing among the mannequins, not moving. No response meant more time for Nate and the rest of the backup to arrive before he made his move.

Meant maybe more time for them to try and save her if he did manage to get his blow in, after all.

"No one ever notices you, do they?" Laura tried. She'd seen it, hadn't she? How lonely this job must be. And now she could see what he was doing with the mannequins. The story he was telling. Those faceless, nameless bodies – they were *him*.

Him, offering a shoulder to cry on to a so-called friend who never even knew he existed. Him, sleeping with a woman who never would have given him a second glance. Him, eating popcorn and watching a movie with a man who would never have allowed him inside the house.

She wanted to sympathize with him. To make him feel seen, heard. But…

166

If he felt like she was sympathizing too much, maybe he would just kill her to get it done with. To fulfil her role in his twisted fantasy, instead of actually having to put in the effort.

No, it was too risky. And she was still none the wiser as to what he was thinking, what he was doing out there in the dark. If she was going to survive *and* get help for the security guard, she needed to lure him out.

She needed to capture him – one way or another.

"It's pathetic," she said, letting the word hit the air like a slap, changing tactic entirely. As far as she knew, he only had a blunt weapon. She had a gun. And her eyes were adjusting more and more with each moment. "They didn't know you at all, did they? They had no idea you even existed. And if they had, why would they have wasted their time by spending it with you?"

She strained, and she thought she heard something – just the edge of something, not enough to identify it fully yet. It was in the vague area that she knew he had to be in, because of what she had seen in the vision. As though he'd made a small, involuntary noise.

She was getting to him.

"You don't really think it gives you any kind of connection, do you?" she asked, turning her voice as nasty as she could make it, belittling and mocking. "You're nothing to them. Even now. They didn't care about you when you were alive, and they still have no idea who you are now. Just some random guy that ended their lives for your own petty enjoyment. Just a loser."

There was a movement ahead at her last word, as though it was the last blow – as though he couldn't take it anymore. She knew this – she had seen this. He would step out and rush towards her, ready to attack. She didn't waste a single moment. She fired.

There was a moment of confusion, something shattering into pieces. Laura processed it a moment later: a mannequin head, exploding into shards of plastic shrapnel. She'd hit a mannequin head. Not the killer. And the shot was ringing in her ear...

She spun, turning from one side of the group of mannequins to the other, trying to identify movement, her gun kept up ahead at all times, ready to fire again. She just had to see him one more time and then she could –

Something hit the back of her head, hard, so hard –

She was spinning, dropping, hitting the floor but trying to keep her gun up –

She was down, her elbow taking the impact, another shot firing off and deafening her –

The gun spiraled out of her reach across the floor, disappearing among the rows of mannequins, gone out of her line of sight until she knew there was no point in even looking for it. It was him and her now, him and his mannequin arm…

She dodged to the side just in time, flinching in reaction to the blur of movement in her vision. Maybe it was the rage, or maybe it was the lingering effects of the gun firing so close to him, but he was slow. Off. Not as strong or as fast as she had expected. Her head was throbbing, but she was used to that, and she analyzed even as she tried to move and scramble away from him that he hadn't dealt too harsh of a blow. Not like the one he had dealt to the security guard.

All she had to do was stay alive until Nate got there.

She just had to stay alive.

He made a sound, a kind of half-sob of rage, and the arm-club was coming down towards her again. Laura shot to the right instead of the left this time, trying to put him off, trying to make him guess. If she only went in the same direction, he'd catch her sooner or later. The blow landed on the floor right next to her head, and she could almost hear the vibrations going up into his arm as it connected with the hard ground.

If he hit the floor instead of her often enough, his arm would tire.

That was how she would keep going. That was it. Every time that she successfully dodged him, it was one more hit to his arm, to his stamina.

And maybe, just maybe, when he finally did hit her – there wouldn't be enough strength in his arm to finish her off.

He howled over her head at the miss and aimed again, the arm hitting the floor so close by her head this time she was sure she was only saved by her last-minute flinch. And she was running out of room. One more roll and she would –

The arm was coming down, and there was no time to think, she had to –

She rolled –

She hit the base of one of the mannequins and it fell, swinging forward, bringing down more, falling on her heavily, several more of them landing around her –

And she was pinned down, couldn't move, and wouldn't luck have it, they'd all missed the killer –

He took aim at her head again and this time she could see it in his eyes, see he knew –

He was going to kill –

A shot rang out, startling Laura into utter confusion because she knew she hadn't fired, and there was a spray of something dark from the janitor's shoulder. The arm he was holding clattered to the ground uselessly as he clutched at his shoulder, crying out in pain.

"Don't move!" Nate yelled, and Laura could have just let go and sunk into the ground with relief, knowing it was over. "You're surrounded by armed police. One movement and I fire again. I repeat, do not move!"

Laura fought her way free of the mannequin, pushing it off herself and slowly testing her strength, putting her hands down on the cold ground and then pushing herself up. Her head swam, throbbed, then cleared a little. She looked up at the janitor. He was clutching his shoulder, looking down, gone totally still. Only his ragged breathing gave away that he was not made of plastic himself.

Nate approached with his handcuffs in his hand, and Laura flashed him a weary, pained, wobbly grin.

"You took your time," she said.

"You know I always like to make a dramatic entrance," Nate shrugged, and then he was making the arrest, and Laura allowed herself to stumble over to a pair of detectives who supported her on each side as they walked back into the light.

CHAPTER THIRTY ONE

Laura shook her head in disbelief. "I can't believe I slept through the whole drive," she said.

"Yeah," Nate replied drily. "It's almost as though you had a recent head injury, or something."

"It wasn't that bad," Laura rolled her eyes at him. "The EMTs said I didn't even need a scan. I got lucky. In the darkness, he completely missed his mark and just glanced the blow off the side of my skull. One of the hard bits. He must have used up all his energy hitting the security guard – and that guy was strong enough to pull through, too. They didn't even tell me not to drive."

"Yeah, well, maybe they were hoping you'd go with common sense on that one," Nate said, pulling a face at her. "I am honestly very happy to drive you home right now. You don't have to do it yourself."

"And then come back tomorrow on the bus and have to get my car anyway," Laura said, shaking her head. She didn't even wince as she did so. The few hours of sleep this morning on top of what had remained of the night in the motel had taken away most of the sting. It was still a blow to the head, of course, but it really wasn't as bad as some of the other ones she'd had.

Either that or she was now so far into the chart of concussions that she no longer felt them. But, hey. There wasn't an awful lot she could do about that after the fact.

"Well," Nate sighed, running a hand back over his short-cropped hair as if he was reaching the limit of his frustration and had no answers left. "Just – text me when you get back, okay? So I know that you made it back safe."

"Will do, Mom," Laura said with a teasing smile. She was glad things were back to normal between them. Better than normal, maybe. Now they no longer had to have any secrets.

She turned around and made for her car across the parking lot, leaving him behind at the door to his.

"Hey, Laura," he called out, when she was only a few steps away.

She turned again, raising her eyebrows.

"Uh." Nate paused, glanced around. They weren't in a private place, here. "Just wanted to say it was, uh, pretty cool. The *technique* you used. It really worked out for us finding the killer."

Laura almost wanted to scream. If he thought it was impressive that she'd seen the killer in the warehouse – even though it hadn't actually led her to right person for such a long time – then he would have been so much more impressed by the way her powers worked when they were actually, well… *working.*

But it was something, and she'd take it. He believed in her. He'd seen it for himself.

And finally, she knew now that it wasn't going to drive him away.

He would keep her secret, and their partnership could go on – just as it always had, but now even better.

"Thanks," she said, with a smile. Then she lifted her hand in a farewell wave. "See you on Monday for the paperwork."

Nate groaned and threw his head back at the mention of the dreaded p-word, and Laura laughed as she walked back to her car.

***

Laura stepped back into the kitchen with a grin, watching Chris trying to supervise a tea party and failing miserably. The girls had already forced him to wear a pair of fairy wings on his back, and now he was being lectured sternly about not holding out his pinkie finger while he drank his tea or offering any of his cookies to the unicorn stuffie next to him.

He glanced up and saw her, and apparently his eyes lit up with the jackpot signs. "Oh, look, girls!" he said, in a tone that was almost desperate. "Looks like Laura wants to join in with our tea party!"

"Come on, Mommy!" Lacey called out. Laura's daughter waved her tiny hands emphatically, the gap between her lower teeth flashing from within her wide grin. "You've got to come. It will fill up the last seat!"

Laura nodded. "Alright, darling," she said, taking her spot on the last 'seat' – one of the cushions from the couch which had been pulled down and arranged in a circle on the floor, around an assortment of plastic teacups and saucers. The spaces between Chris, the girls, and Laura were all filled with various toys and dolls who had also been invited to join them. "What kind of tea is it?"

"It's tea," Lacey said, with such a matter-of-factness and a bewildered tone that Laura had to laugh. The girls probably didn't even realize that different kinds of tea existed.

"Here you go, Mommy," Amy said, handing her a cup, and Laura blinked.

That was new.

"Thank you," was all she managed to say, reeling from the surprise. She looked up and met Chris's eyes and saw the same reaction mirrored in him. The two girls were carrying on playing as if nothing had happened. Maybe they didn't even realize the slip that she had made.

What should she do? Correct her?

But Chris recovered first, clearly deciding to just brush over it. "What should we talk about with our tea?" he asked.

"Makeup," Amy said decisively, making Laura smile again. The girls were just repeating things they'd heard or seen without really knowing anything about it. She was sure neither Amy nor Lacey had ever worn a single touch of makeup in all their young lives.

She watched them both, Amy and Lacey, playing together. They really did look like they could be sisters, with their matching blonde hair and blue eyes.

A year ago, Laura had been estranged from her daughter, fighting for custody in the courts, alone and lost. Now she was sitting here with two girls that looked up to her, a new boyfriend – maybe a second chance at a real family. Her eyes misted up.

"Will you do some lipstick on us, Mommy?" Lacey asked, and Laura quickly sniffed, blinking away the tears and smiling.

"Not a chance," she said, leaning down to kiss Lacey on top of her head. "Maybe when you're a little older." She glanced up at Chris to see him watching her with an expression not dissimilar to her own, and she thought that maybe when he swallowed hard, it was to get rid of a lump in his throat.

Laura's phone buzzed in her pocket, a text alert. She briefly considered ignoring it. After all, this was – well, in a way, it was family time. Considering that she spent almost every weekend here now, maybe it was no surprise that Amy thought of her as a mother figure.

But then Laura knew she might be missing an important message about a case, and she was too much of a believer in her job to ignore it. She slipped the cell phone out of her pocket and checked it quickly, her heart almost stopping in her chest when she saw what it actually was.

"Hey, who wants some real cookies?" she asked.

Chris raised an eyebrow at her as the girls both chorused their predictable *me, me, me!*. She flashed him an apologetic smile and mouthed the word *work* while holding up her phone. If he believed that she was out following a lead or answering a call from her boss, he wouldn't ask many questions. He knew that her work was confidential, after all.

"Alright, I'll be back soon," she said, getting up. She felt bad for leaving Chris looking after the girls alone, but… he could handle it. Just for the twenty minutes or so it would take.

She reread the message from Zach as she stepped outside: *Can we meet? It's urgent.* She fired off a reply with the name of a nearby café and walked there quickly. She was getting familiar enough with the neighborhood that she knew she could get there and back in a short time, so long as she didn't linger too long with Zach. As she walked, she ran through options for excuses to get away from him quickly – anything but the truth. She didn't want to risk Amy's safety, and she didn't quite fully trust Zach yet.

She went past a bakery and made a mental note to stop in on the way back so that she wouldn't forget the fake cause of her departure. It was right next to the café, just a few doors down, a convenient placement that made her thank the stars for a quick moment before heading in.

She grabbed a table at the café and sat anxiously, her leg bouncing up and down as she waited for Zach to appear. She checked her watch. Any longer, and this excuse of hers wasn't going to hold up to scrutiny…

"Laura," he said, his tone sounding relieved as he sunk into the chair opposite her. Laura almost jumped; she'd been looking at the time so intently she hadn't seen him come in. "I'm so glad you could meet me."

"What's going on?" Laura asked, getting right to the point. "I don't have a lot of time. I told them I was going out for cookies."

Zach nodded. "Right. I'm sorry for interrupting your day. It's just – the visions."

Laura leaned forward a little, so they wouldn't have to raise their voices to a level where someone else could overhear them. "What about them?"

"I'm having… difficulty," Zach said. "They seem to be getting darker and fuzzier. Like I'm trying to watch a movie through fog. It's getting harder to see what's going on and actually understand it. And I don't think they're coming as frequently as usual, either."

Laura paused. "That's exactly like what's happening to me," she said breathlessly.

Could it be that they were… losing their visions?

Was that even possible?

Was that why they had found each other now?

"I don't understand it," Zach said. "It's not like the other times when my visions just faded away for a while. This is different. Dark. It's like… like the aura of death, just hanging over everything I see."

Laura's breath caught. The aura of death. The way it would cloud your vision in real life, dark tendrils like smoke everywhere, poisonous and so thick you thought you'd never get out. He was right. It was exactly like all of her visions were being strangled by that same aura. "What does it mean?"

"I don't know," Zach said, and for the first time since she'd met him, he actually sounded scared. Uncertain.

Somehow, that made her feel reassured. Even though it maybe shouldn't have. She knew, now, that she wasn't alone in being afraid for the future. In being confused. Just that fact made her feel better able to face whatever was coming.

"We'll figure it out," she said. The old man looked so worried and dismayed that she reached out to pat his hand on the table, to make him feel better.

And as she did, a spike of a headache hit her, almost as if the visions had heard their fears and wanted to provide an answer. She took a breath –

She was standing some distance away from them, watching, but everything was dim and confused, tendrils of the vision escaping around the edges and even blurring and distorting what she could see. But she could make out enough to see –

To see Zach on the floor, lying flat on his back, his gray hair standing out like a light in the darkness of the vision. She couldn't see his face, his expression, but she knew it was him by his shape. His aura, almost.

There was someone above him. Kneeling over him, bent forward. Moving –

Stabbing. The man was stabbing Zach, plunging his hand down into Zach's chest –

Laura wanted to move forward, to do something, to intervene, but as in all of her visions she was only trapped, watching, unable to move. She couldn't do anything to stop this from happening. To save Zach's life. To even see the damage.

And then the man over him turned and looked at her, looked right at her, and –

Just for a moment, the tendrils cleared, the fog lifted, and she saw his face as clear as day.

Christopher Fallow.

She'd seen Chris stabbing Zach in the chest.

Laura breathed again, staring at Zach's hand on the table with horror, her heart beating so fast she thought she was going to pass out.

NOW AVAILABLE!

ALREADY LOST
(A Laura Frost FBI Suspense Thriller—Book 8)

FBI Special Agent—and psychic—Laura Frost has seen it all. Yet when she encounters a mysterious gramophone left at the crime scenes of a new serial killer, playing old, creepy music, she is stumped. What could possibly be the meaning?

"A masterpiece of thriller and mystery."
—Books and Movie Reviews, Roberto Mattos (re Once Gone)

ALREADY LOST (A Laura Frost FBI Suspense Thriller) is book #8 in a long-anticipated new series by #1 bestseller and USA Today bestselling author Blake Pierce, whose bestseller Once Gone (a free download) has received over 1,000 five star reviews. The Laura Frost series begins with ALREADY GONE (Book #1).

FBI Special Agent and single mom Laura Frost, 35, is haunted by her talent: a psychic ability which she refuses to face and which she keeps secret from her colleagues. While Laura gets obscured glimpses of what the killer may do next, she must decide whether to trust her confusing gift—or her investigative work.

The music, Laura realizes, is the key to a cryptic message the killer is trying to impart. But is it a message meant only for him?

Or for Laura to come and find him?

Laura has only one chance at this. And if she gets it wrong, another woman will die.

A page-turning and harrowing crime thriller featuring a brilliant and tortured FBI agent, the LAURA FROST series is a startlingly fresh mystery, rife with suspense, twists and turns, shocking revelations, and driven by a breakneck pace that will keep you flipping pages late into the night.

Book #9 in the series—ALREADY HIS—is now also available.

"An edge of your seat thriller in a new series that keeps you turning pages! ...So many twists, turns and red herrings... I can't wait to see what happens next."
—Reader review (*Her Last Wish*)

"A strong, complex story about two FBI agents trying to stop a serial killer. If you want an author to capture your attention and have you guessing, yet trying to put the pieces together, Pierce is your author!"
—Reader review (*Her Last Wish*)

"A typical Blake Pierce twisting, turning, roller coaster ride suspense thriller. Will have you turning the pages to the last sentence of the last chapter!!!"
—Reader review (*City of Prey*)

"Right from the start we have an unusual protagonist that I haven't seen done in this genre before. The action is nonstop... A very atmospheric novel that will keep you turning pages well into the wee hours."
—Reader review (*City of Prey*)

"Everything that I look for in a book... a great plot, interesting characters, and grabs your interest right away. The book moves along at a breakneck pace and stays that way until the end. Now on go I to book two!"
—Reader review (*Girl, Alone*)

"Exciting, heart pounding, edge of your seat book... a must read for mystery and suspense readers!"
—Reader review (*Girl, Alone*)

Blake Pierce

Blake Pierce is the USA Today bestselling author of the RILEY PAGE mystery series, which includes seventeen books. Blake Pierce is also the author of the MACKENZIE WHITE mystery series, comprising fourteen books; of the AVERY BLACK mystery series, comprising six books; of the KERI LOCKE mystery series, comprising five books; of the MAKING OF RILEY PAIGE mystery series, comprising six books; of the KATE WISE mystery series, comprising seven books; of the CHLOE FINE psychological suspense mystery, comprising six books; of the JESSE HUNT psychological suspense thriller series, comprising twenty four books; of the AU PAIR psychological suspense thriller series, comprising three books; of the ZOE PRIME mystery series, comprising six books; of the ADELE SHARP mystery series, comprising fifteen books, of the EUROPEAN VOYAGE cozy mystery series, comprising four books; of the new LAURA FROST FBI suspense thriller, comprising nine books (and counting); of the new ELLA DARK FBI suspense thriller, comprising eleven books (and counting); of the A YEAR IN EUROPE cozy mystery series, comprising nine books, of the AVA GOLD mystery series, comprising six books (and counting); of the RACHEL GIFT mystery series, comprising eight books (and counting); of the VALERIE LAW mystery series, comprising nine books (and counting); of the PAIGE KING mystery series, comprising six books (and counting); of the MAY MOORE mystery series, comprising six books (and counting); and the CORA SHIELDS mystery series, comprising three books (and counting).

An avid reader and lifelong fan of the mystery and thriller genres, Blake loves to hear from you, so please feel free to visit www.blakepierceauthor.com to learn more and stay in touch.

BOOKS BY BLAKE PIERCE

CORA SHIELDS MYSTERY SERIES
UNDONE (Book #1)
UNWANTED (Book #2)
UNHINGED (Book #3)

MAY MOORE SUSPENSE THRILLER
NEVER RUN (Book #1)
NEVER TELL (Book #2)
NEVER LIVE (Book #3)
NEVER HIDE (Book #4)
NEVER FORGIVE (Book #5)
NEVER AGAIN (Book #6)

PAIGE KING MYSTERY SERIES
THE GIRL HE PINED (Book #1)
THE GIRL HE CHOSE (Book #2)
THE GIRL HE TOOK (Book #3)
THE GIRL HE WISHED (Book #4)
THE GIRL HE CROWNED (Book #5)
THE GIRL HE WATCHED (Book #6)

VALERIE LAW MYSTERY SERIES
NO MERCY (Book #1)
NO PITY (Book #2)
NO FEAR (Book #3)
NO SLEEP (Book #4)
NO QUARTER (Book #5)
NO CHANCE (Book #6)
NO REFUGE (Book #7)
NO GRACE (Book #8)
NO ESCAPE (Book #9)

RACHEL GIFT MYSTERY SERIES
HER LAST WISH (Book #1)
HER LAST CHANCE (Book #2)
HER LAST HOPE (Book #3)

HER LAST FEAR (Book #4)
HER LAST CHOICE (Book #5)
HER LAST BREATH (Book #6)
HER LAST MISTAKE (Book #7)
HER LAST DESIRE (Book #8)

AVA GOLD MYSTERY SERIES
CITY OF PREY (Book #1)
CITY OF FEAR (Book #2)
CITY OF BONES (Book #3)
CITY OF GHOSTS (Book #4)
CITY OF DEATH (Book #5)
CITY OF VICE (Book #6)

A YEAR IN EUROPE
A MURDER IN PARIS (Book #1)
DEATH IN FLORENCE (Book #2)
VENGEANCE IN VIENNA (Book #3)
A FATALITY IN SPAIN (Book #4)

ELLA DARK FBI SUSPENSE THRILLER
GIRL, ALONE (Book #1)
GIRL, TAKEN (Book #2)
GIRL, HUNTED (Book #3)
GIRL, SILENCED (Book #4)
GIRL, VANISHED (Book 5)
GIRL ERASED (Book #6)
GIRL, FORSAKEN (Book #7)
GIRL, TRAPPED (Book #8)
GIRL, EXPENDABLE (Book #9)
GIRL, ESCAPED (Book #10)
GIRL, HIS (Book #11)

LAURA FROST FBI SUSPENSE THRILLER
ALREADY GONE (Book #1)
ALREADY SEEN (Book #2)
ALREADY TRAPPED (Book #3)
ALREADY MISSING (Book #4)
ALREADY DEAD (Book #5)
ALREADY TAKEN (Book #6)

ALREADY CHOSEN (Book #7)
ALREADY LOST (Book #8)
ALREADY HIS (Book #9)

EUROPEAN VOYAGE COZY MYSTERY SERIES
MURDER (AND BAKLAVA) (Book #1)
DEATH (AND APPLE STRUDEL) (Book #2)
CRIME (AND LAGER) (Book #3)
MISFORTUNE (AND GOUDA) (Book #4)
CALAMITY (AND A DANISH) (Book #5)
MAYHEM (AND HERRING) (Book #6)

ADELE SHARP MYSTERY SERIES
LEFT TO DIE (Book #1)
LEFT TO RUN (Book #2)
LEFT TO HIDE (Book #3)
LEFT TO KILL (Book #4)
LEFT TO MURDER (Book #5)
LEFT TO ENVY (Book #6)
LEFT TO LAPSE (Book #7)
LEFT TO VANISH (Book #8)
LEFT TO HUNT (Book #9)
LEFT TO FEAR (Book #10)
LEFT TO PREY (Book #11)
LEFT TO LURE (Book #12)
LEFT TO CRAVE (Book #13)
LEFT TO LOATHE (Book #14)
LEFT TO HARM (Book #15)

THE AU PAIR SERIES
ALMOST GONE (Book#1)
ALMOST LOST (Book #2)
ALMOST DEAD (Book #3)

ZOE PRIME MYSTERY SERIES
FACE OF DEATH (Book#1)
FACE OF MURDER (Book #2)
FACE OF FEAR (Book #3)
FACE OF MADNESS (Book #4)
FACE OF FURY (Book #5)

FACE OF DARKNESS (Book #6)

A JESSIE HUNT PSYCHOLOGICAL SUSPENSE SERIES
THE PERFECT WIFE (Book #1)
THE PERFECT BLOCK (Book #2)
THE PERFECT HOUSE (Book #3)
THE PERFECT SMILE (Book #4)
THE PERFECT LIE (Book #5)
THE PERFECT LOOK (Book #6)
THE PERFECT AFFAIR (Book #7)
THE PERFECT ALIBI (Book #8)
THE PERFECT NEIGHBOR (Book #9)
THE PERFECT DISGUISE (Book #10)
THE PERFECT SECRET (Book #11)
THE PERFECT FAÇADE (Book #12)
THE PERFECT IMPRESSION (Book #13)
THE PERFECT DECEIT (Book #14)
THE PERFECT MISTRESS (Book #15)
THE PERFECT IMAGE (Book #16)
THE PERFECT VEIL (Book #17)
THE PERFECT INDISCRETION (Book #18)
THE PERFECT RUMOR (Book #19)
THE PERFECT COUPLE (Book #20)
THE PERFECT MURDER (Book #21)
THE PERFECT HUSBAND (Book #22)
THE PERFECT SCANDAL (Book #23)
THE PERFECT MASK (Book #24)

CHLOE FINE PSYCHOLOGICAL SUSPENSE SERIES
NEXT DOOR (Book #1)
A NEIGHBOR'S LIE (Book #2)
CUL DE SAC (Book #3)
SILENT NEIGHBOR (Book #4)
HOMECOMING (Book #5)
TINTED WINDOWS (Book #6)

KATE WISE MYSTERY SERIES
IF SHE KNEW (Book #1)
IF SHE SAW (Book #2)

IF SHE RAN (Book #3)
IF SHE HID (Book #4)
IF SHE FLED (Book #5)
IF SHE FEARED (Book #6)
IF SHE HEARD (Book #7)

THE MAKING OF RILEY PAIGE SERIES
WATCHING (Book #1)
WAITING (Book #2)
LURING (Book #3)
TAKING (Book #4)
STALKING (Book #5)
KILLING (Book #6)

RILEY PAIGE MYSTERY SERIES
ONCE GONE (Book #1)
ONCE TAKEN (Book #2)
ONCE CRAVED (Book #3)
ONCE LURED (Book #4)
ONCE HUNTED (Book #5)
ONCE PINED (Book #6)
ONCE FORSAKEN (Book #7)
ONCE COLD (Book #8)
ONCE STALKED (Book #9)
ONCE LOST (Book #10)
ONCE BURIED (Book #11)
ONCE BOUND (Book #12)
ONCE TRAPPED (Book #13)
ONCE DORMANT (Book #14)
ONCE SHUNNED (Book #15)
ONCE MISSED (Book #16)
ONCE CHOSEN (Book #17)

MACKENZIE WHITE MYSTERY SERIES
BEFORE HE KILLS (Book #1)
BEFORE HE SEES (Book #2)
BEFORE HE COVETS (Book #3)
BEFORE HE TAKES (Book #4)
BEFORE HE NEEDS (Book #5)
BEFORE HE FEELS (Book #6)

BEFORE HE SINS (Book #7)
BEFORE HE HUNTS (Book #8)
BEFORE HE PREYS (Book #9)
BEFORE HE LONGS (Book #10)
BEFORE HE LAPSES (Book #11)
BEFORE HE ENVIES (Book #12)
BEFORE HE STALKS (Book #13)
BEFORE HE HARMS (Book #14)

AVERY BLACK MYSTERY SERIES
CAUSE TO KILL (Book #1)
CAUSE TO RUN (Book #2)
CAUSE TO HIDE (Book #3)
CAUSE TO FEAR (Book #4)
CAUSE TO SAVE (Book #5)
CAUSE TO DREAD (Book #6)

KERI LOCKE MYSTERY SERIES
A TRACE OF DEATH (Book #1)
A TRACE OF MURDER (Book #2)
A TRACE OF VICE (Book #3)
A TRACE OF CRIME (Book #4)
A TRACE OF HOPE (Book #5)